Pure

Catherine Mesick

Copyright © 2011 by Catherine Mesick.
Cover Design by Mirella Santana: mirellasantana.com.br.
Credits: © Yana Bobrykova and Марина Хоменко.

All rights reserved. Published by Scofflaw Publishing.

ISBN: 978-0-9986631-0-4

Pure Series: Book 1

Pure

Catherine Mesick

Chapter One

I leaned my forehead against the dark window, welcoming the feel of the cool glass against my feverish skin.

I could feel the night calling to me, though I didn't exactly know what I meant by that. It had been happening more often lately—it was a strange tugging on my mind.

Something was pulling me out into the dark.

In an unguarded moment, GM had told me that my mother had had visions. The way the night called to me, I wondered if this feeling was the beginning of a vision.

I wished I could talk to my mother. I'd been wishing for that more and more often lately.

I turned away from the window, trying to shake off the feeling that tugged on my mind, and I picked up the framed photograph that always sat next to my bed. In the photo, a man with curly brown hair and a pale, blond woman smiled as they kneeled on either side of a laughing, fair-haired girl of five. The inscription on the back was hidden by the frame, but I knew well what it said. In GM's busy scrawl were the words *Daniel, Katie, Nadya.*

My father, me, my mother.

Though the memories were faint, I did remember those early days in Russia. I remembered the big apple tree and the roses that

1

grew at our house. I remembered playing with my red-haired cousin, Odette.

I remembered, too, the day GM had taken the picture. Little had she known then that her son-in-law and her daughter would be dead soon afterward.

My father had died first in an accident in the mountains. My mother died just a few weeks later of a fever, and GM had moved us to the United States shortly after that. We'd been here for eleven years now, and my old life was beyond my reach for good.

I set the picture down.

The darkness continued to call to me, and I tried to force my mind back to reality—back to what was normal and safe and unrelated to the unknown out in the dark.

I thought of my friends—and school—but even as I did so, I felt a sudden, sharp tug on my mind, and I was seized by an irrational desire to run out into the night—and to keep running until I found the source of the summons.

I closed my eyes and willed the feeling away.

After a moment, the night calling began to subside. I concentrated harder, pushing it further away from me. In another few minutes, the feeling was gone entirely. Relief flooded through me.

I was free.

I stood for a moment, breathing hard and looking around at all the familiar objects in my room, as if to reassure myself. Then I climbed back into bed and turned out the light.

I was just drifting off to sleep when I was jolted wide-awake by the sound of a car tearing down our street. The car screeched to a halt somewhere below my window, and then turned sharply into our driveway.

I sat up. I heard the muffled slam of two car doors outside, and I heard GM, who usually kept late hours, hurrying toward the door.

I got out of bed and fumbled in the dark to find a robe. I was puzzled—who could possibly have come to see us in the middle of the night?

As I hurried out of my room, I heard a heavy pounding on the front door, followed by a woman's cry.

"Anna! Anna Rost! Annushka! Open the door!"

I froze in the hallway. Only GM's oldest friends called her Annushka—and there were precious few of those.

I heard GM quickly unbolt the door and open it.

"Galina!" GM shouted in shock. Her voice rose even higher. "Aleksandr? Is that you, Aleksandr? How tall you are! I scarcely would have recognized you."

I wished I could see who was at the door, but I knew that if I went downstairs, GM would just order me back to my room. She clearly recognized her visitors, and they were clearly people she had known back in Russia.

And GM never allowed me to get involved in anything that had to do with the past.

I crept to the top of the stairs but remained in the shadows— the better to hear without being seen.

"Annushka!" Galina cried. She had a heavy Russian accent— much heavier than GM's. "Annushka! I had scarcely allowed myself to believe that we'd actually found you! Oh, Annushka! After all these years!"

"Hush, Galina, hush," GM hissed. "You'll wake my granddaughter. Come in. Quickly, now."

I could hear the clack of a woman's footsteps in the hall, followed by a man's heavier tread. The door was closed and the bolt reset.

GM led her visitors down the hall to the kitchen.

I tiptoed down the stairs and sat on the bottom step. I wouldn't be able to see into the kitchen from my perch without leaning over the banister, but I knew from experience that I would be able to hear.

GM's voice floated down the hall to me. "Since you're here, Galina," she said, "you and Aleksandr may as well have a seat."

I heard chairs scraping on the kitchen floor.

"You're not entirely happy to see us, are you, Annushka?" Galina asked.

"I am happy to see you," GM said stiffly. "I am not happy about what it is that you bring with you."

"And what is that?" Galina asked sharply.

"Superstition," GM said wearily. "I have a feeling that this conversation is going to be difficult. However, we may as well try to be civilized. May I offer you both a cup of tea?"

"Yes, thank you," Galina said.

I heard water running as a kettle was filled.

A moment later, I heard GM sit down at the table. "I suppose you have a good reason for storming my house in the middle of the night?"

"Annushka, we need your help," Galina said urgently.

"Then why didn't you just call?" GM snapped. "Why fly all the way here from Russia? You did come from Russia, didn't you?"

"Yes, we did."

GM snorted. "Ridiculous. Again, I say, why didn't you just call?"

I figured that everyone in the kitchen was too absorbed in the conversation to notice me, so I risked a look over the banister. GM was sitting with her back to me, and I could see that she had pulled her long silver hair into a ponytail that flowed like silk down her back. She was resting her elbows on the kitchen table as she regarded her visitors.

Facing GM was a woman who was young enough to be her daughter. She was blond, and she wore a nondescript beige coat with brightly colored mittens. Next to her was a young man who seemed to be in his early twenties. He was wearing an olive-green military-style coat, and his hair was an odd shade of brown—sort of a cinnamon color. There was a strong family resemblance between the two of them, and I guessed that Galina and Aleksandr were mother and son.

Aleksandr must have felt my eyes on him, for he transferred his gaze from GM to me.

I felt a flash of panic as Aleksandr's eyes met mine, and for just an instant, a feeling of strangeness—something wildly foreign— washed over me. I quickly pulled my head back behind the banister.

I froze, waiting to hear if Aleksandr would tell GM that he had seen me.

But Aleksandr didn't say a word, and silence settled on the kitchen. I relaxed.

"Why didn't I just call you?" Galina said at last, breaking the silence. "I feared you would not listen. I feared you would hang up on me. Was I wrong about that?"

GM did not reply.

"I tried to keep in contact with you," Galina said mournfully. "You didn't answer any of my letters or phone calls."

"I didn't answer you," GM said, "because you wanted to involve my granddaughter in your nonsense. You wanted to make her believe that nightmares are real."

"I wanted to *teach* her," Galina replied angrily.

"So that's what this is all about, then?" GM snapped. "You, in your great wisdom, have decided that the time has come for you to drag my granddaughter into your world of darkness and ignorance?"

"I did not choose the time, Annushka," Galina said. "It was chosen for me. I feared something like this would happen, and if I'd been working with Ekaterina all the time, maybe we could have prevented this."

I was startled to hear Galina call me by my Russian name—no one ever did that—it was almost as if the name weren't even mine. To my family I had always been Katie—my English father had been responsible for that.

"I don't want to hear your nonsense, Galina," GM said curtly.

5

"Annushka, you have to listen!" Galina cried. *"He's* free! You know who I mean—"

"You will not speak that name in my house!" GM shouted.

Just then the kettle began to whistle, and I jumped.

I heard GM get up, and the whistling soon stopped. There were other noises as GM clattered around, getting the tea ready.

No one spoke.

"I am sorry," Galina said softly, after some time had passed.

I heard GM's chair scrape as she sat down again.

"I will not discuss this if it upsets you," Galina added.

"You don't believe in the supernatural, do you, Mrs. Rost?" Aleksandr asked.

GM snorted. "The mischievous spirits and the vampires? No, I do not. Those are just stories designed to scare people—tales about the supernatural are nothing more than a way to spread fear."

"They aren't all mischievous spirits," Aleksandr said lightly. "They say the Leshi, for example, is actually quite a good fellow. Though you make an excellent point about fear—there are darker things than vampires in Krov."

"You are too young to believe in such foolishness," GM said wearily. "Why can't any of you from the old village have a normal conversation? Look at me. I started over here. I lead a safe, comfortable life now. Can't you do the same?"

"I heard you are a graphic designer," Galina said.

"Yes, I am," GM replied.

"I don't even know what that is," Galina said, and there was a note of wistfulness in her voice.

"There's so much that you miss," GM replied quickly. "How are you doing, Galina? How are you really? Are you happy? You know that in my heart I miss you. And don't you want good things for your son? How about you, Aleksandr? How are you?"

"Still unmarried. Ask my mother," Aleksandr said in amusement.

"Shut your mouth, Aleksandr," Galina snapped, her tone unexpectedly sharp. "Don't be a fool."

"Galina, why don't the two of you move somewhere else?" GM asked.

"We can't leave—"

GM broke in hurriedly. "I don't mean leave Russia. I mean leave the village—leave tiny little Krov. Move to Moscow. Or another big city. Russia is such a beautiful country. You don't have to stay in that dark, tiny corner of it. Move some place where there is life—where there are new things."

"Though you will not admit it," Galina said, "you know why I can't leave."

Silence settled on the kitchen once again.

"Annushka, there are lights on at the Mstislav mansion," Galina said after a time, her voice low and edged with fear. "The house has been deserted for a long time. You know when that house was last occupied—it was eleven years ago."

"Perhaps his son has decided to take over the place," GM said evenly. "It would be nice for someone to sweep out the cobwebs. It was a grand old mansion, and it should be restored to its former beauty. The house itself certainly never did anything wrong."

"They opened the old airfield two weeks ago and began fitting up a plane," Galina said. "That's what made us decide to come here."

GM was unimpressed. "So? It would be nice for everyone in the area to have a proper airfield. It might encourage good things."

"Annushka," Galina said urgently, "*his* house is lit up again. And it was *his* plane they were working on. You know the one I mean—he bought it when he first amassed his fortune."

"I saw his plane myself," Aleksandr interjected. "I believe he reached the U.S. ahead of us—it took us time to get our travel documents in order."

"Quiet, Aleksandr!" Galina snapped. "Annushka, please. It's *him*. He is *free*. And he will seek out—"

"Galina, I warned you not to bring this up." GM's tone was sharp.

"Annushka!" Galina cried.

"He's dead, Galina," GM said sternly. "Enough!"

"He's returned!"

"Nonsense!"

"Annushka! How can you say that? He killed your daughter!"

A chair scraped back violently.

"Superstition killed my daughter!" GM shouted.

"Annushka! You must listen!" Galina wailed.

"Get out of my house!" GM cried.

I heard porcelain shattering against a wall, and two more chairs scraped back.

I got to my feet.

I watched in shock as Galina and Aleksandr ran down the hall to the front door. GM came running after them.

Galina fumbled with the locks, and then she and Aleksandr escaped out into the night. GM ran after them.

I quickly followed.

The cold night air cut through my thin nightclothes as I hurried down the concrete driveway in front of the house.

GM was standing in the middle of the driveway, breathing hard. Strands of silver had worked their way free of her ponytail and settled in scattered array around her head, glinting softly in the moonlight.

Galina and Aleksandr jumped into a car that sat just behind GM's own. The engine roared to life, and the car took off, tires screeching.

I watched the car's red taillights disappear into the night, and then I glanced over at GM—I had never seen her so angry.

"GM, what's going on?" I asked.

She whirled around. She stared hard at me for a moment and then looked down at the silver cross she always wore. She wrapped her fingers around it and gripped it tightly.

"I'm sorry," GM said quietly. "I wanted to spare you all of that. I never should have let them in."

"Are you all right?" I asked. "Who were those people? Why did the woman—Galina?—why did she say a man killed my mother? I thought she died of a fever."

Anger blazed in GM's eyes. "Your mother *did* die of a fever. Galina doesn't know what she's talking about."

GM's expression softened as she continued to look at me. "Come back into the house, Katie. It's too cold out here."

She put her arm around my shoulders and guided me back toward the gold rectangle of light that streamed out of the still-open door.

I stopped suddenly. I'd thought for just a moment that I had seen a tall figure standing in the shadows near the house. I blinked and looked again.

The figure was gone.

"Is something wrong?" GM asked, looking around as if she feared that Galina and Aleksandr had returned.

"No, it's nothing. I thought I saw something, but it's gone now."

GM steered me firmly into the house and locked the door behind us. Then she guided me into the kitchen. "How about a hot drink?"

I looked around the room. Three of the kitchen chairs were standing awkwardly askew. On the kitchen table were two of GM's blue-and-white china cups. One of the cups lay on its side, its contents spilled on the table—a brown puddle on the white surface. I could see shards of a third cup littering the floor, and a brown stain ran down the far wall.

"Did you throw a cup of tea at those people?" I asked.

GM simply made a derisive sound and waved her hand. Then she went over and kneeled down to examine the broken teacup. I knew that she was very fond of that tea set, and she wasn't the type to lose her temper easily.

"GM, what made you so angry?" I asked.

She ignored my question. "It occurs to me now that it was a bad idea to bring you in here. I'm sorry you had to see this."

She straightened up and calmly retied her ponytail. Then she put her hands on her hips and looked over at me.

"I think this will all keep till morning. Never mind about that drink now. We've had enough excitement tonight. It's up to bed for both of us."

"GM!" I cried as frustration welled up within me. "You're acting like nothing happened!"

She gave me a puzzled, slightly wounded look, and I felt a wave of contrition wash over me—I wasn't used to shouting at her.

I went on more quietly. "Why won't you answer any of my questions?"

"I did answer one—about your mother," GM replied, averting her eyes.

I wasn't going to let her get away so easily. "No, you told me something I already knew—my mother died of a fever. You didn't tell me why anyone would believe she'd been murdered. That is what Galina was saying wasn't it? That a man from your old village had killed her? And why wouldn't you allow Galina to say his name?"

GM looked at me, and I could see a distant flicker of pain in her eyes.

She held out her hand. "If you will go upstairs with me, I will tell you a story. It will help to explain."

I hesitated. Too often, GM had distracted me when I had asked questions like these—she had diverted my attention from the past and sidestepped my questions without ever refusing to answer them outright. I feared she would talk around me again.

My questions would evaporate the way they always did.

"Please, Katie, come with me," GM said, her voice low and pleading. "You know the past is difficult for me."

I resigned myself and took GM's hand.

We went up to my room.

GM switched on the light. The lamp by my bed had a faded shade with yellow sunbursts on it. I'd kept it for years, refusing a new one when GM had wanted to redecorate. My mother and I had painted the shade together one summer long ago.

GM smoothed back the quilt on my bed. "Let me tuck you in." She sounded sad and tired.

After I had settled under the covers, GM sat down beside me.

"I will tell you something I have never told you before, Katie. The night your mother died—"

GM's voice quavered, and she stopped.

She composed herself and then went on.

"The night your mother died was the worst of all—for the fever, I mean. It had raged through her body, and she had reached a point at which she could no longer find comfort of any kind. She couldn't eat or drink; she couldn't sleep. She couldn't even close her eyes for more than a few moments to rest—she said closing them made the burning behind them worse. On that last night, she kept calling for your father, and of course, your poor father was already gone—dead in that terrible accident. She was crying out for him to protect you. Even in her delirium, she knew she wouldn't last long."

GM paused again. Her chin had begun to tremble.

She composed herself once more and went on in a low voice. "When I could make her understand who I was—when I could make her understand that I was her mother—she begged me to protect you. She said, 'Swear to me that you will always protect Katie.' She need hardly have asked for that—the desire to protect you had been in my heart since the day you were born. But I swore it to her then, and I swear it to you now. On my life, I will always protect you."

GM stared at me steadily as she said the words, and I felt tears stinging my eyes. Soon they began to fall.

"After I made my promise," GM said, "Nadya seemed to grow calmer. She asked to see you. I brought you in, and she kissed you on the forehead. You were sleeping and didn't wake. Then she sang her favorite piece of music—no words, just a hum. Do you remember it?"

I nodded. When I was a child, my mother had often sung the same melody to me. It was from a piece of music by Mussorgsky.

GM went on. "Not long after she finished singing, Nadya was gone. I swore to her that I would protect you, and I have. And I will. That's why I moved you out of the old village. That's why I moved you out of Russia right after your mother died. I had to get you as far away as I could from people like Galina. She is a good woman, but her thinking is trapped in the Dark Ages. She would warp your mind as she warped your mother's. She has nothing for you but superstition and shadows."

GM rose. "I love you, Katie. Believe me when I say there is *nothing* out there. There is nothing in the dark."

She pressed a kiss to my forehead, as she'd said my mother had once done, and then left the room, closing the door behind her. And I was left feeling less comforted rather than more so.

I was grateful to hear a story about my mother, even though it was painful—I could feel her love reaching out to me across the years. But as I had feared, GM hadn't actually answered any of my questions—instead she'd left me with more.

Why had she said there was nothing in the dark?

What was she afraid of?

Chapter Two

The next morning, I was awakened by the harsh, insistent beep of my alarm. I shut it off and then sat up, brushing the hair away from my face. I sat still for a long moment, unable to think clearly—my dreams were still fogging my mind. Something had come to me in those dreams and was still clinging to me now— it was the same strange longing that called to me every night.

For the first time, I had felt the night calling in my sleep.

And there was something else that was different, too. There had been a presence—a shadowy figure in my dreams.

Someone had invaded my mind in my sleep—I was sure of it.

But even as the thought occurred to me, I shook my head as if to escape from it—I knew the idea was crazy. I pushed the thought away forcefully.

I got out of bed then and found myself swaying dizzily. I was still tired after my too-eventful night, and my eyes were burning and puffy—probably because of the crying I'd done.

I walked to the bathroom and switched on the light.

I turned on the tap in the sink, and I splashed my face several times with cold water. I'd hoped the water would make me feel more awake, but instead it just made me shiver—and the water as it streamed down the drain sounded unnaturally loud.

I shut the water off, and another, more powerful shudder ran through me. The shudder was just passing off when I was hit suddenly by another wave of dizziness.

I feared for a moment that I was going to black out.

I placed my hands on either side of the sink and let my head fall forward. I took several deep, steadying breaths and willed myself to feel normal again.

After a moment, I felt better, and I raised my head. I gave myself a critical look in the mirror.

My face was a little paler than usual, but I didn't look nearly as bad as I felt. I pressed a hand to my forehead and then to my cheek. My skin was cool to the touch and not feverish. I was pretty sure I wasn't ill—that was reassuring at least.

My eyes, however, were a little red, and I leaned closer to examine them. As I did so, I was startled to see something flicker behind me, and I turned quickly to look.

But there was nothing behind me but a wall and a towel rack.

I figured my tired eyes were just playing tricks on me, and I turned back to the mirror.

As I peered at my reflection again, I saw another flicker of movement behind me, and this time I stared at it in the mirror. The flickering continued, and as I watched, it grew and coalesced into a dark shadow that hovered on the wall. I stared at the shadow steadily—it was definitely directly behind me.

I turned and looked over my shoulder. Nothing was there.

I turned back to the mirror—and I was startled to see that the shadow was still hovering just behind me in the glass.

I leaned closer. The shadow remained behind me in the mirror, and as I watched, it began to grow in size. It grew longer and wider, and then thicker and more substantial. Suddenly, there was a man standing behind me. I could see him very clearly over my shoulder— black hair, blue eyes—a handsome face set in harsh lines.

The look in the man's eyes was dangerous.

Panicked, I spun around.

No one was there.

I hurried out of the bathroom into the hall.

My first instinct was to tell GM about what I had seen, but I quickly discarded the idea. Did I really think I had just seen a man standing in my bathroom? Did I really want to tell GM that I had been hallucinating and upset her over nothing?

I took a deep breath and went back in.

The bathroom was empty, of course, and I peered warily into the mirror. The man was no longer there, and the glass reflected only my own face and the wall behind me. I leaned closer to the mirror, keeping my eyes fixed on the area over my shoulder.

Several long moments passed, and nothing strange appeared in the mirror—no shadow, no harsh-looking man.

I straightened up in relief—I had just been imagining things.

I quickly showered and dressed.

As I ran downstairs to breakfast, I could smell cinnamon and sugar, and I wondered what was going on. GM didn't usually approve of sweets.

When I entered the kitchen, I saw that all traces of the confrontation from the night before had been swept away, and GM was busy buttering slices of freshly baked bread.

I couldn't help smiling as I realized that GM had made cinnamon raisin bread for me—it was my favorite, but I didn't actually get to have it very often.

GM looked up at me, and I could see anxiety flicker in her eyes. She clearly felt bad about the scene last night and was trying to make up for it. I was doubly glad now that I hadn't told GM about my seeing things in the mirror—I didn't want her to feel any worse than she already did.

"Good morning, solnyshko," GM said. "Solnyshko" was her pet name for me—a Russian endearment meaning "little sun." "Did you sleep well?"

I pushed all thoughts of my hallucinations aside and did my best to appear unconcerned.

"Yes, thanks," I said. "How about you?"

"I always sleep well," she said, waving the knife she held. "It is hard to disturb a mind like mine."

I glanced at the cinnamon raisin bread. "Did you make this for me?"

"Can there be any doubt?" GM asked gruffly, pushing the plate of buttered bread toward me. "I know how much you like it."

"Thanks, GM."

I got out some milk, and we both sat down at the table. GM cut off two slices of bread for herself, and then she began poking raisins out of the bread with her knife. GM had a strong aversion to raisins—she only kept them in the house for me.

I was just reaching for my milk glass when an image of the man from the mirror suddenly flashed before me.

I pulled my hand back in alarm.

GM looked up at me. "Is something wrong?"

"It's—it's nothing."

"Are you sure?" GM asked, frowning. "You looked startled just now."

I took a deep breath and tried to appear calm.

"It's really nothing," I said. I finished up breakfast quickly and kissed GM on the cheek. "Thanks again."

I hurried to pull on my coat, and then I was out the door.

It was early October, just past my sixteenth birthday, and there was a definite chill in the air. As I walked down the driveway past GM's bright red sports car, the side mirror on the car caught my eye.

Against my better judgment, I paused and looked into the mirror.

For a moment, nothing happened. And then a shadow began to appear over my shoulder. Soon the shadow began to grow more substantial, spreading out and lengthening to reveal a man standing behind me—a man with dark hair, light eyes, and sharply defined features.

I cried out and spun around.

No one was standing behind me.

I looked back at the mirror, but the man was gone.

I hurried away from the car.

As I continued on my walk to school, I ordered myself not to panic. *Act normal*, I told myself. *Just act normal.*

I forced myself to think of the day ahead of me. I had a quiz in English today—which I hadn't studied for, thanks to the distracting night calling. Of course, I knew that Simon would say that I didn't need to study in order to do well.

I felt a sudden, strange tug on my heart as I thought of Simon. Was there something wrong between the two of us? I had a feeling that there was—but what it was exactly, I couldn't pin down.

I hurried on to school, feeling my spirits sinking steadily.

As I neared the fence that surrounded Elspeth's Grove High School, I spotted a brown-skinned, black-haired girl sitting on a picnic table, talking to a tall, pale boy with brown hair that fell over his eyes.

I smiled when I saw them, and the girl noticed me and waved. I was glad to see my best friend, Charisse, and her boyfriend, Branden. Somehow the sight of them made me feel as if everything were back to normal. Surely hallucinations couldn't exist in a place as normal as a schoolyard.

I hurried over to join them.

"Hey, Charisse. Hey, Branden," I said.

"Happy Monday," Branden replied gloomily. "Welcome to the beginning of our prison sentence for the week."

"Ignore him, Katie," Charisse said. "How was your weekend?"

"Pretty good," I said, hoping Charisse wouldn't ask for details. "How was yours?"

"It was—a weekend," Charisse replied, smiling. "Are you ready for the quiz in English?"

I glanced at her sharply. Charisse's smile was bright, but there was something distracted about her tone—it was almost as if she wanted to avoid talking about the weekend as much as I did.

"Don't remind me about the quiz," I said. "I'm really not ready for it."

"Don't worry, overachiever," Charisse said. "I'm sure you'll be fine."

Branden groaned suddenly. "The quiz. I forgot all about it." He sighed and slung his backpack over his shoulder. "I'd better get going."

Charisse looked up at him in surprise. "What? Why? Why are you leaving?"

Branden was rueful. "Katie may be able to get by on a quiz without studying, but I can't. I haven't even read the play yet. I'm going to get some reading done—someplace where there are fewer distractions. I can't study while you're around, gorgeous."

Charisse stood up to kiss him on the cheek. "Okay. I'll see you in first period."

Branden kissed her on the forehead and then loped away across the yard toward the school.

I smiled. "I'm guessing you guys didn't get a chance to talk about the quiz this weekend."

"No," Charisse said. Her voice grew dreamy. "We try not to deal with the real world too much when we're together. We were talking about other things."

"You know, sometimes you two are horrifyingly cute together," I said.

"Some people think you and Simon are pretty cute together, too," Charisse replied.

I felt a blush rise to my cheeks. "Simon and I are friends, Charisse. Close friends. But just friends. You know that."

"I know he likes you. And I think you like him, too. You just haven't admitted that to yourself, Katie."

I felt another strong tug on my heart and an even stronger desire to end this particular line of conversation.

I made no reply, and Charisse didn't pursue the topic any further.

She sat down again, and I stood beside her silently.

After a moment, I glanced at her face. The preoccupation I'd noticed before was still there.

"Charisse, is something wrong? Is it the audition you had Friday?" I paused. "You didn't get the part."

"No, I got the part," Charisse said. "I'll be appearing in our high school's little fall production."

"That's great," I said. "Isn't it?"

"Yes, it's great," Charisse replied. "But it doesn't seem so important right now."

I looked at her. "What do you mean?"

"It's my parents," she said. "They've split up."

"What?" I said, startled.

Charisse sighed—the sound was more wistful than anything else. "They're getting a divorce, Katie."

"Are you serious?"

"Of course I'm serious."

"Oh, Charisse," I said. "I'm so sorry."

I sat down next to her. "Are you okay?"

Charisse gave me an odd little smile. "I'm fine."

"What happened?" I asked.

Charisse sighed again and shrugged. "In a way, it was nothing out of the ordinary—my parents have always argued a lot. They're both stubborn—neither one of them ever backs down. But you know that already."

I nodded. I did know that—but I'd had no idea that things had progressed to this point.

Charisse continued. "So, after yet another argument, my dad left last night. He went to stay at a hotel until he can find an apartment. My mom and I are going to stay at the house."

"I'm sorry, Charisse," I said again. "This must be killing you."

Charisse looked up at the sky. "That's the weird part—I'm okay with it. My parents have been fighting my whole life, and I think they may actually be better off apart. But people are supposed to be devastated when their parents break up, and I'm not. I don't even want to talk about it, really. But I did want you to be the first to know that it happened—you're my best friend."

I was surprised by Charisse's attitude, and I didn't know how to respond. I cast about for a few moments, trying to think of what to say.

"I suppose you have a right to your feelings," I said at last, "whatever they are."

Charisse gave me a wan smile. "There's no need to worry about me, Katie. I'm completely fine with everything."

I glanced around again, once more at a loss for words, and I caught sight of a familiar blond head pushing determinedly toward us through a crowd.

It was Simon. His pale brows were drawn together, and his expression was stormy.

Charisse looked up at him as he approached. "Wow. Simon does not look happy. Did you guys have a fight or something?"

"Of course not," I said. "And you know we're just friends."

I stood up as Simon reached us. He glanced at Charisse and gave her a tight-lipped smile. "Hey."

He turned to me and pushed his hands into the pockets of his jeans, hunching his shoulders. "Can we talk? Alone?"

I glanced uncertainly at Charisse. "Will you be okay?"

Charisse smiled. "Of course. Like I said, I'm all right with it all. I'll see you in English class."

Simon waited with his head bowed while Charisse walked away.

When she was gone, he raised his face to mine—he looked miserable.

"Simon?" I prompted.

"It's my brother, James," he said abruptly. "He's in trouble. *Real* trouble. This time, he's going to jail."

I was startled. Simon's older brother had a habit of getting into trouble with the law, but this sounded extreme—even for him. "Jail? You really think he's going to jail?"

Simon nodded grimly. A muscle in his temple worked as he clenched his jaw. "It's bad. It's about as bad as it can be. The cops came to the house last night looking for him. My parents ordered me to go to my room and stay there. I couldn't hear everything, but I heard enough."

Simon stopped and looked over his shoulder. Then he went on in a low voice.

"Somebody robbed a liquor store last night and shot the clerk. The police think it was James."

Cold fear washed over me. "He shot the clerk? Did he—"

I stopped suddenly. I didn't want to finish the question. I was afraid of what the answer might be.

Simon smiled bitterly. "Did he kill the clerk? No. The clerk is in the hospital in stable condition. They think he'll be okay. Which doesn't change the fact that James shot somebody."

"You said the police *think* it was James," I said.

Simon nodded.

"But they don't know for sure?"

"No—he's gone missing. Nobody's been able to question him."

"Then we don't know it was James yet," I said. "Maybe the police are onto the wrong person."

Simon looked at me miserably. "Then why didn't he come home last night? The police don't know where he is. *We* don't know where he is. Katie, if he's innocent, where is he?"

"Don't assume the worst just yet." I tried to sound reassuring— it was all I could really do. "Maybe James just happened to be near the liquor store at the wrong time. Maybe he was afraid he'd be accused of being involved in the crime when he really wasn't. With a record like his, you can understand how he might get nervous and take off."

Simon nodded, and I could see the taut lines of his face begin to relax.

I went on in the same soothing tone. "James has been trying hard lately to pull his life together. You and I have both seen how he's changed. Just wait till you hear his side of things before you make up your mind."

Simon took in a deep breath and let it out heavily. His expression relaxed even further. "You're right. James has been doing better lately. Maybe it is just a misunderstanding."

"Simon!" A shrill voice suddenly sounded in my ear, startling me.

A girl was wedging herself in between Simon and me, forcing both of us to step back to give her room.

I soon found myself staring at a dark, glossy ponytail.

"Hey, Simon! How are you?" the girl chattered happily. "Are we still on for lunch today?"

I sighed inwardly as I realized that I recognized the voice.

"Irina?" I said. "Is that you?"

The girl spun around. It was, as I had suspected, Irina Neverov. Her dark eyes narrowed maliciously as she looked at me. "Oh, Katie! I didn't see you there. Simon and I have a few things to discuss. Would you mind giving us some time alone?" Irina flashed a smile. "Thanks so much."

I wondered, as I had before, how things had gotten to this point. Irina and I had been good friends once long ago, but now that we were older, we had somehow become enemies.

And as far as I could see, the animosity was all on her side.

Simon broke in firmly. "I'll see you at lunch like I said, Irina. Katie, would you walk inside with me?"

"Sure," I said, glancing at Irina.

She was glaring at me.

Simon took my elbow and steered me across the yard and into the school. He didn't say anything, and I could see that the tension in his jaw had returned.

The two of us continued to walk in silence until we reached my locker, and then I glanced up at Simon. His face had gone impassive.

"Simon?" I said. "I assumed you still wanted to talk, but you haven't said a word."

"There's nothing going on between Irina and me," Simon blurted out. "The two of us were assigned to be partners for a science project—I didn't get to choose. We're going to meet today at lunch, and then we'll meet after school for part of the week. You have nothing to worry about—you're all that matters to me. You have to know that by now."

"Simon, you don't owe me an explanation," I said. "You have the right to be friends with anyone you want."

Simon's expression grew pained. "But Irina and I aren't friends. That's what I'm trying to tell you. We're having lunch together because we're using the time to work on the project. That's all. I should have told you earlier, but I know you and Irina don't get along. I don't want you to think there's anything in it. You believe me, don't you?"

"Simon, of course I believe you."

He looked deeply relieved. "I'll make it up to you, I promise."

"Simon, you don't owe me anything," I said. "It's okay if you want to have lunch with other people sometimes."

"I insist on making it up to you," Simon said, smiling and backing into the crowd of students in the hall. "I'll see you later, Katie."

I watched Simon go. He'd been afraid I'd be jealous—but even after I'd heard he was going to have lunch with another girl, I'd felt no stab of envy.

I liked Simon. I really did. But for me it was definitely a friendship.

All the same, for some reason, I couldn't help but feel a twinge of regret.

By the time I made it to second-period English, I was still thinking about Simon. As I walked in, I was so lost in thought that I didn't realize at first that the room was buzzing about something. I reached my desk and was surprised to see Irina sitting on it, holding court with her friends, Bryony and Annamaria.

"We're meeting practically every day after school this week," Irina said in a loud, clear voice. "Simon says it's just for the project, but I actually think he has an ulterior motive. I think he's using the project as an excuse to get to know me better."

Bryony and Annamaria giggled.

Irina darted a furtive glance at me. "You know, when we're together, Simon can't take his eyes off me. I would say he's working up the courage to ask me out."

I glanced around, and I realized that Irina was attracting the attention of the entire class. People were whispering and staring, and I got the uncomfortable feeling that everyone was eager to see if an argument would break out.

Apparently everyone else thought that Simon and I were a couple, too.

"Excuse me, Irina," I said. "You're sitting on my desk. I wouldn't mind sitting somewhere else, but you know how Mr. Del Gatto feels about his seating chart."

Irina blinked in surprise. That was clearly not the reaction she'd expected.

Several people in the class giggled.

Irina gave me a bright smile. "Oh, Katie. I didn't see you there. It's funny how you seem to be invisible today."

There were several more snickers, and Irina shot me a triumphant look.

I stood where I was, staring at Irina steadily.

At first, Irina returned my gaze defiantly, but as our staring contest stretched on, Irina's gaze faltered, and a flush crept up under her olive coloring.

She slid off my desk and walked away with the eyes of the class upon her. I sat down at my desk. With the spectacle over, the class lost interest in us and went back to talking about other things.

A few moments later, Mr. Del Gatto walked in. Just as he was turning to close the door, Branden and Charisse scurried into the room.

"Miss Graebel, Mr. McKenna," Mr. Del Gatto said, "so good of you to join us."

Branden and Charisse mumbled their apologies and went to their seats.

"All right, ladies and gentlemen, come to order, please," Mr. Del Gatto said.

The class quieted down, and Mr. Del Gatto strode toward his desk at the front of the room. He pulled out a stack of papers and set them on the desk with a slap.

"Ladies and gentlemen, I'm going to call roll, and then I'm going to pass out the quiz. Nothing on the quiz should be a surprise to you. The topic is Lydia Grace's play, *The Maid and the Moon*. We had a lecture about it on Friday, and of course, you should have read the material—though I have my doubts about whether or not all of you have done so."

There was a collective groan from the room.

"There's no use in your complaining to me," Mr. Del Gatto said. "I gave you plenty of warning. Put away your books. You have a few moments to say your prayers while I take attendance."

While Mr. Del Gatto called out names, I took a quick mental inventory of what I knew about the play. The *Maid and the Moon* was a dramatization of the life of our town's founder, Elspeth Quick, who had been born in the early eighteenth century in a small community in New England. As a teenager, she had been falsely accused of witchcraft and had fled south to elude an angry mob bent on her destruction. Her true love, Christian Miller, followed her and eventually caught up with her. Following a thin thread of silver moonlight on an otherwise dark night, Elspeth guided them through the forest to a fresh spring that ran through a grove of fruit trees. The two of them spent the summer in the grove and waited out their pursuers. Eventually, they settled in for good, and a town grew up around them.

Despite Elspeth's eventual prosperity, however, rumors of witchcraft continued to cling to her all of her life, and the grove where she and Christian had hidden was said to be haunted—

Mr. Del Gatto slapped a quiz facedown on my desk, and my reverie was broken.

Before long, everyone had a copy of the quiz, and Mr. Del Gatto moved back to the front of the room.

"In compensation for your great suffering today, after the quiz we will watch a filmed version of the play. While watching the film, the quick amongst you will realize which questions you answered incorrectly. Those less fortunate will watch in blissful ignorance, noticing nothing."

Mr. Del Gatto glanced up at the clock above the door. "Turn your quizzes over. You have twenty-five minutes."

I flipped the sheet over and scanned the questions quickly. I was relieved to see that there were no questions I couldn't handle. I got to work.

Shortly before time was called, I set my pencil down and leaned back in my chair, glad to be finished.

No sooner had I done so than I was seized by a sudden, strong desire to put my head down on the desk and go to sleep. My mind began to grow foggy—and I began to feel as if I were sinking—as if something were pulling me down into unconsciousness.

"Time's up!" Mr. Del Gatto shouted.

I shook my head, trying to clear it.

Mr. Del Gatto walked around the room, collecting the quizzes.

"I expect to give my red pen quite a workout tonight."

Mr. Del Gatto moved back to the front of the room and deposited the quiz papers on his desk. Then he wheeled a TV and DVD player out of a corner to the front of the room. He switched on the movie.

"Mr. McKenna, would you do us the honor of switching off the lights?"

Branden extinguished the lights, and the room was plunged into semi-gloom.

I propped my chin on my hand and tried to ignore the unnatural feeling that was pulling at me. I forced myself to concentrate on the play.

As the minutes passed, I began to feel better. I watched the actors on the screen, and I felt myself being drawn into the drama.

Just as I was starting to relax, I spotted a dark shadow in one corner of the TV screen. As I watched, the shadow began to grow in size and move around the screen.

I wondered if something was wrong with the TV.

I turned and glanced around the room. All eyes were facing forward, and all the faces around me appeared to be untroubled. No one else seemed to have noticed that anything was wrong with the picture.

I turned back to the movie. The shadow continued to move around the screen, growing darker and more distinct. I watched it, feeling a chill run through me. Suddenly the shadow coalesced into a clear shape. It was a man—the same man I had seen looking over my shoulder in the mirror at home.

I bit my lip to stop myself from crying out and jumped to my feet.

I stumbled toward the door. "Mr. Del Gatto, I don't feel very well."

"Go to the bathroom or to the nurse—wherever you need to go," Mr. Del Gatto said, concerned. "Just take the hall pass so no one stops you."

I clutched at the little block of wood that served as the hall pass, and I hurried out of the room.

I ran until I reached the nearest girls' bathroom. Then I pushed the door open and stumbled inside, sinking to the floor in a corner, out of sight of the mirrors.

I closed my eyes, and the man's face rose again in my memory. There was no doubt in my mind that I had just seen him in the TV screen. I had now seen him in three different places.

I opened my eyes and ran my fingers through my hair. What was happening to me?

I leaned my head back against the wall. Whatever it was that was going on, I knew I couldn't tell anyone about it—everyone, GM included—would think I was crazy.

I would have to figure it out on my own.

Using the wall for support, I climbed to my feet. I eyed the row of mirrors and sinks in front of me warily.

I would have to look.

I took a few tentative steps toward the mirrors, and then I forced myself to move quickly. I rushed forward and gripped the edge of a sink for support.

I kept my head down.

After a moment, I raised my head and looked into the mirror. Only my own eyes stared back at me. I was alone in the smooth sheet of glass.

I breathed in and out slowly and released my grip on the sink. I looked down at my hands.

I was shaking.

I heard the door to the bathroom creak open, and I spun around.

Irina stalked into the bathroom, her eyes sweeping the room suspiciously.

"Katie, are you in here? Mr. Del Gatto sent me to find you. He says you're ill."

She sounded like she didn't entirely believe it.

Irina caught sight of me, and her eyes widened in surprise. "You're really pale, Katie. Are you all right?"

My head was swimming, but I gave her a reassuring smile. "Yes, I think so."

Irina took a step closer, scrutinizing my face. "Are you sure? You don't look so good."

I was surprised to see genuine concern in Irina's dark eyes. "I'm not ill," I said. "I just had kind of a spell."

Irina frowned. "What do you mean by a 'spell'?"

"I don't know exactly," I admitted. "But it's happened several times already."

"Maybe you should see a doctor."

I ran a hand across my forehead unsteadily. "I think you may be right."

"Are you well enough to go back to class?" Irina asked. "I can walk you to the nurse instead if you're not up to it."

"I can go back to class," I replied.

The two of us walked out of the bathroom together.

As we made our way back to class, I felt weak and unsure of my footing. Irina kept a watchful eye on me, as if she feared I would collapse.

When we reached the door to Mr. Del Gatto's class, I stopped and turned to Irina.

"Thanks for looking out for me," I said.

Irina's eyes narrowed warily, and she stiffened. She opened the door and swept into the classroom without a word.

I followed her rigid back into the room.

"How are you feeling, Katie?" Mr. Del Gatto asked.

"I'm okay now," I said—though I wasn't entirely sure that was true.

I did know that I wouldn't be able to watch any more of the movie—I didn't want to see that strange man's face again.

The room was dark, and I could hear the actors on the TV speaking their lines. I hurried to my seat and covered my eyes with my hands as surreptitiously as I could.

I had no idea what I was going to do.

Chapter Three

At the end of class, someone tapped me on the shoulder. I jumped.

I looked up to see Charisse standing next to my desk. The lights were on now.

"It's okay, Katie. The movie has been turned off." Charisse was staring at me in concern. "Why did you have your eyes covered? Are you all right?"

"I'm okay." I began gathering up my things quickly. "Let's just get out of here."

"I can take you home if you aren't feeling well," Charisse said. "You don't look so good right now."

"No, I'm fine," I replied.

We walked out into the hall. Charisse was eyeing me just as Irina had—as if I were in imminent danger of collapse.

I made an effort to smile. "I'm better, really."

"What happened in the middle of the movie?" Charisse asked. "Why did you run out of class like that?"

I knew I couldn't tell Charisse that I was losing my mind. "I—I suddenly felt very ill. But luckily, it wore off."

I figured it would be a good idea to change the subject—I didn't want to discuss the weird things that were happening to me right now.

"So where were you and Branden at the beginning of class? It's not like you guys to cut it so close. You were almost late, and you know that's an automatic detention."

Charisse smiled. "Branden and I had something to discuss—something very important."

"About the quiz?"

Charisse's smile deepened. "No."

"Then what was it?"

"I'll tell you later. Right now, it's a secret."

"Charisse!"

"I'll tell you, I promise. I'm not trying to be mysterious. It's just that I told Branden I wouldn't tell anybody until we get everything ready."

"You know you're only making me want to know even more."

Charisse laughed. "The news will be worth the wait, trust me."

We'd come to a parting of the ways in the hallway, and Charisse paused and looked at me closely. "Are you sure you're okay?"

"Yes, I'm fine."

Charisse continued to stare at me.

"Really, Charisse," I said. "I'm fine."

"All right," Charisse said. "I'll see you at lunch. If you still aren't looking good then, I am definitely taking you home."

I spent the next two classes avoiding glass or anything that could hold a reflection. By the time I made my way into the cafeteria for lunch, I was still a little rattled, but I was feeling close to normal again.

My head was much clearer, and I could finally think straight.

I went through the line, and I spotted Charisse and Branden at a table nearby. I began to walk toward them.

Someone stepped into my path, and I looked up to see Simon.

He held up a small envelope. "This is for you."

I looked at the envelope, puzzled. "Thanks."

Simon continued on his way toward a table where Irina sat waiting for him, beaming.

I went over to join Charisse and Branden.

Charisse looked up as I sat down. "I'm glad to see you're looking better."

"I'm definitely feeling better, thanks."

"So what happened to you in English class?" Branden asked. "It looked like you were going to explode."

Charisse frowned and kicked him under the table.

"Hey," Branden said. "There's no need for violence."

"There is as long as you say silly things," Charisse replied.

Branden and Charisse continued to argue good-naturedly, so I opened Simon's envelope, knowing I wouldn't be observed.

I pulled out a card with a big red heart on the front. On the inside Simon had written, "I'm thinking only of you."

I glanced up, looking for Simon. I spied his table and discovered that he was already watching me. When I caught his eye, he smiled and waved.

I smiled back. The card was really thoughtful, and so was Simon himself. I felt a rush of affection for him.

I made it through the rest of the day without any further disturbing visions, and I was in a relatively good frame of mind as I walked home.

When I reached the house, GM was already there as usual—she ran her graphic design business out of our home. But I didn't say anything to her about my strange day at school—I knew she'd be horrified if I told her I'd been seeing things that weren't there. Instead, I hurried up to my room.

I figured I would try to do some research online.

I thought back to the two strange visitors we'd had the other night—the ones GM had chased off. I didn't really know who they were or what it was they'd wanted with us, but they'd both been from Krov, Russia, and they'd both talked about legends. And both my mother and I had been born in Krov, and apparently both of us had seen strange things.

Maybe I could find out something about the visions—and maybe there was a way to stop them from happening.

I searched online for Krov, but all I found was frustration. Not only was there nothing online about the legends or folklore of Krov, there was nothing online about Krov at all.

It was as if the town of Krov didn't exist.

I thought back to what the man—Aleksandr—had said in the kitchen. He'd mentioned spirits, vampires, and something called the Leshi. Searching on spirits and vampires brought up thousands and thousands of results—more than I could possibly sift through. I did read some of them, but none of them seemed to be related to my situation.

Searching on the Leshi simply told me that he was a Russian nature spirit—a green-haired guardian of forests and animals who could change his appearance. Apparently when impersonating a human, the Leshi had unusually bright eyes and wore his shoes on backward. As Aleksandr had said, the Leshi seemed to be a good fellow, but he didn't seem to have anything to do with me.

I did a final search on visions, but that search had more results than I could realistically go through, too. I read through what felt like hundreds of entries without finding anything that sounded like what was happening to me.

I decided to give up on my research.

I sat back in my chair and sighed. There really didn't seem to be any information available on people from Krov who had visions.

I began to wonder—could I have imagined the visions? Maybe I just needed to get some rest and things would get better.

I got started on my homework, and I was able to work for several hours without interruption. When I went down to dinner later that evening, I was feeling clear-minded and even a little relaxed.

GM didn't seem to notice that anything was wrong with me, and I began to relax even further. Maybe everything was going to go back to normal.

Right after dinner, I received a text from Simon saying that James had returned home, and everything was fine—he would give me the details tomorrow.

I was deeply relieved.

As the evening wore on, the night calling remained at bay, allowing me to concentrate on my homework and finish it properly.

I went to bed feeling more normal than I had in weeks.

In the morning, I awoke with the alarm, and I felt a stab of nervousness as I approached the bathroom. But no shadows or strange men appeared in my mirror, and I was able to finish my morning routine without anything unusual happening.

I thought longingly that I could get used to that.

I was in a cautiously good mood as I made my way to school, and as I entered the schoolyard, I spotted Charisse and Branden at their usual picnic table. Charisse was sitting, and Branden was standing, and they were leaning their foreheads together with their hands intertwined.

I decided not to bother them—they didn't look like they were in the mood for conversation.

I turned away from them, looking for Simon. As I did so, I was startled to spot someone who was familiar in exactly the wrong way.

Just behind a small group of students was a dark-haired, blue-eyed man.

It was the man I had seen in the mirror.

In the flesh he was taller and younger than he had appeared in the mirror—he was actually only a year or two older than I was. But his features were still set in harsh lines, and the look in his eyes was still dangerous.

His gaze met mine, and I saw anger flash in his eyes.

A stab of fear ran through me, but I started toward him anyway. Whoever he was, I was going to find out what was going on.

"Katie!"

A familiar voice called my name, and I turned to see Simon walking toward me, grinning.

I turned back quickly, looking over the crowd.

The man from the mirror was gone.

"Who are you looking for?" Simon asked, coming up to stand beside me.

"No one," I said, but I couldn't help glancing back at the spot where the man had been standing. He was still nowhere to be seen.

Could I have been hallucinating?

"So, James is okay," Simon said.

I turned back to him. He was still grinning and didn't seem to have noticed that anything was wrong. I pushed my fears aside.

"I was really happy to get your text last night," I said, making an effort to appear normal. "James is really all right?"

"Yeah." Simon sighed in relief. "It was a pretty weird set of circumstances, but he made it home safely last night. And we know for a fact that he didn't shoot anybody. He's even back at school today. We drove in together."

"I'm so glad to hear that, Simon. What happened?"

"Well, like I said, it was kind of weird. You know Derek Finlay?"

"The guy who takes all the photographs? He's a senior?"

"Yeah, that's the one. He and James are friends, and James went out with him on Sunday night to help with something called a 'mentored advanced project' that Derek has been working on."

"That's the night of the liquor store robbery?" I said.

"Yeah. James and Derek went out to the forest—to that old fruit grove—to take some photos. Supposedly, there's been some paranormal activity in the area. They wanted to see if they could photograph something cool. You know the place—it's the spot where they say that witch Elspeth hid before she founded the town."

"Elspeth wasn't a witch," I protested. "That was narrow-minded superstition on the part of her accusers."

Simon smiled. "Okay, then—so she wasn't a witch. Whatever she was, James and Derek went to her original hiding place in the Old Grove. They found two men in the grove already, and they were standing in front of a huge bonfire. One of the guys was dressed pretty normally, but the other was wearing a ton of furs—he even had a fur hood that covered his face. James and Derek just watched the two men for a few minutes, trying to figure out what to do about the fire. While they were watching, the guy in the furs suddenly took off and ran into the woods, and then the other guy took off after him. James and Derek chased them—you know, trying to get them to come back and put out the fire. But they couldn't catch them, so they went back to try to put out the fire themselves. And that's when the fire department showed up. Followed by the police."

"And the police showed up just in time to get the wrong impression," I said.

Simon smiled ruefully. "Exactly. A woman saw the fire and called the police. And they caught James and Derek with the fire and didn't believe them when they said they hadn't set it. So, the two of them stayed in a holding cell overnight."

"Overnight?" I asked. "They didn't call your parents or Derek's? They just let you guys worry?"

Simon shrugged. "They're both eighteen, and they were both embarrassed. They didn't want anybody to know they'd been hauled in, so they didn't call anyone. On Monday, the woman who originally called the police came in and said they weren't the two she saw start the fire. She described the normal guy and the one in the furs. James and Derek were free."

"In that case, James wasn't anywhere near the liquor store robbery Sunday night," I said.

"Nope."

"Why did they think it was James, then?"

"The guy who shot the clerk was about the same height and weight as James and was wearing a ski mask. And James had been in there several times in the past trying to buy alcohol and had been turned away for being underage. The last time he was thrown out—which was some time ago—he'd gotten really angry and had made threats. The clerk just kind of guessed."

"That's quite a guess," I said. "But I don't understand—if the police had James in custody already for the fire, why were they out looking for him in connection with the liquor store robbery?"

"The state police are the ones who arrested James and Derek in the forest—the forest is a state landmark or something, so it's under their jurisdiction. The county police are the ones who were called about the liquor store robbery. So, it was two separate groups of police who were involved. And since the state police can vouch for James's whereabouts, the county police know for a fact that he's innocent."

"Wow—that really is a weird set of circumstances," I said. "You and your parents must be so relieved."

Simon ran a hand over his hair. "We are. Believe me. Oh, and get this. There was a break-in here at the school on Saturday night. Someone broke into the main office and stole all of the permanent records. Whoever did it broke into the library, too, and stole all the yearbooks."

"Someone stole all of the yearbooks?" I said. "Who would want them? And why didn't anybody tell us? I didn't hear anything about the school being broken into."

"Yeah, well, the school's trying to keep it quiet. I only I heard about it because the police came by again last night to question James about it. They didn't have anything definite—they thought maybe he was trying to get rid of his permanent record or something. Of course, the records are all kept electronically, too, so nothing's really gone. The paper stuff's just backup for people who like things done the old-fashioned way."

I had to shake my head. "This is starting to get ridiculous. James is hardly the only troublemaker in town."

Simon gave me an injured look.

"Sorry," I said. "He's hardly the only former troublemaker in town. Which group of police came looking for him this time?"

"It was county again. But James was with me Saturday night. I was free since you were busy."

I felt a momentary twinge of regret, and Simon continued.

"James and I went out for pizza, and then we came home and played a video game—*Realms of Night*. We could even tell the police exactly where we left off in the game. Our parents were home, too."

"Then James has solid alibis for the Saturday and Sunday night robberies here in Elspeth's Grove."

"Yeah, we're all pretty grateful for that. James has been doing so well lately that we don't want to see anything knock him off track."

Just then the first bell rang, warning us that it was time to head inside for homeroom.

I glanced back at Charisse and Branden.

The two of them remained as before, with foreheads touching and fingers intertwined. As far as I could tell, they hadn't moved at all.

I turned back to Simon. "I think we should leave our two lovebirds over there alone. I have a feeling they'll make it in on time somehow."

Simon glanced back at them, and then looked at me. There was a strange expression on his face.

"They look happy," he said.

I felt uncomfortable under his gaze. "They do."

I looked away quickly.

Simon and I walked into school together, and he followed me as I went to my locker.

"I still have to make it up to you for missing lunch yesterday," Simon said.

"Simon—" I began.

"I insist." He walked off, grinning.

I rested my forehead against the cool metal of my locker and felt another twinge of regret. I liked being with Simon—a lot. But what

I felt for him was warm and comfortable rather than all-consuming. It was certainly nothing like what was going on between Branden and Charisse.

My mind kept drifting back to Simon throughout the morning, and it wasn't until I was on my way to second-period English that I remembered I had a problem.

I paused before the classroom door.

We were scheduled to watch the second half of the Lydia Grace play today. We'd only made it through the first half yesterday.

A flash of panic ran through me. I didn't want to see the strange man in the TV screen again—especially not after I'd hallucinated seeing him out in the schoolyard today. What if I saw him again—what would I do?

I ordered myself not to panic, no matter what happened.

Then I went into the classroom.

As I walked to my seat, I was surprised to see a strange man sitting at Mr. Del Gatto's desk—but it wasn't the one I'd feared seeing. The man at the desk was clearly a substitute teacher. He was young, and his hair was so sleek and flattened with gel that it was hard to tell what color it was. He had a deep tan and wore a large, ostentatious ring with a red stone in it.

Looking at him, I felt my heart sink further. If he was indeed a substitute for Mr. Del Gatto, not only were we going to finish out the play—which wouldn't last the entire period—we might even start another movie so that he wouldn't have to teach anything.

I wasn't going to be free of the TV screen for the entire period.

As I sat down at my desk, the sub looked up at me and flashed me a bright, white smile. I looked away. The man was giving off a decidedly oily vibe.

I glanced around the room. Charisse and Branden hadn't arrived yet, and I figured that the two of them would come very close to being late again. I wondered if the sub was the forgiving type, or the kind who gave out detentions to let everybody know they wouldn't get around him.

I glanced over at the sub and found he was staring at me. I quickly looked away again.

I became very interested in the rest of the classroom.

Turning in my seat, I saw Irina standing by the door, making a show of talking to Bryony and Annamaria, and playing with the silky white scarf that she wore. I thought for a moment that they might be talking about me, but they glanced at the teacher's desk several times and giggled. I realized that they were actually interested in the sub.

For his part, the sub was still looking at me.

I turned back around in my seat, feeling his eyes on me, and I opened a book and hid myself behind it.

I couldn't wait for English class to be over.

Eventually the bell rang, and the sub got up and closed the door. I glanced around quickly. Charisse had made it in on time, but Branden hadn't. His seat was empty.

The sub walked up to the board at the front of the room and wrote "MR. HIGHTOWER," while his big red ring winked at the class. Then he turned to face the room.

He smiled, revealing his gleaming teeth.

"Folks, as you can see, I'm Mr. Hightower. I'll be subbing for Mr. Del Gatto for the next few days. He's going to be out for a little while."

I felt my spirits sink. Mr. Del Gatto must be really sick—and we were going to be stuck with the shiny new sub.

"Now, unfortunately, I'm going to have to ask you to call me Mr. Hightower. School rules. But if you guys were in college, you could call me 'Tim.' And honestly, you guys look a lot more like college students than high school kids to me."

An appreciative murmur rippled through the class.

Mr. Hightower continued. "Since you guys are so sophisticated, I'm going to skip taking roll—they don't always take it in college. And just so you know, I'm likely to skip it tomorrow, too." He winked at the class. "I understand from Mr. Del Gatto's notes that you're finishing up watching a play for the first part of class today. I have to say, you're making it really easy on the new guy."

The class laughed.

Mr. Hightower wheeled the TV and DVD player to the front of the room in one swift movement. Then he flicked them both on and walked to the back of the room to turn out the lights.

I braced myself for what I might see in the screen.

I could feel my heart pounding as the movie resumed, and the actors recited their lines. I waited, on edge, and watched. But no shadows appeared, and there were no faces that did not belong.

As time passed, I began to relax, and the movie continued to run its course. Before I knew it, the play was over, and Mr. Hightower had turned the lights on again.

I blinked in the sudden brightness and took a deep breath. I hadn't seen a single thing in the TV screen that shouldn't have been there.

I was unbelievably relieved.

Mr. Hightower returned to the front of the room and addressed the class. "Folks, we still have some time remaining together, but I have no specific instructions for the rest of this class. So, I propose that we make the rest of the period a free period. But you guys have to promise to keep the noise level down to a dull roar."

A ripple of laughter ran through the class.

Most people began to talk then, and there was rustling and some low laughter as the class relaxed. I got out my Social Studies book and began to read—I had a feeling we wouldn't be doing much work in English class for the next few days.

At long last the bell rang, and I jumped up and swept my stuff into my backpack.

Mr. Hightower's voice rose above the clamor as everyone began to pack up and file out.

"Katie Wickliff, can I see you for a moment?"

I froze. The last thing I wanted to do was talk to the unctuous Mr. Hightower. I pulled on my backpack, fixed a polite smile on my face, and approached his desk.

"You wanted to see me, Mr. Hightower?"

Mr. Hightower gave me another of his gleaming smiles. "You look worried, Katie—don't be. I wanted to tell you something good. Mr. Del Gatto told me that you're one of his favorite students."

Inwardly, I doubted it. If Mr. Del Gatto were sick enough that he was going to be out for several days, I didn't think his students would be on his mind much.

Mr. Hightower went on. "He said you're one of his favorite students because you're one of his best." He leaned forward and rested his elbows on the desk, lowering his voice confidentially. "In fact, he said you're one of his best ever. Since we'll have a few days without Mr. Del Gatto, how would you like to do some extra credit?"

I eyed the man in front of me carefully. His voice was friendly, flattering, but there was something watchful about him.

"What kind of extra credit?" I asked.

Mr. Hightower turned the big ring on his finger in a complete revolution. I watched as the red stone disappeared from view and then made its reappearance.

"You live with your grandmother, right?" Mr. Hightower said.

I nodded, but the question made me feel uneasy.

"Anna Rost?" he said.

I nodded again. I really didn't want to answer his questions— and nodding was easier than speaking.

"Well, everyone knows your lovely grandmother is from Russia. Since your class is doing a unit on local writers and stories, why don't you ask her if there are any old stories from her hometown that she remembers. You could write an essay on that. Does that sound like fun?"

Mr. Hightower was staring at me steadily.

I was growing more uncomfortable by the second. "I don't think so, Mr. Hightower."

Mr. Hightower nodded and smiled—this time concealing his dazzling teeth. "I understand. A great student like you must have a pretty busy schedule. Let me know if you change your mind. The offer's open all week."

I nodded again, and Mr. Hightower unleashed his brilliant grin. "I always like to encourage the brightest students."

I turned to go, and I could see Charisse waiting for me by my desk. Irina was standing just behind her, glaring at me.

As I walked toward Charisse, Irina sailed past me, flinging her scarf over her shoulder.

"Oh, Mr. Hightower," Irina said. "I have a question for you."

"Shoot, kiddo," he replied amiably.

"What did Mr. Hightower want?" Charisse asked as I reached her.

"Let's just get out of here," I said, moving toward the door.

Feeling someone's eyes on me, I glanced over my shoulder. Mr. Hightower was watching me as he listened to Irina.

I turned away quickly.

As we walked out into the hall, Charisse touched my arm. "Katie, you look really freaked out. What happened with Mr. Hightower?"

Now that we were out with the chattering mass of students, I began to feel a little silly. "Nothing really. Mr. Hightower just offered me some extra credit work. He just seems—a little creepy to me."

Charisse giggled. "He is a little over-gelled, isn't he?" She tapped me on the shoulder. "Why did he offer you extra credit? Why not me? I'm the one who could use it."

"I don't know. It was weird," I replied. Suddenly, I drew in my breath sharply. "Charisse, how did Mr. Hightower know my name? I've never seen him before in my life. How did he even know who I was?"

Charisse blinked in surprise. "What do you mean, how did he know? He's a teacher. You're a student in his class. Of course he knows who you are."

My uneasiness was growing. "But Mr. Hightower never called roll. He said we were too cool for it or something—so he doesn't know who any of us are. He also said Mr. Del Gatto told him what a great student I am."

"That must be how he knew you, then."

I shook my head. "Can you imagine Mr. Del Gatto bragging about any of us?"

"Not really, no," Charisse said.

I went on in a rush. "And Mr. Hightower knew I lived with my grandmother."

"A lot of people know that," Charisse said. "Maybe he knows her. Maybe she told him about you."

"Maybe. I don't know. Somehow I can't picture the two of them being friends."

Charisse gave me a concerned look. "What is it that worries you about Mr. Hightower?"

I sighed. Maybe I was just tired from seeing strange men all over the place. "I'm not sure. It's probably nothing—things have just been weird lately. Sorry I've been rambling on about this."

I took a deep breath and pushed my uneasiness away. "So, how are you doing? I didn't get a chance to talk to you this morning. And when are you going to tell me what your big secret is?"

Charisse gave me a conspirator's smile. "I'll tell you tomorrow. I promise. Branden and I will be ready for everyone to know by then."

I glanced around. "Speaking of Branden, where is he? I haven't seen either one of you without the other in ages."

Charisse grinned. "Branden had to see a guy about a thing."

I nodded. "Very enlightening. I must say, so far you've been good at keeping your secret. But then, you've always been good at keeping secrets."

Charisse seemed pleased. "Thank you."

I gave her a serious look. "That may not always be a good thing."

"Katie, there is no way you are tricking me into giving my secret away early. It'll be worth the wait."

"That's not what I'm getting at," I said. "I'm worried about you. You haven't breathed another word about your parents' divorce since you first mentioned it. And it must have been brewing for some time—and you never brought it up until the whole thing erupted."

Charisse laughed. "Is that all? You really had me worried for a moment. My parents have always argued—you know that."

"But Charisse, things must have escalated to cause the breakup of a nearly twenty-year marriage."

"Honestly, Katie, I've been expecting this my whole life. And I'm okay with the divorce. I did think it was weird that I reacted so well at first, but I realized that's just the way I am. I accept things and move on."

As I looked at her, Charisse's eyes softened into sympathy. "I can understand how hard family things must be for you. You barely had any time to spend with your parents before they died. Divorce probably reminds you of that loss. It's not so bad for me, Katie. Besides, I've got it covered."

Something about her tone caught my attention. "What do you mean, you've got it covered?"

Charisse stopped at the hallway that led to her class and smiled.

"I've got to run or I'll be late. Everything will be fine—better than fine. You'll see."

She walked off, and I stood staring after her. After a moment, Charisse glanced back at me.

"Katie!" she shouted. "I have a plan! I know what I'm doing!"

I watched her disappear into the crowd.

There was something very strange about the way Charisse was acting.

Chapter Four

As I got ready for school the next morning, I was feeling very odd. I hadn't been bothered by the night calling at all on the previous evening, and I had been able to sleep without trouble again. And once again, I hadn't seen anyone in the mirror who shouldn't have been there.

All the same, I felt like something was wrong.

GM was in a good mood at breakfast and talked enthusiastically about a new project she was working on. She'd been uncharacteristically subdued since we'd had our visitors on Sunday night, and I was happy to see her acting more like herself again.

After giving GM a quick kiss on the cheek, I left the house and walked to school, avoiding the mirror on GM's car on the way out, just in case. The air was crisp but not too cold, and I couldn't help admiring the red and gold leaves that still clung to the trees. Out in the fresh air everything seemed bright and new.

I began to feel a little better—maybe today would be a good day.

At school, I spotted Charisse and Branden at their usual picnic table. This time they were both sitting on the table, holding hands and smiling at one another. Simon was standing nearby.

As I walked toward them, Simon broke into a grin. He looked so happy that I felt a now-familiar wave of regret wash over me.

I was happy to see Simon—but I wasn't quite as happy to see him as he was to see me.

"Hey, Katie," he said as I reached him.

"Hey." I glanced over at Charisse and Branden, who were now whispering to each other. It was clear there would be no conversation from either one of them this morning—I supposed I would have to wait till later to find out what Charisse's big secret was.

I turned back to Simon. "So, how was everything at home last night? The police didn't come by looking for James again, did they?"

"Luckily, no. It was pretty quiet."

He paused and gave me a serious look. "And how are you? Lately, you've seemed different—kind of faraway. But today you seem a bit more like yourself."

I looked down at my feet. I hadn't realized that Simon had noticed my strange moods—and I certainly couldn't explain what was wrong.

I could hardly tell him that I'd been seeing people who weren't there and feeling the night calling to me.

I had to wonder then—was that all it was that was creating the distance between Simon and me? Was it just my temporary insanity?

Maybe I actually liked him better than I realized.

I looked at Simon closely. "I didn't mean to be distant," I said. "I've just been feeling strange lately. But I'm better now."

Simon's brow creased with concern. "Were you sick?"

"No," I said. "I just had a funny feeling I couldn't shake off."

"You're sure you weren't sick?" Simon said.

He sounded so concerned that I couldn't help smiling a little. "I'm sure."

"You weren't worried about Irina and me and the fact that I've been meeting up with her for our project, were you?"

"No."

Simon smiled then, too. "Well, whatever it was, I'm glad you're better."

He glanced over at Charisse and Branden. "It's kind of cold out here, and I doubt those two will miss us if we leave. Do you want to go inside? I think some business club is running a coffee and tea cart. Maybe we could get something to drink."

"Sounds good," I said.

Simon and I walked toward the school, and I glanced over at him. It felt good to be walking beside him without any awkwardness between us—and I should have felt like things were back to normal. But my uneasiness from earlier in the morning suddenly returned to me in a rush.

Why did I feel like something was terribly wrong?

I pushed the feeling away.

Simon and I went into the school and soon located the coffee and tea cart. As we waited in line, I started to feel too warm, and I took off my coat and draped it over my arm. We were almost at the head of the line when the guy ahead of us turned to leave and tripped, sending coffee flying all over everything.

I looked down and watched as several dark brown spots bloomed on my cream-colored sweater and began to spread out.

"Are you okay?" Simon asked. "You're not burned, are you?"

"No, I'm fine," I said. "Are you okay?"

"Yeah, it's all on my coat. No harm done."

I glanced down ruefully. "I'd better go rinse these stains out before they set in. I'll see you at lunch."

I hurried to the nearest girls' bathroom. The room appeared to be empty, and I briefly considered taking off my sweater so I'd have an easier time getting at the stains.

Just in case, I double-checked all the stalls—I was, in fact, alone in the bathroom.

But it occurred to me that someone could come in at any moment, so I decided to keep my sweater on and just do the best I could.

I tore off several paper towels from the dispenser on the wall and went to a sink. I turned on the tap and began to blot at the stains on my sleeve. To my relief, the stains began to fade.

I was just starting to work on the stain on my collar when I heard a click from the door. The door was hidden by a tiled wall, so I couldn't see who had come in.

I was definitely glad I hadn't taken off my sweater now.

I looked up, but no one came around the wall, and I figured I must have imagined the sound. I realized that the bathroom door didn't click anyway—it creaked—so it probably wasn't the door. I turned back to the stain on my collar.

It suddenly flashed into my mind that there was a lock on the bathroom door—a crescent-shaped tab at the top of the door—and that the lock would probably make a sound like the click I'd heard. But I shrugged the thought off—who would want to lock the door to the girls' bathroom?

I leaned toward the mirror and continued to dab at my collar. As I did so, I caught a flicker of movement out of the corner of my eye. I looked up into the mirror and saw the dark-haired, blue-eyed man from my earlier hallucinations standing behind me once again.

I turned around.

This time, he didn't disappear.

I felt a flash of panic. The strange man I kept seeing in mirrors was actually standing in front of me now. He was staring at me steadily—and I could see anger—even hatred—burning in his eyes.

And yet, he was strangely beautiful. There was something perfect about the shape of his face and the long, lean lines of his body.

Behind me, the water kept running in the sink. For a long moment there was no other sound in the room.

"Who are you?" the man asked at last. His voice was harsh, and he had an accent I couldn't quite place.

"Are you real?" I asked.

The man moved closer to me in one swift movement and leaned in. His face was only inches from mine.

I began to feel light-headed. Was I hallucinating all of this?

"Who are you?" he demanded.

I could feel the warmth from his body, and I reached out a hand to touch his shoulder.

"You feel solid enough," I said. He did indeed feel solid, and I found I was reluctant to move my hand.

I also realized I wasn't hallucinating—somehow an image in a mirror had become real.

"How did you get out?" I asked.

Puzzlement flickered in his eyes. "How did I get out of what?"

"Out of the mirror," I said. "That's where I first saw you."

The man's anger returned. "How do you know that woman Galina Golovnin?"

"Galina Golovnin?" I said. "Is that the woman who came to my house on Sunday? I never heard her last name."

There was more confusion in the man's eyes, but he pressed on, leaning even closer.

"What do you know of Gleb Mstislav?"

I caught at the name. "Mstislav. Galina mentioned a Mstislav mansion. She said the lights were on—she seemed to think there was some kind of danger. Does Gleb Mstislav have something to do with that?"

The man's eyes ranged over my face. "You really don't know, do you?"

"Know what?" I said.

The man stared at me for a moment without saying anything. Then he turned to go.

"Wait!" I said. "Are you a student here? How will I find you again?"

The man turned back.

"I'm sorry if I scared you," he said. "You should forget you saw me."

He turned away again.

"Wait!" I said, feeling panic rising in me. "If you know something about Galina and this Gleb Mstislav, then I need to talk to you."

"No," he said sharply.

"I need to talk to you."

"It's better if you don't."

"But what if I genuinely have to?" I said in a rush. "What if the danger that Galina hinted at actually happens? What if I need to talk to you then?"

Something flickered in the man's eyes that I couldn't quite read.

"What is your name?" he asked.

"Katie Wickliff," I replied.

"Finally you answer a question," the man said, a small smile quirking at one corner of his mouth. "If you need to talk to me say 'Katie Wickliff summons you.' If you do that, I will find you."

The man turned and disappeared around the wall, and I heard the lock on the door click again. I hurried after him, rushing around the tiled wall and running out into the hall. I looked both ways through the crowd of students.

The man from the mirror had vanished.

I glanced back at the door to the girls' bathroom. Something that wasn't quite right had been tugging at my mind, and as I looked at the door, I realized what it was. The lock was on the *outside* of the door—it was designed to keep people out, not lock them in. There was no way the strange man I'd just encountered could have locked the door once he was inside the room. And if he'd locked it from the outside, then he wouldn't have been able to get in.

So—how had the door come to be locked?

I went to homeroom in a bit of a daze.

By first period I had begun to have doubts. Had I really spoken to the man from the mirror, or were my hallucinations getting stronger? But then I remembered the feel of his shoulder under my fingers. He was definitely real.

So who was he? And how did he know about the visitors we'd had on Sunday night?

No matter what was going on, I knew that I couldn't tell anyone that I'd seen an imaginary man come to life.

I knew that no one would believe me.

As I walked into second-period English, I noticed that Bryony and Annamaria were standing listlessly by Irina's desk, and I figured that Irina must be out sick. Without their leader, the two of them didn't seem to know what to do with themselves.

Mr. Hightower was still subbing, but after giving me an over-bright smile and greeting me warmly, he didn't notice me again. Instead, he skipped role, as he had hinted he might yesterday, and gave the class a free period. I had plenty of work to do for my other classes, so I kept busy until the end of the period. I was so deeply engrossed in my work that I was startled when the bell rang.

As everyone started filing out, Charisse came up to my desk, smiling. "Hi."

I looked up at her. "You're cheerful today."

"I have good reason to be."

I stood up and swept my books into my backpack. "Does your good mood have something to do with your big secret?"

"It does."

I slipped my backpack on. "Does that mean you're going to tell me what it is now?"

Charisse moved toward the door. "Not yet."

I hurried after her. "Charisse!"

She looked at me over her shoulder. "What?"

I caught up to her, and the two of us filed out into the busy hallway.

"Charisse, you promised," I said.

She giggled. "I know. I *will* tell you—but just a little later. It's so crowded now. And it'll be crowded at lunch, too. I want to tell you when it's just you and me. Let's make an appointment to meet at the picnic table after school."

"Charisse, I can't believe you're dragging this out."

"Please, Katie. This is really important to me. And I have a question to ask you afterward, so you should prepare yourself."

"All right," I said. "I'll do the best I can to prepare myself without actually knowing what this is about."

"It's nearly the end—I promise," Charisse said. "So how are you doing? I haven't heard much about what's going on with you lately."

I looked away. I wanted to tell Charisse what was going on, but I knew I couldn't. I cast around for something to say.

Charisse seemed to notice my discomfort. "Do you still think Mr. Hightower is creepy?"

She was wrong about what was troubling me, but I was thankful for the diversion.

"I don't know," I said. "Maybe 'creepy' is too a strong word. I'm just a little uncomfortable with how hard he tries to make people like him. And why doesn't he ever call roll? It's like he's encouraging people to cut. I doubt if he even noticed that Irina wasn't in English class today."

Charisse blinked in surprise. "Do you think Irina was cutting class? She's almost as much of a bookworm as you are."

"I don't think she cut," I said. "But what if something happened to her or to someone else? What if it was important to know whether or not a student was in class? I'm convinced he doesn't know the names of most of the people in there."

Charisse shrugged. "Maybe he just wants to make his time as a sub as easy as possible."

"Maybe," I replied. "I just don't think he's doing us any good."

"Don't despair," Charisse said. "Mr. Del Gatto will be back soon, and then you can bask in his sarcasm once again."

She stopped. "Well, this is my hallway. I'll see you at lunch."

As Charisse walked away, I found myself looking over the crowd for the man from the mirror. I both hoped—and feared—to see him again.

The strange man and the light-headed feeling he'd given me were still on my mind when I went to the cafeteria for lunch. I spotted Simon sitting at a table alone, and I made an effort to focus on the real world in front of me.

I couldn't let myself get lost in dreams—no matter how intoxicating those dreams might be.

After I went through the line, I sat down next to Simon and glanced around. "Where's our favorite couple? This is the first time I've beaten them to lunch in ages."

"They're being mysterious again."

"So, you noticed that about them, too?"

"Yeah," Simon said. "Branden said he had something to tell me today."

I looked at him sharply. "Charisse said the same thing to me. Do you have any idea what it is?"

"No." Simon looked down at his tray and stabbed at some lettuce. Then he looked up at me. "They aren't my favorite couple, you know."

I met his gaze. "No?"

"No," Simon replied firmly. "We are."

He went on in a rush. "Katie, I want to make it up to you for my spending so much time with Irina this week. Would you like to go see a movie this Saturday? I really miss spending time with you."

As Simon said the words, I felt a strange tug on my heart—as if something were pulling me away from him. I was suddenly irritated with all of the strange things that had been happening to me lately—especially with the weird feeling that kept pushing me away from Simon. I'd known him forever, and he was a good friend. Why shouldn't I spend time with him?

I smiled at him. "I'd like that."

Simon's answering smile made me feel good.

A moment later, a backpack hit the table with a resounding thud, causing our trays to jump.

"Now who are the googly-eyed lovebirds?"

I looked up to see Branden grinning down at us. With one big hand, he pushed his backpack out of the way and slid his tray into place. Then he sat down heavily.

Charisse sat down next to him.

"So glad you could join us today," Simon said.

"We had business to attend to," Branden replied loftily.

"So, how have you been, Simon?" Charisse asked. "I feel like I haven't seen you much lately."

Simon feigned shock. "I can't believe you're actually talking to me. Don't you and McKenna want to spend the entire lunch period staring soulfully into one another's eyes?"

"Very funny," Charisse said.

"Actually, we have a lot to talk about today," Branden said.

Charisse kicked him under the table. "Don't tell them. I promised Katie I would tell her when it was just the two of us."

"What?" Branden protested. "I was just going to tell them the news about Mr. Del Gatto."

"There's news about Mr. Del Gatto?" I said.

Branden leaned forward. "The rumor is that he's missing."

I was startled. "What do you mean 'missing'?"

"I mean nobody knows where he is," Branden replied. "Travis Ballenski told me—his dad is a cop. It turns out that Mr. Del Gatto's neighbor, Mrs. Hannity, called the police after there was a lot of crashing and screaming over at his house the other night. The police went out and found that the back door had been pulled off its hinges, and Mr. Del Gatto was nowhere in the house. The police have been looking for him since then, but they haven't found him yet."

I stared at Branden in shock. "When did this happen?"

"Monday night," Branden said.

"Was it a home invasion or something like that?" Simon asked.

Branden shook his head. "No one knows exactly. But the cops don't think so. Nothing seems to have been taken—but Mr. Del

Gatto lived alone, so there isn't anyone who can say for sure if anything is gone."

"What happened with the door?" Simon asked. "Do the police know how it got pulled off its hinges?"

"Nope," Branden replied. "They have no idea—but doing something like that would have taken a lot of force—a lot of it. And apart from the door being trashed, there's no evidence. The guy has just vanished."

I felt a strange sense of dread settle over me. The conversation continued on around me, but I was lost in my own thoughts.

I was worried about Mr. Del Gatto—and I had the strangest feeling that I had expected to hear something like this. And then I remembered that the school had called in a sub. They had obviously known that Mr. Del Gatto would be out. I figured that Branden must have gotten a hold of a wild rumor—Mr. Del Gatto was probably okay.

All the same, I was still uneasy.

My uneasiness stayed with me for the rest of the day, but I managed to shake it off as my final class drew to a close.

I had my appointment with Charisse.

When the final bell rang, I hurried out to the picnic table. Charisse was sitting on the bench, already waiting for me, and she jumped up to hug me.

"Oh, Katie! I'm so happy!"

I stepped back from the embrace and looked at her, surprised. "I'm happy to see you, too."

"I really never thought this could happen!" Charisse continued, holding onto my arms and spinning me around. "I hadn't really planned to do this, and yet it's so right!"

"Does this mean that you're finally going to tell me what your big secret is?" I asked.

Charisse stopped spinning and stared at me incredulously. "Can't you guess? I thought it was obvious. I was sure you would figure it out long before I got the chance to tell you."

"Charisse!" I cried in frustration. "I have no idea what you're talking about. Just tell me."

"Katie, what have I always wanted to be?"

"An actress," I said.

"Yes!" Charisse cried. "I'm moving to New York! I'm going to follow my dreams and become an actress."

I was stunned. "What?"

Charisse laughed. "I know! Isn't it wonderful?"

"I don't understand," I said. "Is one of your parents moving to New York now that they're separated?"

"No," Charisse said. "It's just me. At least at first. Branden will follow me later."

"You mean you're running away from home?" I said.

"No, of course not. I'm just moving on to the next phase in my life." Charisse sighed happily. "Katie, it all happened so suddenly. I've got an agent."

"An agent?"

"Yes, he came right up to me here at school on Monday. He actually pulled me out of homeroom. He said he saw me in the schoolyard, and he knew I was a natural—he said he knew star quality when he saw it. Katie, he's going to represent me. Here's his card."

I glanced briefly at the card Charisse handed me before giving it back to her.

"Charisse, are you crazy?"

Her face fell. "You aren't happy for me?"

"Well, no, not exactly."

Charisse looked wounded. "I was going to ask you if you wanted to come with me. You probably couldn't come right away, but eventually you could move up, too, and you could share our apartment."

"You want me to move with you to New York?" I couldn't believe what I was hearing. "Charisse, you're only sixteen. No one will rent you an apartment. And you don't have a job."

"I know," Charisse replied. "That's why Branden and I have been so busy lately. I told him all about my agent, and he's been doing everything he can so we can go up together. We had to arrange to get fake IDs and fake birth certificates—the birth certificates are just in case. But Branden knows some people in New York who need a roommate right now. So, I'll go up first and move in as the new roommate—I won't have to be on the lease or anything. And I have enough money in the bank from my parents to cover my share of the rent for the first few months. And then I'll get a job as a waitress and start going out on auditions. Once I'm established, Branden will come up to join me. We don't have the IDs or the birth certificates yet, but we'll have them soon."

"Charisse, are you crazy?"

She was beginning to grow angry. "You already said that."

"Charisse, you're buying forged documents? Where are you getting them from?"

"Everybody has a fake ID, Katie," Charisse snapped. "It's not a big deal. And I'm certainly not going to tell you who our contacts are. Not if you're going to take this kind of an attitude."

"So that's why you've been late to classes and to lunch," I said. I sat down on the bench by the picnic table.

Charisse stared at me. "You're acting like we're criminals."

"You can't run away from home," I said. "Do you know what happens to runaways?"

"I'm *not* running away." Charisse shook her head, blinking back tears. "You're my best friend. You were supposed to be happy for me. This wasn't how this was supposed to go at all."

"Charisse, I'm sorry," I said. "But I can't think of this plan as anything but a mistake."

"People a lot younger than me are successful actresses," Charisse said frostily. "If anything I'm wasting my time hanging out around here."

I shook my head. "Oh, Charisse, this is not right."

She bristled. "Why? You don't believe that Branden and I know what we're doing? I'm following my dreams, and Branden is going to support me in any way he can. No offense, Katie, but you don't know anything about having a successful relationship, and we know all about it. We can make this work."

"Successful relationships," I said slowly. "So that's what this is all about? You think you can make up for your parents' failed marriage by running away from it?"

"Don't be ridiculous," Charisse snapped. "You have no idea what you're talking about."

"I remember now," I said. "When I asked you about the divorce yesterday, you said you were taking care of it. Is this what you meant by taking care of it?"

"Katie!" Charisse cried. "This is unbelievable. How dare you try to psychoanalyze me?"

"Charisse, please just listen," I said. "You know I'm your best friend. What you're talking about doing will hurt your parents. It will hurt Branden's parents. You can't do this."

The tears that had threatened earlier now began to stream from Charisse's eyes. "I *thought* you were my best friend in the whole world. And I *thought* that you would always support me. But now I see how wrong I was. I can't believe you're ruining this for me."

Charisse turned and ran off.

I stood up and took a few steps after her, but I soon stopped. I realized that going after her would do no good.

Charisse was in no mood to listen.

I sat back down on the bench.

Chapter Five

I walked home slowly, too worn out from my argument with Charisse to think about it.

Too much was going on lately, and the strain was starting to wear me down.

As I walked, the man from the mirror kept crowding into my thoughts—and try as I might, I couldn't keep him out. Suddenly, I'd had enough. There was one person who might be able to tell me what was going on—even if she didn't want to admit it.

I decided I had to talk to GM—I had to get some answers from her about my mother's visions. Even if she thought I was crazy—even if it upset her.

I had to know what was going on with me.

I walked up to my house and stood staring at it. I suddenly felt nervous—talking to GM wasn't going to be easy.

I went inside.

"GM?" I called, and I hoped my voice didn't sound unsteady.

"In the kitchen, Katie."

I found GM standing at the kitchen table. She was spreading peanut butter on cut-up stalks of celery.

"I'm making a little snack," she said. "Would you like some?"

The scene before me was so normal that I felt tears stinging my eyes. Suddenly, I just wanted things to go back to the way they used to be—no runaways, no strange visitors with dire warnings, no unnerving hallucinations.

When I didn't answer, GM looked up and took in the expression on my face. She froze with her knife poised over the celery.

"What's wrong, solnyshko?"

I wanted to blurt out everything, but I knew that wouldn't be fair to GM—I knew how sensitive she was about the past. I decided to approach the topic of visions in a roundabout way.

If I was lucky, maybe I could convince her to talk.

I took a deep breath. "GM, do you remember the visitors from Sunday night?"

GM stiffened. "Yes."

"Are they still here? I mean are they still in town?"

"No." GM's tone was sharp.

I felt frustration welling up within me. This wasn't going well.

"How do you know they're gone?"

GM set her knife down with a clatter. "I know they are gone because I told them that if I ever saw them again, I would call the police. I told them I would have them arrested for trespassing and making threats. They know better than to stay around here."

GM's tone told me clearly that the subject was closed—I wasn't going to be able to get at the topic of visions by a roundabout route.

I would have to try the direct route. I took another deep breath.

"GM," I said, "I know this is hard for you, but I need to talk to you about those visitors—and my mother's visions."

"No," GM snapped. "Again, I say, no."

"No?" I said.

"No."

"GM, I *need* to know."

"Enough!" GM said. "Enough! I will not have it!"

I felt a sudden flash of anger.

"I'm not five years old anymore!" I shouted. "You can't protect me from everything! Something's happening to me, and I don't know what it is. You *have* to talk to me. You have to help me."

GM stared at me for a long moment. Then she seemed to grow resigned to something. "Of course I will help you, solnyshko. I am your grandmother. You only have to tell me what is wrong."

"I've been seeing things," I said. "Things that aren't there. I've been having—visions. And I need to know what you know about them. There's no harm in your telling me the truth."

GM sighed heavily. "Yes, solnyshko. I have always feared that something like this would happen. Let us go and sit down."

She led me into the living room and steered me toward the couch.

"Now tell me what you've seen," GM said.

I quickly ran through all of the times I had seen the strange man's face in glass. I stopped short of telling her that I had actually seen the man in person. I didn't want her to worry any more than she was already going to.

GM nodded. "I believe you," she said quietly. "I have heard stories like these before. From your mother."

"Then you have to tell me what she saw," I said.

GM sighed again. "I will tell you. Though I do so with a heavy heart. Your mother had visions of a man. She saw a man named Gleb Mstislav."

I drew in my breath sharply. "Is that the man Galina believes killed my mother?"

GM bowed her head. "Yes."

"And what do you believe about him?"

"I believe Gleb was a very bad person. I believe he was a mobster. I believe he killed a number of people."

"But not my mother?"

GM shook her head. "No, she died of a fever, solnyshko. I saw it myself."

"But Galina believes that this Gleb is looking for me now—and that I am in some kind of danger."

"Yes. But that cannot be."

"Why not?" I asked. "You just said yourself that Gleb was a bad man."

"It cannot be because Gleb Mstislav is dead."

As GM said the words, a strange coldness came over me. I remembered now that she had said the same thing to Galina.

GM looked at me sadly. "I don't know anything else about what your mother saw—truly I do not. But Katie, believe me when I say that you must work to push these 'visions' away. I don't know where they come from, but I do know they aren't good for you."

"Who is Galina?" I asked. "Why does she believe that she knows anything about my mother?"

"Galina and your mother were good friends from the time they were small," GM said. "Galina, as she grew up, began to believe in the local superstitions of Krov. To my despair, your mother did also."

"Superstitions?" I said. "You talked a lot about superstition the night the visitors were here. I remember now that you told Galina that superstition killed my mother. What did you mean by that?"

GM pursed her lips together. Then she spoke.

"Your mother had the fever that eventually killed her for many weeks. The doctor had urged her to stay in bed. But Nadya kept sneaking out of the house. She would ramble around town all night, and she was always worse when she returned in the morning. She believed she was fulfilling some kind of mission, stopping some great evil. One morning Nadya was found out in a petrified forest on the outskirts of Krov. That is the morning her fever won. Nadya was delirious and too weak to survive after that. She only lived a few more days. I often wonder if she would have lived, if she hadn't believed that she had to force herself to go out and fight monsters in the dark."

"What was it that my mother thought she had to do?" I asked.

"I don't know," GM said. "I know it had something to do with Gleb. But what it was exactly, I truly don't know. And I firmly believe that there was nothing in it. Your mother had no supernatural calling. And neither do you. Trust me, solnyshko."

She gave me a long, level look.

I met her gaze. "Thanks for telling me all of this," I said quietly. "I know how hard this has been for you."

GM hugged me tightly then, and in that hug I could feel just how much she feared to lose me.

That evening we had a quiet dinner, and afterward, I went up to my room to do some homework. But as I worked, my mind kept drifting. I thought of Charisse, but I pushed the thought away quickly. Her angry words still stung, even in memory. And there didn't seem to be anything I could do anyway—I had tried calling and texting her, but she wouldn't answer.

I thought then of the man from the mirror—and about what GM had said. She wanted me to forget about the visions I'd had—she wanted me to push them away. But I couldn't do that—not now that they'd become real. So the question was—who was the man from the mirror?

A possible answer began to form in my mind—and it was a disturbing one.

According to GM, my mother had had visions of Gleb Mstislav—and according to Galina, that same man had killed my mother.

And I had been having visions of a strange man.

I had to wonder—was I now seeing Gleb Mstislav, too?

I realized then that that was impossible—Gleb was dead, and I had actually seen the man from my visions in the flesh. I had even touched him.

So he couldn't be Gleb Mstislav.

And then a chill spread through my body—*unless he isn't what he seems*, a small voice whispered.

A stab of fear lanced through me, and I stood up and went to the window. I opened the curtains and stared out into the darkness.

I thought back to the night calling that had plagued me until recently. It occurred to me that the night calling had stopped when the visions had started. And the visions themselves had stopped when the man from the mirror had come to me in person. Though the idea was crazy, I began to wonder if the man from the mirror was setting a trap for me.

Entirely unbidden, a question popped into my mind. *What if the man from the mirror is Gleb Mstislav, somehow returned from the grave to kill you just like he killed your mother?*

I took a deep breath. The idea was completely ridiculous. It just wasn't possible.

But it occurred to me that there was a way I could find out.

I could ask the man myself.

As crazy as it sounded, the man had said he would come if I called him—*Say "Katie Wickliff summons you."*

I decided I would do it. I would call him.

I stood very still and listened. GM was still up and would be up for hours. I didn't want her to be around when I tried summoning the man from the mirror—though I wasn't sure why. After all, it probably wouldn't work—how could it?

There was no way the man could hear me speaking over any distance. The only way he could hear me was if he were hanging around my house at night, hoping I would go outside and call him. And if he did that, he was probably a psycho.

I told myself not to think that way—it was only leading me down a different dark path. I resolved to go outside after GM was asleep and call for the strange man. Then, when he didn't show up, I could prove to myself that he was neither vengeful murderer nor psycho.

I sat down at my desk again and forced myself to concentrate on my homework.

Time seemed to crawl by. But at long last I heard GM settle into her room for the night. I waited a little while longer, just to be sure she was asleep, and then I crept out into the night.

I stood in my driveway, looking up and down the street. Everything was quiet. There was no one to see my little experiment.

Even though it seemed unlikely to me that the man from the mirror was hiding out in my yard, it occurred to me that I really should check—just to be sure.

With that in mind, I went over the yard thoroughly with a flashlight. Our house didn't have shrubbery, but it did have a few trees, and I shone my light up into their scantily clad branches. No one was hiding in the trees or anywhere else in our yard that I could see. I even went out to the shed in the back where we kept the lawn mower.

No one was in the shed, either.

Just to be sure I was covering all possibilities, I walked from one end of my street to the other slowly, going over my neighbors' yards with my flashlight. As far as I could tell, no one was hiding on my street—or if someone was, there was no way he was hiding out close enough to my house to hear me speak.

I returned to my yard and went to the back to stand under my bedroom window.

Feeling slightly foolish, I glanced around me one last time and prepared to summon the strange man from the mirror.

There's no way this'll work, I told myself.

I took a deep breath. Then, in a whisper, I spoke the words he had told me to say.

"Katie Wickliff summons you."

There was a ripple in the air around me, and then a short sharp breeze. The man from the mirror was suddenly standing before me, his face pale in the dim light.

He grasped me by the wrist.

"What is it?" he demanded. "What's wrong?"

Without waiting for a reply, he pulled me away from the house. "Is he here?"

I was stunned. All I could do was stare up at him.

"Katie, answer me," he said urgently.

"How—how did you get here?" I stammered. "I searched my yard. I searched the street. You weren't there. You weren't anywhere. You couldn't possibly have heard me."

His grip on my wrist tightened. "Is he here?"

"Who?" I asked.

He looked toward the house. "Gleb Mstislav."

I forced myself to focus. No matter how the man had gotten here, I had called him for a reason.

"Gleb Mstislav," the man repeated. "Is he here?"

"You tell me," I said.

He blinked and then stared at me, puzzled. "What are you talking about?"

"Tonight, my grandmother told me that my mother once had visions of Gleb Mstislav. And I've been having visions, too—visions of you. And then today you suddenly appeared to me in the flesh. So who are you? Are you Gleb Mstislav? Have you returned to haunt me just as you haunted my mother?"

The man seemed startled by my words. "No, I am not Gleb Mstislav."

"Then who are you?" I demanded.

"My name is William," he said. "William Sursur."

"Anyone can make up a name," I said. "How do I know you aren't Gleb?"

"Because I am here to kill him," William replied.

"My grandmother told me he's already dead."

"He is."

I felt a chill steal over me. "How can you kill someone who's already dead?"

"That's not something you need to worry about."

"If he's dead," I said, "is he a ghost?"

"No."

"Then what is he?"

"That's not something you need to worry about, either."

I looked down. "You're still holding my wrist," I said.

William's hand moved, and he wrapped his fingers around mine. His skin was warm and his palm pleasantly calloused. I felt a tingle run through me where his fingers touched.

"Tell me more about your visions," William said.

It was a difficult subject to start in on, and I was feeling strangely light-headed.

"I saw you in the bathroom mirror," I said slowly.

William's lips twitched into a half smile. "I *was* in the girls' bathroom."

"I saw you before that—in my mirror here at home. You were standing behind me. When I turned around, you weren't there. I saw you again in the side mirror of my grandmother's car. And in a TV screen. I even saw your face once as I reached for a glass. I kept seeing you everywhere."

"And what did you think?" he asked quietly.

"It was frightening, at first."

"And now?"

"Not so much. You're much more pleasant in person."

I thought I saw a reddish tinge suffuse William's face, but in the dim light, I couldn't be entirely certain.

"You mentioned your mother," William said. "You said she had visions of Gleb. Why didn't you ask her to describe him? Gleb and I are nothing alike—I'm sure she could have told you that."

"My mother died years ago," I said. "I'd always been told she died of a fever. But Galina said a man killed her. She didn't say his name when she visited us, but tonight my grandmother told me that Galina believes Gleb was the man responsible."

William nodded once, and his face took on the same harsh lines that I had seen when he'd first appeared in my mirror.

"I don't want to alarm you," he said. "But I have to tell you the truth. Your life may be in danger. Promise me you won't go anywhere alone at night. You're safe enough during the day, but at night you need to be very, very careful."

The tone of his voice made me shiver. "What do you mean I'm in danger?"

He shook his head. "I can't tell you. I've got to go now. But you'll see me again." He glanced around. "You should go inside now."

William was still holding my hand, and he began to pull me back toward the house.

I followed him. "You know, you may think you're helping me by not telling me anything, but you're actually making the fear worse."

"You wouldn't believe me, even if I could tell you," William replied.

We walked up to the house, and he released my hand.

"Go on in," William said. "I'll stay until I see the door close behind you."

Though I was strangely unwilling to go, I turned toward the door.

"Wait just a moment," William said.

I turned back toward him.

"You summoned me here thinking that I might be the person who killed your mother."

"Yes," I replied.

"Why?" he asked. "Why would you do something so dangerous? Why would you summon your mother's killer?"

"I called you because I didn't want it to be true," I said.

A smile twitched at one corner of William's lips.

I was still thinking of that half smile when I fell asleep.

Chapter Six

B y all rights, I should have been afraid of William.

As I walked to school on Thursday morning, I told myself that over and over again. But I couldn't bring myself to fear him, no matter how many times I went over the facts.

He'd first appeared to me in a mirror, and he could hear whispers over long distances. He could move with impossible speed.

So I was left with an uncomfortable question—not so much who was William?

But what was he?

As ridiculous as it sounded, I had to admit to myself that William could not possibly be human.

So what else was there? So far I didn't know enough about William to make any kind of a guess. What I had witnessed up to now didn't point to anything I knew of, and searching online for mirrors and whispers didn't bring up any useful results.

So I would just go on believing that I was safe with William— whatever he was.

I didn't want to believe anything else.

Safe without him, however, was a different story. If I believed what William had told me, then there was a dead man named Gleb Mstislav who was somehow still walking around out there.

And he might be after me.

I shivered inside my coat as I realized that I did, in fact, believe William.

So what did Gleb want? And had he really killed my mother?

As I drew closer to school, my thoughts turned to Charisse—and I wondered what type of reception I would get when I saw her.

But when I walked into the schoolyard, I realized that I need not have worried about my reception. The picnic table Charisse had staked out since the beginning of the year was empty.

Not far away, I spied a familiar blond-haired figure with his hands stuffed into the pockets of his jeans. His back was to me, and his head was down.

I walked over to him. "Hey, Simon."

Simon turned and looked at me, and I was startled by his appearance. There were dark circles under his eyes, and his skin was pale. But the look on his face was the worst part—he was clearly miserable.

"Simon, what's wrong?"

A muscle worked in his jaw, and it was a moment before he answered. He grated out one word.

"James."

"Maybe it's just another misunderstanding," I said quickly. "Maybe there's a good explanation."

Simon shook his head, and his face contorted. "It's not the police this time. It's James himself. He's gone."

"Gone? You mean he ran away from home?"

Simon shook his head again and looked down at his feet. "He was taken."

"Taken?" I said. "What do you mean he was taken?"

Simon looked up at the sky. "This is going to sound crazy, but I swear to you it all happened. Katie, our house was attacked last night."

"Attacked?"

Simon nodded grimly. "Just a little past eleven. James was out on the mud porch at the back of the house. He goes out there with his laptop sometimes—for the wireless reception. I was up in my room, and I heard this serious crashing and screaming downstairs. I ran down to find out what was going on, and I found my mom and dad staring out into the mud porch. The back door had been torn clean off its hinges, and James was gone. I ran outside, but I couldn't see him anywhere. I ran into the woods behind our house, but I couldn't find any sign of him there, either. Eventually, I had to give up and go back home. In the meantime, my parents had called the police—"

Simon broke off, and he stood for several moments not saying anything. Then he looked at me.

"Somebody took my brother, Katie. Somebody *took* him. Some freak broke into our house and dragged him into the forest. Who would do that?"

"Oh, Simon," I said. "I'm so sorry."

"The police say they have no leads. They even think some of James's former friends might have come after him, or helped him to stage this. But Katie, you didn't hear those screams. Something really horrible happened last night—there was nothing normal about it."

"Why didn't you call me?" I asked.

"I couldn't do that to you," Simon said. "I wanted you to sleep. Besides, there was nothing you could have done."

"You should have called me anyway," I said. "And why did you come to school today? You should be at home."

Simon shook his head. "I'd rather be at school. Both of my parents are at work anyway, and I didn't want to be home alone. Sitting around doing nothing won't do James or me any good. I know my parents will call me the second they hear something."

It was hard for me to see the pain in Simon's face. "Simon, you know that if there's anything I can do—"

He interrupted. "You're doing me a world of good. Just by being near me."

I took Simon's arm, and we stood together in silence.

"Simon, is it possible the police could be right?" I asked carefully after some time had passed. "Maybe some of James's old friends did come after him?"

"Not a chance. I can understand why you would ask, though. But James *is* different. He's severed his old ties. And he told me that he doesn't owe anybody anything. He said he made right with everybody. And I really believe he did."

Simon's voice trailed off.

Then he went on in a rush. "But you know what? This does remind me of what Branden told us yesterday."

"What was that?" I asked. The only thing I could think of was Branden and Charisse's impending move to New York, but it didn't seem very likely that that was what Simon was referring to.

He noticed my confusion and gave me a wry smile. "Don't worry. I know about Branden and Charisse's crazy plan—Branden told me yesterday after school. That's not it. What I was thinking about was something he said earlier in the day. Do you remember what he said at lunch? About Mr. Del Gatto?"

"Yes," I said. "Branden said he'd heard that Mr. Del Gatto had disappeared."

Simon went on urgently. "He also said that someone had pulled his door off its hinges. That's the same thing that happened at our house."

"I don't quite understand," I said. "You think someone is going around kidnapping grown—or nearly grown—men?"

"I haven't seen Mr. Del Gatto around recently, have you?"

"I'd wondered about Mr. Del Gatto, too," I replied. "But the sub for his class said Mr. Del Gatto would be out for a few days. He already knew the absences were coming, so Mr. Del Gatto must still be in contact with the school. Maybe his house just got broken into and vandalized while he's out sick, or hospitalized, or whatever it is that's taken him away from school."

Simon sighed in exasperation. "I don't know. Maybe."

I recognized the stubborn set of his jaw—he'd made up his mind. I tried to think of something soothing to say, but I couldn't come up with anything. Eventually I decided that words wouldn't really help anyway.

"Simon," I said, "why don't you come over here and have a seat?"

I pulled him over to the picnic table, and we sat down on the bench. I rested my head on his shoulder, and he rested his head against mine.

We sat that way until the warning bell rang. Then we went inside.

I went to homeroom and had to be nudged when my name was called. I was worried about James, and even though I'd tried to reassure Simon, I was far from being reassured in my own mind. What could possibly explain the attack on James?

I was still in a daze when the bell rang to signal the start of classes.

But as I filed out into the hallway with everyone else, I suddenly felt strangely alert—I felt like someone's eyes were on me. Moments later, I heard a now-familiar voice.

"Katie."

I turned. William was standing by the wall next to a bank of lockers.

My heart fluttered when I saw him, and I drew apart from the crowd to stand beside him.

"Katie, I have to talk to you."

I took in the look on his face. "William, what's wrong?"

"There have been—disappearances," he said. "And they've been getting worse. Three people from this school are now missing."

"Three people?" I said. "I just heard about James Krstic—he's a student here. Who are the others?"

"There was another student—a girl named Irina Neverov."

"Irina?" I said, incredulous. "She's disappeared?"

"Yes, she's gone," William said grimly. "And they've all gone the same way—the door torn off, the victim dragged out. A teacher from this school named Anthony Del Gatto was the first one—he was taken Monday night."

"So, Branden was right," I murmured. "The rumors were true."

William nodded. "And a pattern is emerging. Irina was next after the teacher—she was taken from her father's home Tuesday night. James was taken from his parents' house Wednesday night. There was one disappearance each night."

"What's going on?" I said. "How do you know all this?"

William ignored my questions and pulled a box out of his coat pocket. "I want you to keep this with you—at all times."

I took the box from him and opened it. Inside was a metal cross on a thin leather cord.

"A cross?" I looked up at William, and some strange thoughts flashed through my mind.

William had warned me about going out alone at night—but he'd said I would be safe during the day.

There was someone out there who was dead—and yet was still walking around.

And now people were disappearing.

My words came out haltingly. "Are you saying the missing people were taken by—a vampire?" I could barely force the words out. "Is it Gleb Mstislav? Is he a—a vampire?"

William winced as if something had hurt him. "No, he isn't. It isn't the shape of this charm that's important—it's the material. The cross is made from iron—iron from a very old source."

"But it was Gleb, wasn't it?" I persisted. "He's the one who's taken everyone?"

"Katie, you don't need to know—I want you involved in this as little as possible. Just promise me that you'll keep this charm with you at all times."

"But—" I began.

"Promise me," William said sharply.

"I promise," I said.

William seemed to relax.

"You should get to class," he said more gently.

"What about you?" I asked. "Do you have to get to class? You never did tell me if you were a student here."

William gave me his little half smile. "No, I'm not a student here."

I paused—what I had to say next was more difficult. "William, when I mentioned vampires just now, you didn't laugh—you took the idea seriously."

William winced again. "Yes, I did."

"Have you ever seen a vampire yourself?" I asked.

"Yes, I have," he said quietly.

I took a deep breath. "William, who are you exactly?"

William's expression grew bleak. "You wouldn't believe me if I told you who—or rather what—I am. You really should get to class."

The obvious pain in his eyes compelled me to drop the subject. I took a few steps down the hall and then turned back to look at him.

William was gone.

I hurried on to class.

By the end of first period, my nerves were frayed—the whispers around me confirmed what William had told me. Mr. Del Gatto, Irina, and James were all missing. On Monday, Tuesday, and Wednesday nights, someone in our town had disappeared.

Everyone was wondering who would be next.

And I still had to wonder about William—I didn't know who he was or how he knew so much about what was going on.

And even though William hadn't actually admitted that Gleb Mstislav was behind the disappearances, it seemed pretty clear to me that he was.

So what was Gleb that he could be dead and yet still alive? And how had I wandered into a nightmare?

Of course, it wasn't just my nightmare. I thought then of Simon and his brother. I wanted to talk to Simon—I wanted to tell him about Gleb Mstislav.

Even if he thought I was crazy, Simon deserved to know everything that I knew.

I realized suddenly that Simon deserved even more—he deserved my help.

William wasn't telling me much, and he'd made it very clear that he didn't want me involved. But if I talked to Simon—told him what I knew—then maybe the two of us could come up with some way to save the people who had been taken—after all, I had information that the police didn't.

And I certainly couldn't go to the police and tell them what I knew—they'd never believe me.

As I made my way to second-period English, I had another sudden, strange feeling that someone was watching me. I turned quickly, hoping to see William again. But instead of William I saw— or thought I saw—a pair of disembodied eyes, floating in the air, watching me.

I blinked and looked again.

The eyes were gone.

I shook my head. The last thing I needed was to start hallucinating again.

I hurried on to English class, and as I walked in, I spotted Bryony and Annamaria huddled together, looking miserable. As I went to my desk, I glanced toward the seats that were assigned to Charisse and Branden—they were empty.

I wondered with a pang what they were up to.

When the bell rang, Mr. Hightower got up from his desk to close the door. As he did so, Branden and Charisse hurried into the room.

I was relieved to see them.

Mr. Hightower smiled at the two of them as they took their seats, and then walked to the front of the room.

"Folks, may I have your attention, please?"

After having two free periods with Mr. Hightower, the class had grown accustomed to doing what they wanted, and most people were talking and not listening to him.

Mr. Hightower's voice rang out, unexpectedly loud and stern.

"Everybody, shut up! Eyes up here. Now."

The chattering stopped, and all eyes turned to him, startled.

Mr. Hightower flashed his now-famous grin—I had heard more than one girl in the class swooning over his smile.

"From what I've heard in the halls," Mr. Hightower said, his tone genial once more, "most of you already know that there is a police investigation surrounding the disappearance of Mr. Del Gatto."

A ripple of surprise ran through the class—teachers didn't usually acknowledge the rumors that swirled around in the halls.

Mr. Hightower held up his hands for silence. "Since Mr. Del Gatto will be gone for an indefinite period, the vacation is over. I'm afraid we'll have to get back to work."

The class groaned.

"I know, I know," Mr. Hightower said, his voice full of amused sympathy. "But it won't be too painful, I promise. Now, let's get out the tools of our trade."

The class rustled as everyone pulled out textbooks, notebooks, pencils.

Mr. Hightower sat on the edge of his desk. "So, folks, where were we? I believe you've been working on a unit devoted to local storytellers, and you just finished Lydia Grace's play, *The Maid and the Moon,* about the life of Elspeth Quick."

The class reluctantly acknowledged that he was correct.

Mr. Hightower began to twist his ostentatious ring around his finger. "I thought we'd start with something fun and easy. Since we're talking about local storytellers, let's talk about some of the stories in our own lives. What are some of the stories that you have in your own families?"

Bryony raised her hand.

Mr. Hightower pointed to her. "Yes, the lovely lady there. Remind me what your name is, please."

I wasn't surprised to discover that Mr. Hightower didn't know Bryony's name—and I was reminded unpleasantly of the fact that he did know mine.

"I'm Bryony Carson, Mr. Hightower."

"Well, you're on, Bryony," Mr. Hightower said amiably.

Bryony didn't speak in class often, and her voice was high and thin. "My grandmother says there's a ghost in her house."

Mr. Hightower beamed. "Intriguing."

He pushed himself off his desk and walked to the blackboard. With a stubby piece of chalk, he wrote "BRYONY, GHOST" in neat capitals on the board.

He turned back to Bryony. "So, Miss Bryony, did I spell your name correctly?"

"Yes," Bryony replied in her small voice.

"Marvelous. And what's the significance of your particular family ghost?"

"Well, my grandmother lives in an old farmhouse near the woods where Elspeth Quick's original fruit grove was—the Old Grove," Bryony said shyly. "The ghost lives in the house with her. She says the ghost was a friend of Elspeth's, and she watches over the woods."

"This is good stuff, kiddo," Mr. Hightower said enthusiastically. "Your family has a personal tie to area history."

Bryony blushed, pleased.

Next to "BRYONY, GHOST," Mr. Hightower wrote "LOCAL HISTORY."

Bryony continued. "The ghost even told my grandmother about a fire in the Old Grove on Sunday night. My grandmother then called the police and the fire department."

Mr. Hightower laughed. "A useful friend to have."

He turned to the class again. "All right. Who's next?"

A boy named Grant Settle raised his hand.

The class giggled in anticipation.

Mr. Hightower pointed. "Yes, Mr.—"

"Settle. Grant Settle. At your service, sir." Grant stood up and sketched a bow.

The class laughed, and he sat down again.

"What have you got for us, Mr. Settle?"

"I saw something strange one night," Grant began in a dramatic voice.

Mr. Hightower wrote "GRANT" on the board and glanced over his shoulder. "Please go on."

"It was during a full moon," Grant intoned. "In fact, it was a full moon. It was hanging out the back window of a car full of my brother's friends." Grant gave an exaggerated shiver. "Scariest thing I ever saw."

The class laughed again.

Mr. Hightower threw Grant a friendly, exasperated look. "Very funny, Mr. Wiseacre."

He erased Grant's name and then surveyed the class. "Let's try somebody serious next. Katie, how about you?"

I jumped when Mr. Hightower called my name—it had been a little while since he'd spoken to me, but the uncomfortable feeling he always gave me came back in a rush.

Mr. Hightower gestured with his chalk. "I know you said your grandmother was from Russia. Do you have any family tales from the old country?"

As far as I could recall, I had never volunteered the information that my grandmother was from Russia—Mr. Hightower had discovered that on his own and had brought it up himself on Tuesday.

"My grandmother is from Russia," I said slowly. "But she's never told me any stories."

Mr. Hightower gave me his most winning smile. "Aw, come on, K. Don't leave me hanging here."

He continued to stare at me, as if willing me to speak, and a long silence stretched between us. I glanced around. The class was staring at me, too, and I felt a blush rising to my cheeks.

"I'm sorry, Mr. Hightower, I don't have anything to tell you. My grandmother doesn't talk about the past much."

He persisted. "Your grandmother is from the town of Krov, right?"

I felt even more uncomfortable—I knew for a fact that I had never told him that. "Yes."

Mr. Hightower tilted his head and gave me a look of friendly skepticism. "You mean your grandmother never told you the story of the Little Sun? That's a local legend from the town of Krov."

I began to wish fervently that the conversation with Mr. Hightower would end. "No, my grandmother never told me the story of the Little Sun. But she does call me that."

"What?" Mr. Hightower asked. He looked startled.

"She calls me 'solnyshko.' It means 'little sun' in Russian."

Mr. Hightower's brows rose. "Does she really?" He stared at me for a long moment, saying nothing. Another uncomfortable silence ensued.

My face was blazing now. "It's a common Russian endearment. It's not important."

A voice interrupted. "Mr. Hightower, I've got a story."

I glanced around at the speaker. It was Branden.

Mr. Hightower looked over at Branden and flashed his big smile. "Well, let's hear it. But first, tell me your name again."

"It's Branden. I have a family story from World War II."

Mr. Hightower turned to write on the blackboard, and I silently thanked Branden. Hope rose in my heart that maybe Charisse and Branden were no longer angry with me.

The rest of the class dragged on, and I couldn't help worrying that Mr. Hightower would return to me to continue his questioning. To my relief, he went through the rest of the class one by one, asking them for stories from their families, and he didn't speak to me again.

When the bell rang signaling the end of second period, I swept my things into my backpack and leapt to my feet. I turned expectantly toward Branden and Charisse, but Charisse grabbed Branden by the hand and dragged him out of the room.

She didn't even glance in my direction.

I felt my heart sink.

I dragged through the next two periods and went to lunch, half-hoping and half-fearing to see Charisse.

In the cafeteria, I picked up a tray and went through the line, coming out on the other end with a grilled cheese sandwich and tomato soup.

I found Simon sitting by himself, and I slid into the plastic seat next to him.

His face was pale and drawn, but he smiled when he saw me. "Hey."

My heart went out to him—I knew how much he must be worrying about his brother. "How are you?"

Simon nodded and looked down at his sandwich. "Good."

"Any news about James yet?"

"No. Not a word."

I placed a hand on his arm. "Don't give up."

Simon smiled. "I know you're here for me. Thanks."

The two of us began to eat in silence.

I had wanted to talk to Simon about the disappearances and about Gleb Mstislav, but I couldn't bear at the moment to trouble him with anything else—he really looked worn out and unhappy. I figured I would call him later that night, and then maybe the two of us could work out something to do.

There had to be a way I could help.

Simon looked up suddenly, and I followed his gaze.

Branden and Charisse were just leaving the line and walking out toward the tables, and Branden caught sight of Simon and me.

He smiled and began to walk toward us.

"Branden!" Charisse called out sharply. "Over here."

Branden turned, surprised, but didn't protest.

I watched as Branden followed Charisse to a table on the other side of the cafeteria.

I set my grilled cheese sandwich down on my tray and pushed it away.

Suddenly, I wasn't very hungry anymore.

Chapter Seven

That night, I climbed into bed and called Simon. The dejection in his voice when he answered tore at my heart.

"Hey, Katie."

"Hey, Simon. Is there any news yet?"

He sighed heavily. "No—nothing. It's like James just vanished completely."

He paused.

"Katie, what if he—what if James is *really* gone? What if he's—"

"Simon, don't think it," I said quickly. "You don't know what's happened. Don't imagine things."

"Hoping is hard, Katie. Every hour feels endless now. I can't help staring at the clock, wondering if the next minute will bring bad news."

I wanted very badly to help Simon, but I knew that would have to wait. He was too tired and too hurt to do any planning tonight. I would talk to him tomorrow at school—then the two of us could figure out what to do.

"Simon, try not to worry," I said. "I know that sounds crazy, but worrying won't help. You don't know how things will work out. You don't have to expect the worst."

He sighed again. "I suppose you're right. I guess I should try to get some sleep now."

"Call me any time if you need to talk," I said. "Even if it's three in the morning."

Simon chuckled a little. "Thanks. Don't be too grouchy if I take you up on that. Good night, Katie."

"Good night, Simon."

I sat for a long moment, holding the phone to my heart. I had a feeling Simon was going to stay awake all night worrying about James, no matter what advice anyone gave him.

I wished again that I could help him.

I thought briefly of going to GM and telling her about the disappearances—maybe there was something else she might be able to tell me about Gleb Mstislav. But I hesitated—I knew the discussion would be hard for her—and the disappearances would frighten her.

I decided I would stick to my original plan and just discuss everything with Simon. After that, we could investigate the disappearances ourselves—he could look into his brother's disappearance, and I could work on the others.

If we didn't come up with anything, then I might go to GM. But I wouldn't bother her if I didn't have to. I knew GM didn't mean to be closed off—she just wanted me to be safe.

Safe. I thought suddenly of William and the look on his face as he had insisted that I keep his charm with me at all times. He had certainly seemed concerned about my safety, too.

I set my phone down and got out of bed. Then I took the little charm out of its box and examined it.

As I remembered, the charm was gray and uneven—a roughly hewn cross with a loop at the top for the cord. The charm was cool to the touch, and its craggy surface had a slight sheen to it—I remembered that William had said it was iron. Following an instinct I didn't entirely understand, I sniffed gingerly at it and caught a faint, familiar scent.

The charm smelled like rust or blood.

I brought the charm back with me to bed and climbed in again. I lay still for several minutes, turning the cross over and over in my fingers. It was, in its own way, a beautiful thing, and I found holding it to be comforting. I wondered where the charm had come from.

And if the charm was mysterious, William was even more so. He seemed to appear and disappear at will. He knew things about the man who had supposedly killed my mother. And he definitely knew more about the disappearances in town than he would admit to.

All the facts pointed to his being a dangerous person.

And I remembered how William had reacted to the word *vampire*.

A chill spread through me as I thought back to the question I'd had about Gleb when William had given me the cross.

Is he a—a vampire?

What if that question actually applied to William?

But William's skin was warm to the touch, and he could walk in the daylight—so he couldn't possibly be a vampire.

But what do you really know about vampires? asked a small voice in my head.

Could such a thing really exist?

I did believe in Gleb, so why were vampires any harder to believe in?

But I couldn't really believe William could be something like that—vampires were dark creatures that fed on—human blood.

William only wanted to help me.

Or did he?

I pushed my fears away forcefully. I cared about William—I believed in him.

I couldn't believe he was a monster.

The sound of GM's footsteps in the hall roused me from my thoughts, and I glanced at my bedside clock. It was getting late. Reluctantly, I set the charm down next to my phone and switched off the light. I settled under my covers.

After several moments lying in the dark, my eyes grew accustomed to the gloom, and I turned to look at the charm on the table. A thin shaft of moonlight filtered down over the cross, causing it to shine dully.

I lay still, gazing at the charm, until sleep came to claim me.

In the morning, I awoke just a minute before my alarm sounded, and I quickly switched it off.

I stretched, feeling strangely full of hope. Today, I would talk to Simon—and then, if he agreed—the two of us would start to investigate the disappearances. I would have to tell Simon about Gleb Mstislav, and though I'd been planning to do that all along, it suddenly occurred to me just how strange the Gleb story would sound. I hoped Simon would believe me—at the moment, I didn't have a lot of proof to offer him.

I hurried to get ready for school, and as I was leaving my room, I caught sight of William's charm.

I slipped the charm on over my head and hid it under my sweater—I had a strange feeling that GM might object to it.

I'd keep it hidden until I got to school.

Then I picked up my backpack and ran downstairs. As I walked down the hall toward the kitchen, I was surprised to hear GM talking to someone on the phone in hushed, tense tones.

"Yes, I agree wholeheartedly—it is necessary to take precautions. Thank you for letting me know. My granddaughter will not leave my sight this morning."

I walked into the room. GM was standing with her back to me.

"Yes, thank you," she said. "Goodbye." She clutched the phone to her heart.

I walked closer. "GM? What's wrong?"

She whirled around. Her face was pale, and she was still clutching the phone in one hand. Her other hand was closed tightly over the silver cross she always wore.

"You are not walking to school today," GM said firmly. "There will be no argument."

I was surprised by the fear on her face. "Sure—if that's what you want. Did something happen? Who was that on the phone?"

"Oh, Katie," GM said, "that was the secretary from your school. She said two students and two teachers have gone missing. She said they fear that the school's staff and students are being targeted, so they are warning all parents not to let their children go anywhere alone. Katie, I am going to drive you to school and everywhere else. I could not bear it if something were to happen to you."

"Don't worry, GM," I said. "Nothing will happen to me. And I'll be happy to have you drive me anywhere."

She threw her phone onto the table and dropped her cross. Then she put her hands on either side of my face and kissed me on the forehead. "You have always been a good girl. I should have known not to worry about your making a fuss."

GM stepped back and grasped both of my hands. "I shall make you breakfast. What would you like?"

I smiled. "Thanks. But I don't want to risk being late. A bowl of cereal and a glass of juice is really all I need."

"I will pour it out for you, then," GM said, pushing me toward the table. "Sit! Sit!"

I sat down, and she quickly furnished me with everything I needed for breakfast. Then she sat down across from me and watched me anxiously as I ate my cereal.

"I won't disappear right in front of you," I said.

GM waved a hand. "I know."

She continued to watch me.

I finished my breakfast as quickly as I could and moved to clear the dishes away.

"Just leave everything where it is," GM said, rising. "I will take care of it later."

"But it'll just take a minute," I protested.

GM interrupted. "No. Leave it. Now we go to school."

I picked up my backpack and followed her out of the house.

As I settled into GM's red sports car, I couldn't help glancing into the side mirror, hoping to see William's face there. I had a feeling I wouldn't see him—my visions seemed to have stopped completely—but I wanted very badly to see him anyway.

As I expected, William's face did not appear in the mirror, and I sat back against the seat, disappointed.

The driver's side door opened, and GM slid in behind the wheel, pulling the door closed with a solid smack. She threw her purse into the back seat and pushed the key into the ignition. The car purred to life.

GM pulled on her seat belt and gave me a smile. "Just for you, I will drive slowly today."

I resisted the impulse to giggle. GM never drove slowly—she had a drawer full of speeding tickets to attest to that fact. I doubted she could slow down, even on a day when she was worried.

If anything, the worry might make her go faster.

GM's eyes flashed to the rearview mirror, and then she backed down the driveway swiftly and expertly. She pulled out onto the road and then shot forward, the engine humming as she shifted smoothly and pushed the accelerator to the floor.

I couldn't help smiling to myself. I was right—GM was driving even faster than usual.

I rested comfortably in my seat, watching the neighborhood flying by and thinking over what I would say to Simon. I wasn't worried about the speed—GM was an expert driver and had unusually quick reflexes.

As we drew to a halt at a stop sign, I marveled as I always did at the way GM could bring the car down from its great speed and ease it into a stop so smoothly that I could barely feel it. I would be taking Driver's Ed soon, and I hoped when I learned to drive that she would teach me how to do that.

In the span of a few minutes, GM brought me to school, and I was just getting out of the car when she stopped me.

"Katie!"

I leaned back in. "Yes?"

"Go into the school. Right now. I will watch from here."

"But there are plenty of people out in the schoolyard," I protested.

"There are also plenty of people missing," GM replied. "Two students and two teachers. Go inside now. If you do not, I will escort you in myself. And give me a call when you're ready to come home tonight."

I sighed. "Yes, GM."

I shut the car door and headed into the schoolyard. I looked over toward the picnic table, and my heart sank as I saw that Charisse and Branden were absent once again. But Simon was standing nearby, his shoulders hunched, his hands in the pockets of his jeans. He looked tired, but he smiled when he caught sight of me.

As I walked toward him, GM's parting words suddenly came back to me—and I stopped short. Had she said two students and two teachers were missing? I was pretty certain that that was what I'd heard earlier, but it hadn't really sunk in before. The two students were James and Irina, and I knew one of the teachers was Mr. Del Gatto. So who was the other one?

Simon hurried over to me.

"Hey, Simon." I was glad to see that he was looking a bit better than he had yesterday. "We'd better get inside."

He blinked in surprise. "Okay. Why?"

"GM is watching me from the car. She received a call from the school this morning about all of the missing people. Your parents probably got the same one. She told me to go straight into the school or she'd walk me in herself."

Simon's eyebrows rose. "Oh." He turned and spotted GM's red sports car. He knew it well and had admired it on many occasions. He raised a hand in a wave. "I guess we'd better get inside, then."

We both headed toward the school.

"How did you sleep last night?" I asked.

Simon gave me a wan smile. "Not great. You can probably guess that we haven't had any news about James."

"He's smart," I said. "We've always known that about him, no matter what he got up to. And he's tough, too."

"That's true enough," Simon said wryly.

"What I mean is, if anyone can find his way home again, it's James. He won't give up."

Simon nodded. "I hope that's enough."

We passed through the large double doors at the front of the school.

"Do you mind if we go to the cafeteria?" I asked. I suddenly felt nervous. I had no idea how Simon was going to take what I had to tell him. I thought my plan was good—but I didn't know what he would think of it. "I have to talk to you about something."

Simon shot me a worried look. "What's this about? Is it something about us?"

"No," I said, "it's not about us. It's about James, Irina, Mr. Del Gatto, and me."

Simon frowned a little. "Okay. I don't know where you could be going with that, but sure. Let's talk."

"Oh! And who's the fourth person?" I said suddenly. "Do you know?"

"What's that?" Simon asked.

"GM said the school told her four people were missing—two students and two teachers. I know Mr. Del Gatto is one of the teachers—but who's the other one?"

Simon's brow cleared. "Oh yeah. I heard about that before you got here. It's a sub named Mr. Hightower."

I felt a ripple of shock run through me. "Mr. Hightower?"

"Yeah, do you know him?"

"Yes," I said. "He's the sub for Mr. Del Gatto. How did you find out it was him?"

"I was talking to Travis Ballenski—I think you know his dad's a cop. Apparently, it happened last night. Hightower's house was pretty messed up."

I took a deep breath and fought the chill that stole over me. Things were getting scarier—Simon and I had to do something.

We reached the cafeteria, and I led the way to a table in an unoccupied corner of the room. At tables closer to the kitchen, students sat eating breakfast and talking. I could smell eggs and toast.

I shrugged off my backpack and sat down. Simon did the same, seating himself next to me.

I looked around the cafeteria one last time, just to make sure that no one was nearby.

As I did so, I thought I saw a pair of eyes floating in the air—just as I had yesterday. I blinked, and they were gone. I shook my head and turned back to Simon.

As I looked at him, I felt my nervousness growing. I knew that what I had to tell him was going to be hard to believe. I did care about him, and what he thought of me mattered.

I steeled myself and looked into Simon's eyes. "Simon, I need your help."

His brow creased with concern. "Of course, Katie. Anything you need. You can depend on me. Always."

His concern warmed me, and it made me feel brave enough to go on.

"Simon, strange things have been happening to me. And I think there may be a connection between what I've been going through and the people who have gone missing, including James."

"Go on." Simon's tone was encouraging.

I plunged into my tale, starting with the night calling and the visions. I told Simon that the visions had become real, and that I had met William—though I omitted some of the details. I told him that two visitors from Russia had shown up suddenly on Sunday night, and that one of the visitors—Galina—believed my mother had been killed by a man named Gleb Mstislav, who was now deceased. I also told Simon that both Galina and William seemed to believe that Gleb had returned from the dead.

And I told him that I believed Gleb was behind the recent disappearances.

While I spoke, Simon sat quietly, listening. From time to time, confusion and disbelief flickered across his face, but he didn't interrupt.

"So, that's everything," I concluded.

Simon sat back in his chair. "That's quite a story, Katie."

"GM can back me up," I said. "On parts of it, at least. Simon, you and I have to work together—we have to investigate this. You and I are the only people who know about Gleb Mstislav—apart from GM and William. But GM refuses to believe there's a problem, and William insists on doing whatever he's doing on his own. We have to help James and the others—because no one else can."

Simon rubbed his chin. "You say you've been seeing things, and these things have become real."

"Yes," I said firmly. "And I'm really not crazy. The only reason I'm bringing this up at all is so that we can help the people in this town."

Simon looked down at his hands. His face was unreadable.

I waited nervously. He had yet to say whether or not he would help me.

"If I understand you correctly," Simon said slowly, "you believe there's a man out there named Gleb, who died and came back to life in Russia. And he may have killed your mother there, for reasons which are not very clear—but may have something to do with visions or some kind of powers. Gleb may be here in the U.S. now, looking for you so he can destroy you, too. And he may have taken everybody who's missing so far in this town while looking for you. And you believe all this because two strangers named Galina and William told it to you."

"Yes," I said—Simon's skepticism was not lost on me. At the same time, a chilling thought struck me. "Simon, you've explained the situation well, and you've made me realize something—I know everyone who's disappeared."

"So do I," he replied.

"You don't know Mr. Del Gatto."

"I know who he is," Simon countered, "even though I've never had a class with him."

"You don't know Mr. Hightower," I said. "He was a sub, and I've never seen him before as a sub in any other class. He may be completely new to our school district."

"It's true that I don't know Mr. Hightower," Simon said. "But Charisse does, and so does Branden. They also know Mr. Del Gatto, Irina, and James—so do a lot of other people in your English class."

"But Charisse and Branden haven't had visions," I said in frustration. "And my visions led me to William, to a specific person who gave me information—although it wasn't much information, and he was reluctant about it."

Simon shook his head, and I went on quickly.

"From what I've heard, the police don't have any suspects or any lines of inquiry. I've at least got a place to start from. Let's forget the supernatural stuff for a moment. Let's just say my mother knew a bad guy back in Russia—even GM acknowledges that he was real and a criminal. She said, too, that my mother tried to stop him. Maybe he didn't really die—maybe he just hid out or something. And maybe he didn't kill my mother, and she did just die of a fever.

"But Simon, what if my mother knew something that was detrimental to Gleb? And what if he thinks that I know it, too? Galina and Aleksandr did come all the way from Russia to warn me."

Simon stared at me for a moment, and then he looked away and sighed. "When you put things that way, it does sound more likely."

He thought for a moment and rubbed his chin again. "But if this Gleb guy is after you, why is he taking other people? Why hasn't he come for you?"

"Maybe he doesn't know where I am," I replied. "My mother's married name is Wickliff, and my last name is Wickliff. But GM's last name is 'Rost.' If you looked in the public records, there would be no Wickliffs listed. I don't think there are even any other Wickliffs in this town. And if you did a search online, you certainly wouldn't find me. You know I'm allergic to social media."

"Then why did Gleb—if he is here—even come to Elspeth's Grove in the first place if he doesn't know for sure that you're here? And like I said, why take other people?"

Simon's objections made sense, and I tried to tease out a logical way to counter them. "Maybe Gleb followed Galina and Aleksandr to Elspeth's Grove," I said.

But as I said the words, doubt tugged at the back of my mind—Galina and Aleksandr seemed to believe that Gleb had preceded them, not followed them. But I pushed the doubt aside—I didn't want to ruin my argument.

I continued. "Maybe once they were all here, Gleb lost track of them and didn't know which house they went to. And even though I know everybody who disappeared, I don't know why Gleb is taking other people. That's why we have to investigate."

Simon continued to look skeptical.

"Simon," I said, "the disappearances started right after Galina and Aleksandr came to my house."

He smiled a little. "Okay. You've made a good point. I'll give it to you that your visitors and their news do coincide with the beginning of the disappearances. It's possible that you may be onto something."

I felt hope flicker in my heart. "So, you'll help me investigate?"

Simon sighed. "Yes, I'll help you investigate. And for what it's worth, I don't think you're crazy. At least not all the way. At least not yet."

"Oh, Simon!" I breathed. "Thank you, Simon! Thank you!"

He looked at me seriously. "I don't like the sound of this William guy, though. I think you should stay away from him."

My heart fluttered a little at the mention of William's name. "I really haven't seen him all that often."

"Good," Simon said firmly. "You should keep that trend going."

I ignored the comment. "Thanks, Simon, really. It means a lot to me that you're going to help me."

"So where do we go from here?" he asked.

I felt some of my earlier nervousness returning. I had to ask Simon to do something that I knew would be difficult for him.

"It's possible the police aren't telling us everything," I began carefully.

Simon snorted. "It's more than possible, Katie. It's certain. The police can't tip their hand if there's a psycho out there."

"Yes, exactly," I said. "Simon, I need you to find out everything you can about James's disappearance—everything the police may not be telling you."

He shook his head. "I don't know about that, Katie."

"Simon, I know this won't be easy for you, but I'm only asking you to do this because I want to get James back. I want to save him and Irina and the teachers. And I want to stop this from happening to anyone else."

Simon ran a hand over his face. "What do you need me to do?"

"Talk to your parents. See if there's anything they know that they haven't told you. Talk to the police. Talk to Travis Ballenski, even. Find out if he's heard anything. Anything at all. Maybe there will be a clue in there somewhere."

Simon smiled tolerantly. "Okay. I'll go looking for clues. I assume you're hoping I'll find out something that will point toward this Gleb guy?"

"Yes."

"And what about you? What are you planning? Nothing too dangerous, I hope?"

I took a deep breath. "I'm going to talk to Irina's parents—carefully, of course. I'll see if they've heard anything. As for the others—it sounds like Mr. Del Gatto lived alone, and I don't know anything about Mr. Hightower. So, I don't know how to investigate those two at the moment."

"That's probably a good thing," Simon replied. "I think you should stay away from the teachers. Talking to other students and their parents is one thing, but asking questions about men you don't know very well is probably not a good idea. What do we do after we're done asking all our questions?"

"We meet up and share everything we've learned," I said. "And I do mean everything—no matter how disturbing or unimportant it may seem. Any little piece of information may turn out to be the key to the whole thing."

"Okay," Simon said.

"Simon, Katie, what are you two still doing here?"

A new voice broke in on our conversation.

I looked up to see Mr. Hodges, the gym teacher, standing beside our table. He was wearing sweats in the school colors of blue and white, as he often did, and he was holding a carton of milk and an orange.

"Hi, Mr. Hodges," Simon said.

"Hi, yourself," Mr. Hodges replied, incredulous. "The bell rang a little while ago. The two of you are late for homeroom."

"Sorry," I said. "We were talking, and I never even heard the bell ring."

I glanced around. The cafeteria was empty except for the three of us.

Mr. Hodges sighed in exasperation. "It's no big deal, Katie. I know you two are good kids. And everybody's a little distracted and on edge lately. If you give me a sheet of paper and a pen, I'll write passes for you both."

I quickly furnished Mr. Hodges with pen and paper. He tore the sheet in half and wrote out a pass for each of us. "Now get to homeroom. You're going to miss all of the announcements if you don't hurry."

"Thanks, Mr. Hodges," I said.

Simon and I quickly rose and moved toward the door. Mr. Hodges followed us out into the hall, and then turned off, heading in the direction of the gym.

Simon and I hurried on through the empty halls.

When we came to a parting of the ways, Simon stopped and smiled at me. He stood for a moment, not saying anything.

I looked up and down the corridor. It was strange being in the halls when no one else was around.

"Well, I'll see you at lunch," I said.

"Thanks, Katie," Simon said.

I was puzzled. "For having lunch with you?"

"No. Thanks for wanting to help James."

In one swift movement, Simon leaned down and kissed me softly on the lips. His hand lingered for just a moment under my chin.

Then he turned and headed off to his classroom.

I was left staring after him, pressing my fingertips to my lips.

Chapter Eight

I had trouble concentrating during first-period Social Studies.
Mr. Fehr stood at the front of the room behind a podium like he usually did, lecturing from his notes. I really liked the class, but this morning I had too much to think over to be able to pay attention.

Simon's kiss had chased everything else out of my mind.

We'd known each other for a long time, and we'd always been friends. After the night calling had died away, I'd tried to open my mind to the possibility that we could be more than friends.

Had my feelings for him changed? We'd certainly never kissed before.

I let my pen trail down the sheet of notebook paper in front of me, watching but not really seeing, as the pen drew a long, blue line across the page.

The kiss had been nice, but somehow it made the two of us seem more like friends than ever.

I didn't know what I was looking for in a kiss—but something was missing.

When the bell rang to signal the end of class, I was jolted out of my reverie. I packed up my things quickly and told myself to focus—I had a problem to solve.

As I filed out into the hall to go to second-period English, I realized that there was one snag in my plan to investigate the disappearances—GM wasn't going to let me out of the house on my own.

But maybe she would let me go out with Simon. Simon and I were planning to meet up for the movies on Saturday night, and GM knew about that. So, maybe she would let me go out with him in the afternoon, too. But there was a problem there also—Simon was supposed to be doing his own, separate investigation.

I sighed to myself—it was too bad that asking Charisse was out of the question.

When I reached English class, I was surprised for some reason to find that Mr. Hightower was indeed gone. Mrs. Swinburne, a substitute I had had many times, sat behind the teacher's desk in a print dress, her fluffy hair standing out in a brown cloud around her face. Prim, proper Mrs. Swinburne was as different as it was possible to be from the flashy Mr. Hightower. Mrs. Swinburne glanced up at me as I sat down and smiled. Then she went back to the papers she was looking through.

As more people came into the classroom, I kept glancing over my shoulder, hoping to see Charisse or Branden. I wondered how they were doing and whether they'd show up—or if today was the day one, or both of them, would be gone.

Soon, the class was full except for the two of them and the missing Irina. I glanced anxiously at the clock. Charisse and Branden were seconds away from being late.

The bell rang, and Mrs. Swinburne got up to close the door.

Just as she was swinging it shut, Charisse and Branden came running into the room. Charisse's eyes widened in surprise when she saw Mrs. Swinburne. She and Branden hurried toward their seats.

"Not so fast, you two." Mrs. Swinburne's voice was sharp.

All eyes in the class turned toward her.

Branden froze where he was. Charisse continued on to her seat.

Mrs. Swinburne started toward her desk. "Step this way, please, Mr. McKenna, Miss Graebel."

Branden hung his head and followed her. Charisse remained seated where she was.

Mrs. Swinburne pulled a pad of orange slips out of her desk drawer and began to write on the top slip.

"I don't know what your previous substitute was like," she said stiffly, darting an angry glance first at Charisse and then at Branden, "but the rules of this school state that any student who is not inside his or her classroom *before* the bell rings will be considered tardy. The rules of this school also state that the penalty for tardiness is automatic detention. I intend to follow those rules."

Branden groaned. "Oh, come on, Mrs. Swinburne."

"No arguments, Mr. McKenna." Mrs. Swinburne tore the top slip off the pad with a snap and handed it to Branden. She began writing on the next slip as he slouched away and slumped in his seat.

"Miss Graebel, approach my desk, please." Mrs. Swinburne's head was bent as she continued to write.

Charisse didn't move.

The class waited breathlessly, anticipating a confrontation. I hoped that Charisse wasn't going to do anything that would get her into any more trouble than she was already in.

Mrs. Swinburne raised her head. "Miss Graebel, I have known you since you were in the second grade. Don't think you'll get around me."

I glanced back at Charisse. She was staring at Mrs. Swinburne defiantly.

"Miss Graebel," Mrs. Swinburne said sharply. "My desk. Now. Or I might start thinking about extending your detention for several days."

Charisse stood up sulkily and walked up to the teacher's desk.

I breathed out, relieved.

Mrs. Swinburne tore off another orange slip and held it out to Charisse.

Charisse took it wordlessly and returned to her seat.

"Now, class," Mrs. Swinburne said, "I am going to be your substitute for the foreseeable future. I am Mrs. Swinburne. I know most of you, and most of you know me. Please don't doubt me when I say I do things by the book. I will start by taking roll."

Mrs. Swinburne was strict, but I was glad that someone who would pay attention to the class was in charge. She, at least, would know who was in her class and who wasn't. That was definitely reassuring when people were disappearing.

Mrs. Swinburne ran through the roll and then rose from her seat. "Class, your last substitute left no notes, so I'm going to go back to Mr. Del Gatto's lesson plan and follow it exactly."

She went to the corner of the room and pulled out the stand with the TV and DVD player. "According to the lesson plan, you were watching a movie on the date when Mr. Del Gatto became indisposed. So we will go back to the movie and then continue on with the lesson plan from there."

The class protested.

"It's no use your complaining," Mrs. Swinburne said firmly. "I don't care if you have seen this before or not. I get the impression that things have been getting lax over the last few days. The best way to get back on track is to go back to the lesson plan and proceed in an orderly fashion from there."

The class continued to grumble as Mrs. Swinburne switched the movie on and went to the back of the room to turn off the lights. She remained standing at the back of the room to keep an eye on the class.

For my part, I was happy that we were going to watch the movie again. I hadn't seen William in a reflective surface in several days, and I knew it wasn't likely that I would see him there now—but I hoped I might see him anyway. As the familiar music of *The Maid and the Moon* filled the room, I scanned the screen eagerly, watching for any trace of his face.

But minute after minute went by, and there was no sign of William. I tried to will him to appear—but nothing happened.

I gave up and concentrated on the movie.

Suddenly, an image flashed in front of my eyes, blotting out the TV screen.

I found myself standing in the dark. Suspended in the air in front of me was something I'd never seen before—a bright light—a glowing sphere of red and gold. Next to me was William. He was staring at me with a look of wonder on his face.

The image vanished as quickly as it had appeared, and I felt a shudder run through me.

I blinked and looked around. I was still at my desk in English class, and we were still watching a movie.

Nothing had changed.

I realized that I was breathing hard, and I worked to calm myself—I was really shaken. What had just happened to me? The image that had flashed before me was more vivid than any of the brief visions I had seen in glass.

Were things going to get worse?

And what did the image I'd seen mean?

I tried to get the image to return, but no matter how hard I concentrated, I couldn't bring it back.

Before I knew it, the bell was ringing, and Mrs. Swinburne was switching on the lights. I quickly packed up and left the room. This time I didn't bother to look for Charisse and Branden.

I knew they wouldn't wait for me.

As I walked to my next class, I felt foggy-minded and a little dizzy.

I had the strangest feeling that something was speeding up.

By lunchtime, I was still having trouble concentrating, and I hoped that eating something would make me sharper. I had to keep my mind clear—I had a lot to do after school.

As I made my way through the hall, I once again had the feeling that someone was watching me. I looked around, half-expecting to see the floating eyes that I had seen a couple of times already.

But nothing was there, and I was deeply relieved.

I didn't need any more visions or hallucinations at the moment.

As I walked into the cafeteria, I spotted Simon, already seated, and I waved to him. Then I went to join the line.

I thought back to the kiss again, and I wondered if Simon would mention it. I didn't much feel like discussing it, and I hoped his mind would be on other things.

Simon smiled at me as I sat down, and I looked away quickly. I had to force myself to think of something other than his kiss.

I thought instead of Irina.

I realized that I still didn't know how I was going to get to see Irina's parents, since I wasn't allowed to go anywhere alone, and Simon would be busy with his own work for James. I decided that I would take my chances with GM herself—since she was planning to pick me up after school anyway, maybe she wouldn't mind taking a little detour.

I realized then that I didn't actually know where Irina lived. Maybe I could look her up online—there couldn't be too many Neverovs in Elspeth's Grove.

"You're awfully quiet," Simon said. "And you haven't touched your food yet."

I looked up at him. "Sorry. I was just thinking ahead to tonight. I want to go see Irina's parents, and I realized that I don't know where she lives."

Simon took a bite of his pizza. "I think her parents are divorced. I don't know where they live, though."

I took a bite of my pizza, too. "I think you're right about the divorce. I remember now that William told me she was taken from her father's house. I guess that means her parents live separately. I should probably go see both parents."

Simon frowned at the mention of William's name. "I really think you should stop talking to that guy."

"I haven't seen him at all today," I said. *At least not in person*, I thought to myself.

Simon seemed mollified by that. "You could ask Annamaria or Bryony where Irina's parents live."

"That's true," I said. I glanced around the cafeteria then—I didn't see either one of them.

While I was looking around, Simon suddenly looked up himself. He sent a friendly nod to someone over my shoulder.

I turned to see who it was. Branden was walking by and had a hand raised in a wave. Charisse was pointedly not looking at us.

I turned back to Simon. "Does Branden still talk to you?"

"Yeah, of course," Simon said. He suddenly became very interested in his pizza.

"He does?" I asked.

"Yeah. It's no big deal."

"It's a big deal to me," I said. "Has Branden told you anything?"

"Like what?"

"Like what? What have they been up to? Are they still going to New York? When is Charisse going to talk to me again?"

"Everything's fine," Simon said. "Don't worry about it."

"What does that mean?" I said.

"It means don't worry. Things will work out."

I sighed and bit into my pizza. I didn't understand why Simon was being so calm about it all.

After lunch, I kept an eye out for Annamaria and Bryony. I didn't have any more classes with them, and the rest of the day passed without my seeing either one of them. As the final bell rang, and the halls flooded with students, I waded out amongst them, craning my neck, frantically trying to spot someone who could give me information about Irina.

I didn't see Bryony or Annamaria, so I hurried outside. I figured I could watch the yard as people left for the day—that way I might be able to spot at least one of them.

I found a good vantage point—on a little hill with a tree—and the minutes ticked by as I watched students streaming out of the school.

There were a lot more people being picked up by their parents today.

As I watched the crowd, a guy in a plain white T-shirt paused and stared at me. I wondered briefly why he wasn't wearing a coat or a sweater—the afternoon was pretty cold—and I found myself staring back at him. Something in his gaze made me uncomfortable, and I soon looked away. I turned to look over the other side of the schoolyard.

I didn't see Bryony or Annamaria on that side either, and I began to wonder if maybe I'd missed them.

"Come on," I whispered to myself. "Where are you guys?"

I turned back to face the school. The guy in the white T-shirt was gone.

The feeling that I was being watched hit me suddenly, and I glanced around quickly. As I did so, a piece of paper fluttered down from somewhere above me and hit me on the nose. Then it floated gently to the ground.

I picked it up. Scrawled on a piece of notebook paper were two names: "Dolores Silver" and "Ivan Neverov." Each name had an address beneath it, and next to "Ivan Neverov" there was a note: *out of town.*

I looked around me and then up into the branches of the tree I was standing next to. No one was there.

The information I needed had literally fallen out of the sky.

I stood for several moments, stunned. Then I looked around one last time just to be sure—but there really was no one near me.

Since I had what I needed, I decided to go with it. I got out my phone and called GM.

She answered immediately. "Katie, are you ready to come home from school now?"

"Yes," I said. "I'm ready." I was a little startled by just how quickly she had answered the phone.

"Stay in the schoolyard," GM said firmly. "Stay inside the fence until you see me."

"GM—"

She hung up.

I sighed and put my phone away. I'd wanted to ask GM about going to see Irina's parents, but she hadn't given me a chance—and I knew there would be no use in calling her back. GM wouldn't answer—she would be entirely focused on getting to the school.

At least that would give me a few minutes to think.

If the mysterious note could be trusted, then Mr. Neverov was out of town. So, even though Irina had been taken from her father's house, I figured I should go to see her mother first. Irina's mother surely would have been told everything that had happened the night Irina disappeared, and she would also know about any recent developments. Maybe she would even know when Mr. Neverov was coming back.

All I had to do was make the visit sound reasonable to GM.

I glanced up at the road beyond the fence just in time to see her gliding to a graceful stop in front of the school.

I hurried over, reflexively checking to make sure that the iron charm from William was tucked under my sweater—in my haste to get out of the school to look for Annamaria and Bryony, I had neglected to put on my coat. I still didn't know exactly why I hid the charm, but a half-formed suspicion lingered that GM would not approve of it.

I got into the car.

GM looked at me disapprovingly. "You should have put on your coat while you were waiting for me. It is too cold for you to go without it."

"Sorry," I said. "I just didn't think of it."

I pushed my backpack off my lap and started to pull my coat on.

"No, no," GM said. "Don't bother with that now. I will get you home quickly."

She turned the heater on and eased the car away from the curb in preparation for her usual rapid acceleration.

"GM, wait!" I cried.

She hit the brakes and turned to look at me in surprise.

"I didn't mean to startle you," I said apologetically. "That came out a lot louder than I had intended it to."

"Is something wrong?" GM asked.

"No, nothing's wrong. Can we go somewhere else? Before we go home, I mean?"

"Where?" GM asked.

I was relieved that she didn't sound angry—she simply sounded puzzled.

"There's a girl—Irina Neverov," I said. "She's one of the two students who disappeared. I wanted to go see her mother—to talk to her."

GM smiled sympathetically and patted me on the hand. "Of course, solnyshko. I remember Irina has been your friend ever since the two of you were little girls."

I sighed inwardly—it had been a long time since Irina and I were friends. GM probably thought that I wanted to console Irina's mother—when I actually wanted to question her.

"Where does Irina's mother live?" GM asked.

I consulted my heaven-sent sheet of paper and gave her the address.

"I'm afraid I don't have any directions," I added.

"We'll find it, Katie. Don't worry."

GM pulled away from the curb gently and then took off like she usually did.

I had to smile. Even when she didn't know exactly where she was going, GM still drove like she was on a racecourse. And she never used GPS, preferring instead to rely on what she called her "inner map"—and it seldom steered her the wrong way.

GM guided the car through traffic expertly, and very soon we slowed for a moment near a worn and faded sign that read "Hunter's Glen."

"I believe we will find the address you gave me in this development," GM said.

She drove into the neighborhood and after a few turns, we pulled onto the street that was listed on my note. We stopped in front of a small house with green siding, and I glanced up at the number. We had found the right place.

"I think this is it," GM said quietly. "Would you like me to come in with you, or would you like to go in alone?"

"I'd like to go in alone."

She nodded. "I'll wait, Katie. Do not hurry."

"Thanks, GM." I got out of the car.

I walked up the short concrete drive toward the house, pulling on my coat, and I began to feel nervous as I approached the door.

I realized I wasn't entirely sure what I was going to say to Irina's mother.

I knocked at the door tentatively.

There was no answer, and my nervousness increased.

I knocked again.

This time, I could hear someone hurrying toward the door, and after a moment, it flew open.

A woman in a drab skirt and blouse with frazzled hair escaping from a ponytail appeared in the doorway.

She looked at me suspiciously. "What do you want?"

I was about to speak when the woman darted a glance over my shoulder, and her eyes narrowed angrily.

I turned and followed the woman's gaze. She was staring at GM's red sports car, which was gleaming in the fall sunlight.

"You're another one of Irina's fancy friends, aren't you?" the woman asked.

"No—I mean—yes," I stammered. "You don't understand. That's not my car."

"Spare me," the woman snapped. "What do you want?"

"I'm sorry," I said. "I don't mean to intrude. I'm hoping I can talk to you about Irina. May I come in?"

The woman's stony expression did not change, but she stepped back to allow me to enter.

I followed the woman into a small living room. A pile of neatly folded laundry sat on one chair, and stacks of newspapers and mail sat on a coffee table.

The woman sank onto a floral sofa and crossed one leg over the other. She stared at me steadily.

I stood awkwardly by the coffee table. I wasn't sure exactly how to begin, so I just plunged ahead. "Mrs. Neverov—"

"Dolores," she interjected sharply. "It's Dolores Silver. But just call me by my first name."

I felt myself coloring—I had known that her last name wasn't Neverov, but I'd forgotten it in my nervousness.

"Dolores," I said. "I know you've been over everything with the police, but is there anything you can tell me?"

"About what?" Dolores asked impatiently.

I shifted from one foot to the other uneasily. "Is there anything you can tell me about the night Irina disappeared?"

Dolores shrugged. "She was at her father's house, and then she wasn't. That's all I know."

"Isn't there anything else?" I asked. "Anything at all that you've heard? Even something that seems insignificant may be important. I'm trying to help Irina and all of the others who have disappeared."

"I know nothing about my daughter," Dolores said stiffly.

"Dolores, please, help me," I said. "Irina is missing."

Dolores sat forward, suddenly animated. "Irina is *not* missing."

"What do you mean, she's not missing?" I said.

"I mean she's not missing *this time*," Dolores said heatedly. "She's been missing all along. The fact that she's missing now doesn't make any difference."

I was starting to get worried. I wondered—was Dolores Silver crazy?

"I still don't know what you mean," I said.

"Irina went missing from my life when she went to live with *him*." Dolores spat out the last word with venom.

She leaned forward and her face began to grow red. A vein began to pulse in her neck.

"She chose him! She chose to live with her father! That's when she disappeared from my life!"

I felt my face begin to burn. I understood what she meant now.

"If her father had cared about her, this never would have happened!" Dolores shouted. "And if *she* had cared about *me*, this never would have happened. She would have been at home with me where she belonged. *I* would have kept her safe!"

Dolores slumped back against the sofa and buried her head in her hands. She began to cry.

"I'm sorry," I said quietly.

I went to the door and let myself out.

Chapter Nine

That night I got ready for bed early.

I took off William's charm and set it on the table by my bed. Then I set my phone down, too, and climbed under the covers. I put my elbow over my eyes.

I wasn't quite ready to sleep yet, but I was tired—and I needed to lie down. My encounter with Dolores had been draining, and I was no closer to discovering what was going on with the disappearances.

My phone rang, startling me. I glanced over at it. It was Simon.

I picked up the phone. "Hey, Simon."

"You sound tired," he said. "Did I wake you?"

Simon's words were casual, but there was a note of anxiety in his voice.

"No, I wasn't sleeping," I replied. "Is everything okay? You sound like something's bothering you."

There was a long pause before Simon answered.

"Katie, I don't want you to get upset. But I think we should call off the investigation, and I mean both of us. My parents don't know anything about James's disappearance and—"

Simon broke off.

"And what, Simon?"

He sighed heavily. "Katie, don't you ever watch the evening news?"

"No, I was a little too worn out to watch the news. I went to see Irina's mother, and things didn't go so well."

"Maybe that's for the best," Simon said. "I really think you should stop looking into things."

"At the moment, I'm inclined to agree with you," I said. "But why won't you tell me what's wrong? Did something happen?"

"Katie, they found one of the missing people."

I felt a rush of excitement. "Simon, that's wonderful. Maybe they'll all be found now."

"Not this way, I hope," Simon said grimly. "When they found him, he was dead."

A chill spread through me. "Oh, Simon. It wasn't—"

"No, it wasn't James," he replied quickly.

"Then—"

"It was Mr. Hightower."

"Mr. Hightower?" I said.

"Yeah. They found him near the Old Grove. The body wasn't in good condition, but they identified him by a large ruby ring he used to wear. Katie, they said most of his bones had been broken, and his face and body had been torn apart. Whoever killed him was a real psycho."

The chill in my body deepened. "He was torn apart?"

"Yes," Simon replied grimly. "Do you see now why I think it's a good idea to stop the investigation?"

"Yes, I do see why," I said.

"I'm glad you agree."

"You must be terrified for James," I said.

"I'm worried about James and you. I don't want to see either one of you end up like Mr. Hightower. It's best that we stay out of the police's way and let them do their job. I care about you, Katie, and I want you to be safe."

"I want you to be safe, too," I said.

"Are we still on for tomorrow night?" Simon asked.

I was startled by the question. "You mean you still want to go to the movies, even after what happened to Mr. Hightower? And with James still missing? Are you sure you feel up to it?"

"Yes, like I said before, sitting at home won't do anyone any good."

"Okay," I replied. "Then I guess we're still on."

"Good night, Katie."

"Good night, Simon."

I set the phone down and pulled my covers around me more tightly.

Hearing about Mr. Hightower's gruesome death had left me feeling shaken.

I could definitely see Simon's point—stopping the investigation certainly seemed like a good idea. But I could also see that it was even more important for me to keep going.

I had to find out what was going on before anyone else got killed.

I tried to make sense of what I'd heard. If I believed that Gleb Mstislav was behind the disappearances, then did I also believe that he was responsible for Mr. Hightower's death?

I most definitely did.

Considering how badly Mr. Hightower's body had been mutilated—what could I do? What could anyone do against a creature like Gleb? And what exactly was he?

I looked over at William's cross where it lay on the table, reflecting the light from my lamp faintly. William had said that the charm would protect me.

I wondered if that were true.

And I wondered where William was.

Unfortunately, I had a lot to do before I could even begin to think about seeing William.

First I had to find a killer.

I reached over and switched off the light and resolved to get back to work tomorrow—with or without Simon.

And I hoped that no one else would be torn apart during the night.

Saturday morning, I showered and dressed quickly and hurried downstairs.

GM was already seated at the table, drinking a cup of tea, when I walked into the kitchen.

"Good morning, Katie. Would you like me to make you some eggs? Or maybe oatmeal?"

"No thanks, GM. I'm just going to have some yogurt and fruit."

I got what I needed and sat down at the table across from GM. I shot her a furtive glance.

She would have read the paper already and would know that Mr. Hightower's body had been found. I didn't know if she would agree to drive me around now that she knew there was a killer in town. I did know that walking around on my own would be out of the question.

"GM," I said, trying to sound casual as I stirred my yogurt, "there are a couple of places I would like to go to today. Would you mind driving me?"

"Where is it that you wish to go?"

Before I'd fallen asleep last night, I had worked out a plan, and I hesitated for just a moment as I prepared to lay it out for GM.

"You know how I went to see Irina's mother yesterday? I'd like to go see her father today, too. I'd also like to go see Mrs. Hannity. She's the neighbor of Mr. Del Gatto—he's my English teacher. He's one of the people who disappeared."

I waited, scarcely daring to breathe.

"What time would you like to go out?" GM did not sound troubled.

I relaxed. "We can go whenever you want. Whenever it's convenient for you."

GM smiled. "All right. How about after lunch?"

"That sounds great. Thanks. I was afraid you wouldn't want to go out after—the news."

"Do not fear. We should be safe enough during the day. Terrible things only seem to happen at night—and of course, you will be with me."

After breakfast, I went up to my room to finish making my plans. I still needed to look up Mrs. Hannity's address online—if I remembered correctly, her house was near the Old Grove. I hoped that I was right about that—it was an important part of my plan this afternoon.

I found her address and mapped it out. Luckily, I was right— her house was where I thought it was.

I turned to my homework then, and I forced myself to concentrate, telling myself it wouldn't help to obsess over what I had to do.

All the same, I was relieved when lunch was finally over, and GM and I went out to the car.

"Where to first?" she asked, as she settled behind the wheel.

"Let's go see Irina's father," I said. I gave her the address.

"That should be easy enough to find," GM replied.

She backed the car down the driveway and zoomed off.

Before long, we were pulling up to a big brick wall that surrounded a community named Sherwood Estates. We slipped through the entranceway and glided past stately homes with expansive, well-kept lawns. We continued on past the Estates' country club and golf course to a set of even larger homes.

GM soon brought the car to a stop. "This should be the place."

I looked up at the large, imposing house before us.

"Wow," I said.

"Would you like me to go in with you this time?" GM asked.

"No thanks. I'll be quick. I promise."

I got out of the car and stood for just a moment, staring down the long paved drive toward the monumental house. Then, I glanced at the equally impressive houses on either side.

Truthfully, I wouldn't have minded if GM had come with me, but I knew I couldn't let her find out what I was up to.

I walked up the drive to the front door and took a deep breath. I knew Mr. Neverov was out of town—thanks to the mysterious note I'd received—but I hoped that someone might be home anyway. Maybe I would still be able to find out something useful.

I reached for the big brass knocker on the door and gave it a few short raps. The sound was much louder than I had expected, and I couldn't help wincing.

Nothing happened, and after a moment, I knocked again.

Once again, nothing happened, and I began to look around for signs that someone might be home.

As I glanced around the front of the imposing house, I noticed very faint trails of black smoke. Surprised, I blinked and peered at the smoke trails more closely. They were hard to see, but they were definitely there—writhing in the air and forming bizarre and grotesque shapes. The effect was strangely hypnotic.

I blinked again and looked away. I knocked once more.

Just as I was starting to think I should give up, the door opened a few inches, and a woman with black-rimmed glasses and a severe bun looked out at me.

"Hi," I said, feeling very unsure of myself. "I'm from Irina's school, and I was wondering—"

"If this is about selling Girl Scout cookies," the woman said impatiently, "Mr. Neverov's household already has a source. We certainly don't need another one."

The woman withdrew.

I put out a hand to the door. "Wait! This isn't about Girl Scout cookies—and this is the wrong time of year for those anyway. It's about Irina."

The woman leaned out again, looking more impatient than ever. "What about Irina?"

"I—I'm worried about her. May I come in?"

The woman sighed. "Very well."

She let me into a highly polished hall and then led me past a large, ornate room with immense sofas and fragile-looking curios.

I paused to look.

"Come along, now," the woman said sharply. "You are not to go in there. The items in that room are too delicate to be handled by children."

"But I'm not—"

"Come along," the woman said.

I followed her dutifully.

"I don't have the faintest idea where to put you," the woman muttered as she led me through the expensive-looking house, her heels clicking sharply on the floor. "I'll have to place you somewhere where you can't break anything."

Eventually, the woman led me to a room and opened the door.

The woman waved a hand. "In you go. Putting you in here isn't ideal, but it's the only place where Mr. Neverov's antiques will be safe from little fingers. This is Mr. Neverov's office. Do *not* touch anything."

I walked into a bare-walled room with a desk, three chairs, and a row of metal filing cabinets. The lack of decoration in the office was in stark contrast to the rest of the house.

The woman turned to go and then turned back abruptly. "I almost forgot. What's your name? There's no point in my talking to Mr. Neverov if I don't have your name."

"It's Katie Wickliff," I said. "What's your name? Just in case I need it for some reason?"

"I am Ms. Finch. I'm Mr. Neverov's executive assistant."

The woman turned to leave again.

"Wait!" I said. "Is Mr. Neverov back, then? I'd heard he was out of town."

"Mr. Neverov is on vacation," Ms. Finch replied stiffly.

"He's on vacation?" I asked, startled.

Ms. Finch regarded me coldly. "Mr. Neverov is a very busy man and deserves his rest. His coming home will not bring his daughter back. He is in constant contact with the police, and they keep him apprised of each new development."

"So there have been developments?" I said.

"I'm going to call Mr. Neverov," Ms. Finch replied shortly, "and see if he wishes to speak to you about his daughter. And that is all I'm going to tell you at this time. As I said, do not touch anything while I'm gone."

Ms. Finch left the room.

As the door closed firmly behind her, I was left with the realization that Mr. Neverov would most likely refuse to speak to me. I looked around the room quickly—there were no papers or other kinds of evidence in sight.

I had only a few minutes at most if I wanted to search the room.

I knew I probably shouldn't, but I hurried to the desk and began to open the drawers. The first two drawers contained labeled folders, which I rifled through quickly—there was nothing about Irina in any of the folders.

In the third drawer, I found a clear plastic bag filled with white cloth. I opened the bag and pulled the cloth out, turning it over. I realized I was holding the white scarf Irina had been wearing the last time I'd seen her.

There were rust-colored stains on it.

I had a terrible feeling I was looking at dried blood.

I quickly pushed the scarf back in the bag and set it on the desk, and then I turned back to the drawer. A folder and two long, flat books sat in the bottom. The folder was labeled "Irina," and I pulled it out and flipped it open.

Inside were notes written in a small, neat hand. At the top of each sheet of paper was written the heading "From discussion with the police," and I scanned each sheet as quickly as possible. The first one documented the break-in at the school from the preceding Saturday night and the theft of the student records and yearbooks. The next sheet documented the disappearance of Mr. Del Gatto.

The one after that documented the disappearance of James. And the final sheet documented the disappearance of Irina herself.

I read over the Irina sheet quickly.

On Tuesday night, a cleaning woman had heard a crash, the back door had been pulled off its hinges, and Irina had not been seen after that. The door to Irina's bedroom had also been damaged, and her scarf had been found on the back lawn.

There were no further notes on Irina.

I turned next to the two long books in the drawer. They turned out to be yearbooks from our freshman and sophomore years.

I was puzzled as I looked over the yearbooks. I had forgotten about the break-in at the school—and Mr. Neverov not only had notes about the break-in, but he also had copies of the yearbooks themselves.

Was the theft of the records and yearbooks related to the disappearances?

I heard Ms. Finch's heels clicking down the hall toward me, and I quickly pushed everything back into the drawer and shut it.

I had just made it to the other side of the desk when Ms. Finch entered the room.

She raked suspicious eyes over me and then cast about the office, looking for signs of disorder. Apparently, she didn't find anything to comment on.

"I was unable to reach Mr. Neverov," Ms. Finch stated flatly. "Since I cannot confirm that you are, in fact, a friend of Irina's, you are not entitled to receive any news about her. I will escort you out."

Ms. Finch twitched her hand in an impatient gesture, and I hurried out of the office. She closed the door firmly behind me.

Ms. Finch then marched me through the house, her heels clacking sharply on the floor, and I felt just a little bit like a prisoner being taken to a new cell.

I was vastly relieved when we reached the front door, and I was shunted out.

I hurried back to the car.

"How was it?" GM asked.

"I didn't really get to speak to anybody," I replied, pulling my seat belt on. "Irina's father is away on vacation."

"On vacation?" GM looked surprised. "Where?"

"I don't know," I said. "GM, you'd come back from a vacation if I went missing, wouldn't you?"

She waved the question off. "Don't be silly, Katie. I would never go anywhere without you. So, where to next?"

"Mr. Del Gatto's neighbor, Mrs. Hannity," I replied, feeling a twinge of nervousness returning. I actually expected this part of the plan to be the most difficult. In reality, I wasn't all that interested in talking to Mrs. Hannity—though I would ask her a few questions. Instead, I was going to use the visit as a cover to search the Old Grove where Mr. Hightower's body had been found.

I knew GM would never take me over there.

"And where does Mr. Del Gatto's neighbor, Mrs. Hannity live?" GM asked, starting up the car.

"She lives in those town houses not too far from the Old Grove," I said. I gave her the address.

GM gave me a strange look as she put the car into gear. "You are certainly doing a lot of consoling, Katie, if you are consoling a teacher's neighbor."

I felt a little guilty about the whole thing—GM was right to wonder what was going on.

"It's as much for me as it is for them," I said a little lamely.

"I understand," GM said. "These are troubled times. You must do what you can to affirm your belief in human goodness."

I hoped I could do more than that—I hoped I could catch a killer.

GM drove over to the town houses quickly.

As we pulled into Mr. Del Gatto's neighborhood, I was able to pick out his place before we even stopped in front of it. I had seen his house last year on Mischief Night—the night before Halloween when pranksters were known to go out. That night I had gone to the movies with Branden and Charisse, and afterward, Branden had heard that a senior with a grudge against Mr. Del Gatto had covered the teacher's house with toilet paper. He had then dragged Charisse and me out to see it.

We had walked through the darkness to find it, and when we reached it, it was indeed all wrapped in toilet paper that stood out pale and ghostly in the night.

Branden had been overcome with laughter.

Mr. Del Gatto's house had been attached to its neighbor, and I remembered that the neighbor's half of the house had received the toilet paper treatment, also. I recalled admiring in amusement the plastic sheep that grazed peacefully in the neighbor's little patch of garden in the front.

The sheep had seemed blissfully unaware of the assault on their home.

I could see the sheep now, looking just as peaceful as ever.

We drew to a stop, and I slipped off my seat belt. "I'll be as quick as I can."

I hurried up to Mrs. Hannity's door and knocked, my heart pounding. I hoped she would be home—and I hoped I could pull off my plan.

As I waited on the porch, I glanced over at Mr. Del Gatto's door. I was surprised to see the same faint black smoke I had seen at Mr. Neverov's house swirling in grotesque shapes around Mr. Del Gatto's half of the house.

I turned and looked over Mrs. Hannity's place—her half of the house was free of the smoke.

I turned back to Mr. Del Gatto's and watched the smoke, twisting and turning in on itself like a tortured soul. The tormented motion was hypnotic, and I found myself unable to look away. The spell was broken abruptly when Mrs. Hannity's door opened, and the woman herself looked out.

Mrs. Hannity had a cloud of white hair and wide, good-natured eyes—I had seen her around town before.

She passed an oven mitt-clad hand over her forehead. "Yes, dear, what can I do for you?"

"Hi, Mrs. Hannity, I'm Katie Wickliff," I said, still feeling a bit distracted by the smoke. "Before I tell you why I'm here, may I ask you a question?"

Mrs. Hannity's wide eyes registered mild surprise. "Yes, you may."

"What's all that smoke on Mr. Del Gatto's porch?" I asked.

Mrs. Hannity stepped out and peered over at Mr. Del Gatto's half of the house. "I don't see any smoke, dear."

I felt a chill steal over me. I had been afraid of that.

"It must just be my eyes playing tricks on me," I said. "I'm one of Mr. Del Gatto's students. May I come in and ask you a few questions about him?"

Mrs. Hannity glanced over her shoulder. "Certainly you may, dear, but just for a moment. I'm baking for my church bake sale, and I'm very busy."

I stepped inside, breathing just a little easier. I was relieved to be past the first hurdle.

Mrs. Hannity led me back to a very warm kitchen where I was surrounded by the scent of sugar and baking dough.

She picked up a spatula and began moving chocolate chip cookies from a baking sheet onto a cooling rack.

"Would you like a cookie, dear?"

"No thank you, Mrs. Hannity. Can you tell me what happened the night Mr. Del Gatto disappeared?"

"That was Monday night." Mrs. Hannity frowned as she worked. "I was in the kitchen here. And do you know—I've never heard such a terrible racket in all my life. There was banging and crashing, and then a loud wrenching—I think that was Mr. Del Gatto's back door coming off its hinges. Then there was the most horrible screaming."

She paused and looked up at me. "You may not think it of me, but I'm very brave. I ran right outside to see what was the matter. Nobody was in the backyard, though—no intruder, no Mr. Del

Gatto, no one at all. There wasn't even any further screaming. It was as quiet in the night as if nothing had happened. All I saw was the door lying on the ground, and I called the police right away. They're the ones who told me poor Mr. Del Gatto had disappeared without leaving any clues—they didn't even find any fingerprints. Well, none aside from Mr. Del Gatto's own."

"And that's all you witnessed?" I asked.

"I'm afraid so," Mrs. Hannity replied. "Now, I really must get back to my baking. It requires precision and care, you know."

"Thanks for your time, Mrs. Hannity," I said, feeling my nerves rising again. "Do you mind if I go out the back door here?"

It was an ordinary request, but I feared Mrs. Hannity would refuse and insist I go out the front. If that happened, GM was definitely going to see me, and there was no way I would be able to sneak out to the Old Grove.

"Certainly, dear," Mrs. Hannity said, as she began spooning a fresh batch of cookies onto the baking sheet. "Have a good day."

I hadn't realized I was holding my breath until I started breathing again.

"Thanks, Mrs. Hannity," I said. I hurried to the door—I knew I wouldn't have much time to search the Old Grove for clues.

I ran out the door and across Mrs. Hannity's back lawn toward the forest.

As I ran, I couldn't help but notice that Mr. Del Gatto's half of the lawn was full of black smoke.

Chapter Ten

As I ran through the trees toward the Old Grove, I seemed to be following a trail of writhing black smoke.

I knew I was headed the right way, so I tried not to let the smoke distract me. But there was definitely something unnerving about the way it twisted—the shapes it formed were not familiar, but they were unwholesome—even threatening.

As I continued to run, I passed a white farmhouse in a small clearing—and I couldn't help but wonder if that was the house that Bryony's grandmother lived in with her ghost.

The smoke continued to trail ahead of me all the way to the Old Grove. When I finally reached it, I stopped abruptly and stared around me in shock.

There, in the circle of trees, I found myself standing in the middle of a thick, twisting cloud of the black smoke.

It swirled around me and rose up in a column. As I watched the smoke turn in on itself, I was startled to hear a faint whispering in the dark vapor. It was unintelligible, yet it seemed to draw me in, making me feel like I was drowning.

I shook my head to clear it—I was letting my imagination get the better of me.

I told myself that there was no whispering.

Suddenly, the feeling I'd had before of being watched came over me once again. I spun around, but I couldn't see anyone.

I decided to hurry up and get moving—GM was waiting, and I had to look around quickly.

I pushed through the smoky haze and tried to examine the grove—though the smoke made that more difficult. As I walked, my shoe caught on something, and I looked down to see a line of yellow police tape lying on the ground.

A chill ran through me as I realized that I must be close to the spot where Mr. Hightower's body had been found. Unfortunately, that was exactly what I was looking for—it was important for me to search the site where he had lain.

I figured I might find something the police had overlooked—after all, they hadn't been searching for anything supernatural.

I bent down close to the ground and brushed my hand over the cold leaves and dirt on the forest floor. I doubted that I would find the place where the body had actually lain—the police would hardly have drawn a chalk outline of it in the dirt—but if I were close, a clue of some kind might jump out at me.

I stayed close to the ground, searching for anything unusual, but the smoke was thicker here, and it clouded my vision. I tried to brush it out of the way, but it remained stubbornly in place. I squinted through it as best I could and continued to search.

Not too far from the base of a tree, I found a large patch of charred earth that extended in a circle—clearly a large fire had been set on this spot not too long ago.

As I examined the burned ground, I heard a rustling in the tree overhead. I looked up but couldn't see what was moving in the branches through the haze of smoke.

Then, from above me, came a short, sharp scraping sound—as if someone were striking a match.

I watched the tree nervously for several moments, fearing that fire was about to rain down on me.

But then I realized I was being paranoid—surely there was no one up the tree.

Who would climb a tree just to light a match?

I turned back to the burnt area and ran a finger over it, picking up a smudge of dark soot. I remembered that Simon's brother James and his friend had been accused of setting a fire that had actually been set by two strange men.

I wondered if this was the spot where the fire had been.

After a few moments, I stood up in resignation. Nothing was really jumping out at me, and the black smoke was making it difficult for me to search the grove properly—it was a complication I hadn't anticipated. I had been out in the grove for a little while now, and GM must have begun to wonder about me.

I decided I'd better get back—maybe I would get another chance to search the grove later.

As I turned to go with the black smoke swirling all around me, something fluttered down from the tree above, brushing softly against my cheek.

I watched as a scrap of paper settled down by my feet.

I bent to pick it up.

The scrap of paper was actually a black-and-white photo that was charred around the edges. The black edges of the photo were still warm, and the burnt scent rising off of it tickled my nose.

I peered at the photo, puzzled. It was a picture from my sophomore yearbook: Mr. Del Gatto, Irina, James, and I were standing against a wall at school—all with strained expressions on our faces. I remembered the day well.

Irina and I had been having an argument in the hall. Mr. Del Gatto had heard the raised voices and had come over to break things up and berate both of us. James, who was in danger of being late, had gone running by. Mr. Del Gatto had corralled him, too. Running in the halls was, after all, against the rules.

Mr. Del Gatto had been lecturing all of us when a student photographer had happened by and had asked to snap our picture, not quite realizing what was going on. Mr. Del Gatto had been thrown off by the appearance of the photographer and had let us all go after that.

I had been out sick the day the formal yearbook photos were taken, just as I had been my freshman year, so this candid photo was the only one of me in the whole yearbook.

I had been mortified when the photo had popped up originally, and as I looked at it now, I was struck by a jarring realization. The picture showed the first three victims of the recent disappearances—and it showed them in the exact order in which they had disappeared. Mr. Del Gatto had gone first, then Irina, then James. The only victim missing was Mr. Hightower—but as a substitute teacher, he was unlikely to appear in any yearbook photos.

And in his place in the lineup was me.

I was struck by an unpleasant thought—could I be next?

I looked back up at the tree. I still couldn't see anything in the branches above me through the swirling smoke. Was someone up there? Perhaps someone trying to warn me?

"Hello?" I called. "Is anyone there?"

But there was no answer, and the smoke continued to swirl with its faint whispers.

I backed away from the smoke into the surrounding trees. The smoke did not follow me—as I had half-feared it might—and once I was clear of it, I could see that it was concentrated in the open space of the grove. I looked over the whole mass of the dark, writhing vapor, and I saw that there was a line of the smoke trailing back the way I had originally come.

There was also another line running deeper into the woods.

I had seen the smoke at Mr. Neverov's house and at Mr. Del Gatto's—was it possible the smoke trail had something to do with Gleb? It certainly wasn't anything normal. I wondered then if I already had the clue I had been searching for—the smoke. I had a strange feeling that the police wouldn't have been able to see it— just as Mrs. Hannity hadn't been able to see it.

I knew I should be getting back to GM, but I wanted to find out what was going on with the smoke. I folded up the yearbook photo and put it in my coat pocket.

Then I followed the smoke trail deeper into the trees.

I hurried along as fast as I could, dodging branches. I had been to these woods many times, so I knew them well, and I knew there was a cave up ahead.

I had an uneasy feeling that I knew where the smoke trail led.

Following an impulse I didn't quite understand, I grabbed for my neck, searching for the iron charm William had given me. I realized with surprise that my neck was bare—I had forgotten to put the necklace on that morning.

I felt a brief stab of panic that I quickly pushed aside. I told myself that I was just being foolish—there was no reason for me to be concerned about not wearing a necklace.

I hurried on, and soon I could see a clearing ahead. Not long after, the cave came into view.

As I had feared, the trail of smoke wound down into the cave mouth.

I hesitated for just a moment and then plunged into it.

The cave was dry—not dank as I had thought it would be—and there was light to see by at first. I followed the smoke deeper into the cave, and as I moved farther from the mouth, the light grew dimmer.

As the light dimmed, the smoke changed, turning white and luminescent—it gave off just enough light for me to follow it.

I continued to follow the writhing white smoke deeper into the darkness, feeling along the cold stone walls with my hands. Twice I scraped my fingers across sharp rocks, and shortly after that I stumbled badly, falling on the unforgiving cave floor. My elbow hurt, and I could feel that I'd torn the knee of my jeans.

I got up and kept going.

Eventually, I spied a bright light up ahead, and a thick, whispering voice filtered up to me.

I could see that there was a chamber up ahead, and I crept closer.

Concealing myself behind an outcropping of rock, I peered into the chamber.

A large man, heavily swathed in furs, was sitting on a flat rock with his back to me. On the floor in front of the man was a lantern that cast a bright, harsh light up toward the ceiling. The smoke that I had followed wound into the chamber—it was white in the darkness and black where it touched the light.

It whirled in a ghostly, windless tornado, concentrating particularly around the man in furs.

Across from the man, I could see the shoulder of a second figure—it looked to be another man—though I couldn't be sure. The face of the far figure was blocked by the bulk of the man in furs, but I was pretty certain that the second figure was the one doing the whispering. Now that I could hear better, the whispered words had a harsh, malevolent sound.

I felt a chill steal over me.

I strained to listen, but I still couldn't understand what was being said.

I would have to go closer.

I had just begun to edge my way into the chamber when I felt fingers lace around my wrist, and I was pulled backward forcefully. I stumbled.

I nearly cried out, but I quickly thought better of it—the two figures in the cave chamber didn't seem terribly friendly. In the dim light, I could just make out a large, dark shape looming beside me. I tugged on my wrist, but I found that I was held in a grip of iron.

I was pulled forcefully to my feet and then dragged back along the cave tunnel away from the brightly lit chamber.

The tunnel was soon dark again except for the luminescent smoke trail.

As I was dragged on, the pace of my captor was too fast for me, and I stumbled again.

A hand encircled my waist and pulled me to my feet. I was pressed firmly against a strong, hard body and half-carried up the tunnel. My heart was hammering painfully—I feared what I would discover when we broke daylight.

The mouth of the cave soon yawned up ahead of us, and I was dragged out into the clearing in front of the cave, the now-black smoke swirling around me once again.

My captor released me, and I whirled around to face him. I was shocked to see who it was.

"William?" I said breathlessly.

"What are you doing here?" he demanded. "Do you know what's in that cave? Do you have any idea?"

I felt a flash of anger. William had interrupted me when I was on the verge of making a discovery. Now I would have to spend more precious time creeping back down the cave tunnel. There was no way I was going to go back to GM without finding out what was going on in that chamber.

"I'm going back in," I said. I turned and walked back toward the cave mouth.

William followed me and grabbed me by the arm, pulling me back.

He leaned close to me. "This is not a joke. That thing will kill you. I will not allow you to go back into that cave."

He began to pull me away from the cave mouth.

I tried to pull out of his grasp. "Where are you taking me?"

"Back to your house," William said.

"How did you know I was in there?" I asked.

"It's my business to know," he said, and he continued to pull me along.

"You have to stop," I said, digging my heels into the earth. "My grandmother is waiting for me. If I go home without her, she'll be worried."

William stopped and let go of my arm. "Go to her then. As long as you are wearing the charm I gave you, you'll be safe."

I shifted my weight uneasily. "What if I'm not wearing it?"

"Then get out of here," William said sharply. "You and your grandmother should get out of here immediately. The creature is weak during the day, but it's still strong enough to kill you. And it can track you at night."

"What creature?" I said. "What is it? Was that Gleb in there? And what is all that smoke?"

William stared at me in surprise. "You can see the smoke?"

"Yes," I said. "It's white in the dark and black in the light."

"I can't see the smoke," William said, staring at me searchingly. "I know it exists, and it clouds my senses. But I can't actually see it."

"Does the smoke come from Gleb?" I asked.

My question seemed to shake William out of his shock.

"Forget the smoke, Katie. Get out of here. Now. It's for your own safety."

I cast a mutinous glance past his shoulder in the direction of the cave.

William took an ominous step toward me as if he expected me to try to skirt around him.

I knew I wouldn't make it.

I turned resignedly and walked back in the direction of Mrs. Hannity's house.

I stopped once, looking over my shoulder to see if William was still there. I could see him, just at the edge of my vision, standing guard over the path to the cave.

I turned and ran the rest of the way.

Just as I spied Mrs. Hannity's backyard up ahead, a figure stepped into my path, and I was forced to stop.

I looked up to see a man standing in my way.

"Hello, little one," he said.

The man had chin-length hair, a short beard, and strangely antique, almost medieval clothes. He definitely looked out of place.

I tried to step around him. "Excuse me," I said.

132

The man stepped into my path again, and there was a hint of amusement in his clear, light-colored eyes.

"I will require just a moment of your time," he said evenly.

I glanced at the man sharply—he had a pronounced Russian accent.

"What do you want?" I asked.

"I am here to offer you some advice, little one."

The man's stare made me feel distinctly uncomfortable—I felt like a rabbit that had stumbled into the path of a wolf.

"I really have to go," I said. "Someone is waiting for me."

The man smiled—a truly disturbing sight.

"You look nervous, little one," the man said. "I am not here to harm you. I am merely here on behalf of some interested parties that shall remain nameless. Certain events have been set into motion, and I can say without exaggeration that you are in a great deal of danger. I am here to recommend to you that you stay close to William."

I began to feel very afraid of the man before me. "You mean William Sursur?" I said.

"The very same."

"You know him?" I asked.

"Yes, very well, little one. He is the one who is best equipped to protect you. I wish I could do it myself, but alas, William has abilities that I do not."

"I don't understand," I said.

"It is not necessary for you to understand," the man replied. "Just follow my advice. As I said, stay close to William. But though you stay close, at the same time, do be careful. It wouldn't do for you to become too fond of him—that is, if you were inclined toward such a thing."

"Why not?" I said.

"Sometimes the people we love aren't telling us the whole truth. Has William told you, for instance, who he is?"

"He told me his name."

The man in front of me smiled.

"Has he told you *what* he is? Surely, you must have noticed by now that William can do things that are, shall we say, unusual?" The man tilted his head. "Perhaps even superhuman?"

"No—he hasn't told me what he is," I said.

"Well then, I will tell you," the strange man said. "I believe you deserve to know. Though he denies it, William knows in his heart of hearts that he is a vampire."

Panic stabbed through me. "A vampire?"

"Yes. I can see that you aren't entirely surprised. That's good. You'll need to keep your wits about you."

"What do you mean?" I said.

"Be careful, little one. Sometimes the people we love can betray us. Be alert for—signs. In everyone. A monster is always a monster."

"Do you mean William?" I asked.

The man simply shook his head. "I've said all I am allowed to say. Good day, little one. And don't let William know that you know what he is. It wouldn't be wise."

The man turned to go. Then something seemed to strike him, and he turned back.

"There is one other thing. And this time I'm speaking purely as myself and not in any official capacity. Don't be too upset with your friend. It's not her fault. She's vulnerable at the moment, and she's being—influenced."

"Do you mean Charisse?" I said. "Charisse is being influenced? By whom?"

"Charisse," the man said. "What a lovely name. Just remember what I said. A monster is always a monster, no matter how attractive the outward appearance may be."

He turned away again.

"Wait," I said. "Who are you?"

The man glanced back at me in amusement. "I'm someone who should know."

He gave me one last disturbing smile, and then he melted into the trees.

Chapter Eleven

William was a vampire.

As the strange man had said, I wasn't entirely surprised.

I hurried on to Mrs. Hannity's backyard, and then I ran on, racing around to the front past the grazing plastic sheep.

I ran up to GM's car and threw myself into the passenger's seat.

GM frowned at me. "What have you been doing in there? It's been well over an hour."

Her expression changed to one of horror as she took in my appearance. "You're scratched and bleeding. What happened to you?"

I took a deep breath—I had to think quickly. Though I felt bad about making up a phony story to tell GM, there was no way I could tell her about the cave—or about the man I had just met.

"I—I was helping Mrs. Hannity clean up her backyard."

I was pretty sure that the backyard was obscured by the house, and I resisted the urge to turn and look to double-check that fact.

I continued. "She had a lot of leaves and branches that needed to be cleared out and placed into lawn bags. I fell while reaching for a loose branch on a tree."

GM was incredulous. "She had you clean out her backyard?"

I shifted uneasily. "Yes."

GM shook her head and started the car. "Unbelievable. The nerve of that woman. To ask you to do something like that when you are visiting her to cheer her up. No more visits for you—today or ever again. You have done enough already."

I was tired and was inclined to agree with GM about the visits.

I felt a wave of frustration wash over me—if only I knew what was going on and how to stop it. It seemed pretty obvious to me that the two men in the cave were involved in the disappearances somehow. Or at least I thought they were two men—I hadn't been able to see the faces of either of them.

William, the vampire, had rather firmly gotten in my way.

GM drove us home quickly, and I went upstairs to change my torn jeans and clean my cuts and scrapes. I made sure to put the iron charm on, too.

Then I sat on my bed.

William was a vampire.

Of course, there was no reason why I should believe the strange, rather unnerving man who had appeared out of nowhere and stepped into my path.

But I did believe him.

And I had suspected the same thing myself.

So, did I believe William was a monster?

I couldn't believe that of him—no matter what the facts might say to the contrary. I believed he was a vampire—but I had looked into his eyes, and I had not seen a monster there. Was it possible for someone to be both a vampire and a good person?

I didn't know for sure.

But I loved William anyway.

I was startled to realize that that was true—I knew what William was, and I loved him.

I sat still for a long time.

Eventually, I forced myself to stir. I still had the Gleb problem to worry about.

I got up and pulled the charred photo I'd found out of my coat pocket. As I stared at the four faces before me, I couldn't help but think once again that this was a lineup of victims.

Mr. Del Gatto, Irina, James, me.

I sat down on my bed, still holding the photo.

Clearly someone had meant for me to find the yearbook photo, and I wondered who it was who had dropped it from the tree. Since William had been in the area, he was the most likely candidate to have dropped it. But if it had been him, why hadn't he spoken to me about not going into the cave at that very moment? Why would he wait till later to waylay me in the dark as he had done?

It seemed to me very unlikely that it had been William.

Whether or not William had dropped the photo, he certainly seemed to know who was down in the cave. I thought back to the words he had used—"that thing" and "the creature."

What was it that was hiding in that cave?

I thought back, too, to the strange smoke I'd seen at two of the victims' homes and down in the cave. I wondered where Mr. Hightower had lived, and I wished now that I could go see the place—I had a feeling that I would see the smoke there, too.

The smoke trail seemed to be exactly that—a trail.

If I could see where Mr. Hightower had lived, and I spotted the smoke trail again, I would know for sure that the smoke marked the perpetrator's passage.

Of course, I could check Simon and James's house for the smoke, too—maybe I could suggest to Simon that we stop by his house before going to the movies.

Thinking of Simon and James reminded me that James had seen two men—one of them in furs—burning something in the Old Grove. Had I seen the same two men? And what had they been burning?

I looked down at the charred yearbook photo. Could they have been burning pages from our high school yearbooks? And why would they do such a thing?

I set the photo down on the bed, and I tried to organize my thoughts, but ultimately, I didn't know what to think. I just hoped that William was safe—whatever it was he was doing back at that cave.

All I could do right now was wait to see what I found at Simon's house.

Eventually, GM called me for dinner, and as I walked down the stairs, I realized that there might be a snag in my plan to check Simon's house for the smoke trail—GM might not let me go out to see Simon tonight.

She had agreed to it earlier in the week, but I realized now that she might have changed her mind about letting me go.

As we sat down to dinner, I decided to broach the topic.

"GM," I said uncertainly.

"Yes, solnyshko?"

"Simon had asked me to go to the movies with him tonight—do you remember? Is it still all right for me to go?"

GM shook her head. "No. I don't think it's safe. Not at night—not since that poor man was murdered. Going out during the day is one thing, but the night is another matter entirely. Once the terrible person who is stalking our town is caught, you may go out again after dark. But not while it is so dangerous. You'll have to call Simon and tell him you can't go."

I started to object but stopped when I saw the look on GM's face. I knew that there was no way I would be able to change her mind. Maybe I could ask her later if I could go over to see Simon tomorrow afternoon. I just hoped that would be soon enough.

After dinner, I went up to my room and sat on my bed to call Simon.

He answered on the first ring. "Hey, Katie."

"Hey, Simon."

"So, what do you want to see tonight?" he asked.

Simon sounded so happy that I suddenly felt really terrible.

"I'm sorry, Simon," I said. "I was just talking with GM, and she said I can't go with you to the movies tonight. She's asked me to stay at home at night until things get better in town. I think Mr. Hightower's death really upset her."

There was a long pause on the other end.

I felt even worse as the silence stretched—I couldn't think of anything to say.

"I understand," Simon said at last. His voice was low and mournful. "I'm going to miss seeing you, though."

"I really am sorry," I said. An apology didn't feel like quite enough. I wished Simon didn't sound so sad.

"Have a good night, Katie," he said. "Stay safe."

"I will. You stay safe, too. Good night, Simon."

"Good night, Katie."

After Simon hung up, I fell back against the pillows and lay still for a moment, clutching the phone.

Charisse had been in the back of my mind since I'd come home. The cryptic remarks the strange man in the forest had made about her were still with me, and I'd had a strong feeling that I should warn her—but at the same time, I had a feeling that she wouldn't listen.

I decided I had to try, and I quickly dialed her number. I waited anxiously, listening to the phone ring.

As I feared, the phone rang and rang and then went to voicemail.

"Charisse, I received a—warning—about you today," I said. "I just want you to be okay. Give me a call when you get this. It's important."

I sent her a text then, but I had a terrible feeling that she'd just delete it.

I considered going over to Charisse's house, but that might just result in a scene—and she still wouldn't listen. I leaned my head back and closed my eyes and tried to think of another way to get a message to her.

But as I rested with my eyes closed, I began to relax, and I suddenly realized just how tired I was. Before long, I sank into sleep.

Some time later, I awoke with a start, and I sat up.

I had a strong feeling that some loud sound had woken me, and I held my breath, listening.

The house was still.

I glanced at the clock next to my bed, and I was shocked to see that it was a little past eleven thirty. I'd intended only to take a nap and had ended up sleeping for hours.

I'd left the light on when I'd settled down for my nap, and as I looked around my room, I felt unnaturally alert. I continued to listen for signs of movement in the house.

But there were no sounds, and I figured I'd been awakened by GM coming up to go to bed.

I got up and stretched and decided to get ready for bed myself. I changed into my nightclothes and stood for a moment with William's charm in my hands. I typically took it off and set it on my nightstand, but tonight I decided to keep it on.

The necklace made me feel as if William were close somehow, and I didn't want to be parted from it.

I wondered what William was doing at this very moment, and I wondered if he was all right.

I settled the charm around my neck, and I turned to my mirror.

As I was running a brush through my hair, there was a scrabbling sound on the roof above me, and I froze.

Though I could not have said why, my heart began to beat very fast.

There was a long stretch of silence, and then the scrabbling sound came again. It was followed by a series of short, sharp stomps.

It sounded very much like someone was on the roof.

The stomping sounds ran all the way across the roof and then disappeared.

I stood still, hoping very hard that the noises would stop.

Somehow I knew I wouldn't be that lucky.

The house was mercifully silent for a few moments, and then a rhythmic rattling began at the back of the house.

I hurried to my door and stepped out into the dark hall, every nerve in my body raw and tingling.

I glanced toward GM's door, but everything was quiet in that direction. As I stood listening, the rattling continued—it was coming from below.

I crept down the stairs.

The rattling grew louder and more forceful.

I reached the bottom step and stood in the dark hall with a bone-deep chill spreading through me. I could hear the rattling very clearly now, and I looked toward the back of the house. Someone was at the back door, trying to get in.

I remembered with a sharp pang of fear that all of the missing people had been stolen from their homes at night after their doors had been torn off. Was that about to happen to me?

Suddenly, there was a loud pounding on the front door.

I was closer to the front door, and I whirled to face it.

The rattling in the back grew louder—and the pounding in the front grew heavier and heavier.

My blood turned to slow ice in my veins. Both exits were being attacked.

There was no way out.

With a terrifying crash, a section of the front door splintered, leaving a small hole in the center.

I felt a cry rise to my lips, but I stifled it, my heart pounding painfully.

"Katie!" cried a voice from the front door.

Through my haze of fear, I realized the voice sounded like William's.

"Katie!" the voice cried again.

More of the front door splintered, letting in the light from the street, and I inched toward it on shaking legs.

"William? Is that you?" I asked.

William's face appeared in the gaping hole in the broken door.

I felt relief flood through me. How had William seen me in the dark through that first small hole in the door? But then again, I supposed vampires had no trouble seeing in the dark.

There was one more terrific crash from the front door, and William battered his way through it. He was beside me in an instant.

His fingers dug into my arms.

"What are you doing here?" he whispered fiercely. "Why didn't you leave like I told you to?"

"What do you mean?" I asked. "I left the Old Grove just like you said."

"When I told you to leave," William whispered angrily, "I meant you should leave town—get as far away from Elspeth's Grove as possible."

Disappointment lanced through me sharply. "I didn't realize that's what you meant. Why don't you want me here?"

"It isn't that I don't want you here," he hissed. "It's for your own good. After you went into the cave, the creature caught your scent. It hunts you now."

"But I put on the charm," I protested. "How did it find me?"

"You left a trail when you weren't wearing the charm. The creature followed that trail to your house. It can't scent you now that you wear it, but here in the house it won't need to. It can hunt by sight."

"What is it?" I demanded. "If it's hunting me, I think I have a right to know."

William sent a worried glance over my shoulder. "If it will help to convince you to leave, then I will tell you. The thing out there is a kost—an evil spirit. It inhabits the body of a man who was named Gleb Mstislav, and it has an active grudge against the living. It seeks only to kill. It is more than capable of tearing you and this house apart. Right now, it is just toying with you. It's trying to scare you before it finally decides to attack."

A cold so profound that it shook me from head to toe spread through my body. "What can we do?"

The rattling at the back door grew louder still.

William began to pull me toward the broken front door. "I have to get you out of here now."

I struggled in his grasp.

"I have to get GM," I said frantically. "She's upstairs."

"I'll see that you both get out of here," William said. "But you have to hurry. You won't have time to pack anything—you'll both just have to get in the car and go."

He took my hand and ran with me up the stairs. When we reached the top landing, he released me.

"Go to your grandmother and bring her out quickly. I'll go back downstairs to guard your exit."

I switched on the light and hurried down the hall. I flung GM's bedroom door open.

In the dim light, I could just make out her sleeping form, and I stumbled across the room to her bed. Though GM liked to keep late hours, when she did sleep, she slept deeply. I could hear the rattling downstairs, and I marveled incredulously at her ability to sleep through it.

"GM, wake up," I said, panic rising in my voice. "We have to get out of here."

She did not stir.

For one brief moment, I feared that somehow the creature below had already gotten to her and that she was dead. I forced my fear away and shook her firmly by the shoulder.

"GM, wake up!"

To my relief, she turned over and blinked, shading her eyes against the light in the hall.

"Katie, what's wrong?"

I tried to keep the trembling out of my voice.

"GM, you have to get up," I said. "We have to get out of the house right now."

She sat up. "What? Why?"

I didn't have time to be diplomatic. "Because if we don't, we're going to die."

"Katie," GM said, concerned, "what is wrong with you?"

"Someone's downstairs trying to get in," I said. "It's the same person who took all the people from school. He's come for us now."

GM's eyes widened with horror. She hastily shoved her feet into a pair of shoes by the bed.

"I'm coming—I'm coming. Katie, grab some shoes and a coat to wear."

I hurried to my room to comply.

Soon, GM and I ran out into the hall in coats, shoes, and nightclothes.

As I reached the ground floor, I could hear a horrible splintering sound.

"He's breaking in!" William cried from the kitchen.

"I'll get your purse, GM," I shouted. "Just run for the front door."

I grabbed the purse and turned to look for GM. Instead of running, she was standing in the hall, staring toward the back of the house.

There was another splintering sound, followed by short, sharp screams. The screams continued.

"What is that?" GM asked, her eyes wide. "What is going on?"

"He's ready to attack!" William shouted. "Both of you need to get out of here! Now!"

I looked for William. All I could see was his dark outline in the kitchen.

"We'll go to the police," GM said.

"No!" William shouted forcefully.

Anger flickered in GM's eyes.

The screaming escalated. There was a loud crash.

"Why not?" GM demanded.

"That's one of the first places he'll look when he finds you're gone!" William shouted. "And the police can't stop him. Get out of this town. Go—run! If I survive, I'll find the two of you."

A sharp stab of terror ran through me. "*If* you survive?"

"Yes, 'if!'" William shouted. "If not, then you'll have to keep running."

The house was shaken by an even louder crash, and I heard a triumphant shriek.

Luminous white smoke began to swirl into the kitchen, and over William's shoulder, I could see a large, dark shape moving toward us. The dark shape suddenly charged into the hall, and I caught sight of a man's face—ghastly, pale, and bloated—a face from a nightmare.

William lunged at the creature and brought it to the ground, shrieking.

I was rooted to the spot in horror.

"Katie, run!" GM cried. She grabbed me by the hand and dragged me out through the broken front door.

I risked one last look back. William looked up, and his eyes met mine for just a moment.

My own eyes filled with tears as GM dragged me away.

Chapter Twelve

We ran to the car, and GM sped off into the night.

"Where's your phone?" I asked urgently. "Do you have your phone?"

"It's in my purse, Katie," GM said, turning a corner sharply. "It fell to the floor by your feet."

Of course that's where it was—I was the one who had dropped it. I found the purse and then fumbled with the clasp. I managed to get it open, and I riffled through it frantically for the phone.

"Who are you calling?" GM asked.

"The police," I said.

"The boy in the kitchen told us not to go to the police."

"I know," I said. "I'm not calling for us. I'm calling for him. The police should go out to the house to help him. Maybe they can scare the creature off."

I found the phone, and I dialed 911 with trembling fingers. A woman answered, and I told her that our house was being attacked. Then I gave her the address.

She told me help was on the way.

I considered calling Charisse next to tell her that GM and I had to leave town and not to worry, but I was afraid she wouldn't answer. I considered calling Simon, too, but I knew he would answer—and he might try to come after us.

I didn't want him getting mixed up in this.

"Who is he, Katie?" GM asked after I put the phone away.

I looked over at her. Though the light was dim, I could see that her face was carefully neutral—it was the face she wore whenever she talked about troubling subjects.

"Who do you mean?" I asked.

"The young man at our house," GM replied. "Who is he?"

"He came out of nowhere and broke down the front door," I said carefully. "He came to warn us about the attack. He's the only reason we got out of the house in time."

GM was silent.

I hoped she wouldn't ask me any further questions about William—I didn't want him to become something else that would be off limits.

I thought back to the horrible, distorted white face I had seen in the hall back at the house, and I felt sick with fear for William.

"GM, have you ever heard of a creature called a 'kost'?" I asked.

"Yes, I have," she said. "Did the young man say that's what that was?"

"Yes," I replied. "And he gave me this iron cross." On impulse, I took it out to show her. "He said it would prevent the creature from tracking me."

GM fingered her own silver cross—I knew that she usually slept with it on.

"Is a kost one of those things that you don't believe in?" I asked.

GM simply sighed.

"Will he—the young man—be okay back at the house?" I asked.

GM looked over at me then. "I hope so, solnyshko."

I turned to stare out the window. The streets were deserted as we drove on, and the streetlights flashed across my eyes from time to time, the only source of light out in the night.

As the miles flew by, I continued to think of William and that horrible creature, and I was afraid for him. Was it even now tearing him apart? I closed my eyes and felt tears stinging my eyelids.

GM switched on some music, and I heard the opening strains of Mussorgsky's *Pictures at an Exhibition*. The piece had been my mother's favorite, and I always found it soothing. GM favored the original arrangement for piano.

I listened, and the music worked its usual charm. Time passed, and I began to grow calmer. By the time we got to *The Great Gate of Kiev*, I couldn't help but smile a little.

"Behind the great gate of Kiev," I murmured. "That's what my mother always used to say whenever I asked where anything was. If I lost a toy or wondered where someone had gone, she always said that what I was looking for was 'behind the great gate of Kiev.'"

GM smiled, too. "I remember her saying that. Kiev is actually in the Ukraine, you know, though it was Russia's ancient capital."

"I know." I'd looked the city up on a map when I was a child—after what my mother had told me, I'd once hoped to go there to find all my lost things.

I sat up straighter in my seat and peered out into the darkness. "We've been driving for a long time. Where are we going?"

"The airport," GM replied.

"The airport?" I was startled. That could mean only one thing—we only had ties to one other place in the world apart from Elspeth's Grove. "Are we going to Russia?"

"Russia is our ultimate destination," GM said. "But we will fly to Georgia first—to Tbilisi. Georgia in Europe, of course. Not the Georgia in the U.S."

"Georgia? Why?"

"We would need a visa to enter Russia from the U.S, and we don't have time to obtain one. Luckily, I do have our passports—I always keep them in my purse. But we don't need a visa to enter Georgia. We'll fly into Georgia and then cross the border."

"Illegally?" I asked.

"Illegally," GM replied.

"Are we going to see Galina and Aleksandr?" I asked.

"Yes."

"But you don't believe in their superstitions," I said.

GM gave me an uncharacteristically bleak look. "We need to get answers, Katie. Nothing is the way it should be."

We drove on through the night, and eventually I fell into a light sleep.

I was dimly aware of GM calling the airport to inquire about flights to Georgia, but for the most part, I passed through troubled dreams that always ended the same way—with a hulking white-faced monster battering down a door.

I had just started awake for what felt like the hundredth time, when bright lights passed over my eyes, causing me to blink in their glare. I sat up in my seat and looked out the window. GM was pulling into a large, well-lit parking lot.

"Where are we?" I asked.

"We're at a mall not too far from the airport," GM replied.

I was puzzled. "A mall? What time is it?"

I looked around—though the lights were bright in the parking lot, there were no other cars, and the mall was clearly closed.

"It's a little past three in the morning," GM replied. "The mall will not be open for many hours yet, but luckily our flight doesn't leave till the afternoon. We were lucky, too, that we will be leaving today. There is only one flight to Georgia from here, and it only leaves every other day."

"But why are we at the mall?"

"We will need regular street clothes, amongst other things. Otherwise, we will look very suspicious trying to board a plane in our nightclothes with no luggage. Also, you may need to brush your hair."

I couldn't help smiling a little. We probably did look a bit of a fright.

"You should try to get some sleep, solnyshko," GM said. "It's been a long night for you. I will keep watch, and you will be safe."

"You're the one who's been doing all the driving," I said. "You should sleep."

"Katie, you know I don't sleep much," GM said firmly. "And I won't sleep at all knowing that you are awake. Go to sleep. Now."

"You're a tough one to argue with," I said.

GM smiled. "I like to win. Now close your eyes."

I did as she asked, and GM started *Pictures at an Exhibition* again from the beginning. The car was warm, and I was really worn out, so despite the bright lights in the parking lot, I found myself drifting off to sleep again. Though the movement hadn't started yet, my mind lingered on *The Great Gate of Kiev*. Behind it, my mother had said I would find anything.

I wondered dreamily—if I looked behind it, would I find her there?

I woke up some time later, and for a moment, I wasn't quite sure where I was. I looked around at GM and the car and the parking lot, and the events of the night came flooding back to me. After I realized where I was, my first thought was of William.

Whatever was going to happen to him back at the house was surely over by now.

I hoped with all my heart that he was safe.

GM turned to look at me. "How did you sleep, solnyshko?"

"Pretty well, considering." The fact that I had had no dreams this time around had helped.

"I'm glad to hear it. Do you think that you would like some breakfast?"

"Yes, that sounds good," I said.

"Excellent," GM said. "The food court in the mall opens at eight a.m., and it's a little past that now. We can go in and maybe find something healthy."

She took in her reflection in the rearview mirror. "I hope our appearance won't cause too much comment."

The two of us got out of the car, and I could see that the parking lot lights were off, and the sky was sunny and cloudless. The morning was pretty chilly, and my bare feet were cold in my shoes. The two of us did look a little strange in our nightclothes and coats—GM was wearing light blue silk pajamas, and I was wearing a thin pink nightshirt.

We hurried into the mall through the nearest entrance.

Soon I could smell coffee and eggs, and GM and I walked into a sea of tables and plastic chairs that was ringed by narrow restaurant stalls. Most of the stalls were dark—but a handful were open, and small groups of people were scattered around the tables eating breakfast.

"What are you in the mood for, Katie?" GM asked.

"I think eggs and orange juice sounds just about perfect," I said.

GM smiled. "Eggs and orange juice it is."

Before long, GM and I were seated in plastic chairs of our own, with scrambled eggs and juice. GM had also insisted on oatmeal.

While we were eating, I thought about the trip ahead of us.

"When we get to Russia, will I get to see my cousin again?" Over the years I had wondered what had become of my laughing, red-haired cousin, Odette. She had been a few years older than I, and I had admired her in that innocent, worshipful way that a small child admires an older one.

"Odette?" GM said. "Yes, I believe we will see her."

"I thought she was really wonderful—beautiful like a princess."

GM smiled. "I remember."

"I don't have very clear memories of my aunt and uncle, though. Odette did have parents, right? My father's brother and his wife?"

"You are being facetious, solnyshko. Yes, of course, Odette had parents. But there's a reason why you don't remember them—a good reason."

I waited for GM to continue, but she simply sipped her juice.

"So, there's a good reason why I don't remember them," I said, "but you aren't going to tell me what it is?"

"No. It doesn't affect our situation. It has nothing to do with visions, superstitions, or mysterious dead men."

"More secrets," I said quietly.

"Sometimes secrets are good, Katie."

After breakfast, we walked around the mall until the shops opened at ten. We went to buy clothes first, and I was happy to have socks again. GM bought more things than I thought were really necessary, and I began to wonder how long she thought we would be gone.

"We have to be prepared for everything," she said.

We bought toiletries next, and in the mall bathroom, I brushed my hair and brushed my teeth. Then I changed my clothes. Though our situation was unusual to say the least—we were on the run from a reanimated corpse—doing simple things like brushing my teeth made me feel a little more normal.

Finally, GM and I went to buy luggage. GM went straight for a set of designer luggage for me, but all I really wanted was a backpack. I figured I could fit everything I had into it, even if I had to squish things a little, and then I could just have a carry-on.

GM allowed me to have the backpack but insisted that I have a rolling suitcase with a handle as well. GM purchased two larger suitcases for herself, and she also bought flashlights, batteries, blankets, travel pillows, a thermos, and a first-aid kit.

"Just in case, solnyshko," she said.

At last we were done shopping, and we took all our stuff out to the car.

"Let us do our packing now," GM said. "That way we can walk into the airport like normal people."

I had to smile at that, and we began to place all our things on the hood of the car.

I stopped suddenly. "You're not worried about all this scratching the paint on your car, are you? I know how much it means to you."

GM waved a hand airily. "No, no, solnyshko. Looking normal is more important than a few scratches at this point."

We got to work packing. It took us about twenty minutes, but we got everything to fit. We put our bags in the trunk.

"It looks like we're normal now, GM," I said.

We got into the car and drove to the airport. GM had purchased our tickets over the phone, so we went in and checked in. We still had several hours to wait until our flight, so we had a leisurely lunch in a restaurant at the airport.

Our table was right next to a window, and from where we sat I could see planes arriving and taking off. As I started on my ravioli, I began to feel a little nervous. I hadn't been on a plane since I was five years old—and that was when I was coming to the U.S. from Russia with GM. We had no relatives in the U.S. to visit, and GM had certainly never taken us back to Russia. She also seldom went on vacation or took breaks from her work.

"What's being on a plane like?" I asked. I watched as a huge passenger jet taxied down a runway and took off.

"It's not such a big deal," GM said. She gave me a sharp look. "Are you worried about the flight, solnyshko?"

"A little."

"Do not fear. You'll be fine. I know that you are brave."

"What about your work?" I asked. "Didn't you just start a new project?"

"The project will be fine, too," GM said. "That's the last thing you need to worry about. What's most important is finding out what's going on."

I watched a few more planes take off. Soon GM and I would be on one of them. We were very genuinely flying into the unknown.

Before I knew it, it was time for us to board our flight. We walked down a long tunnel into the plane where a cheerful blond woman greeted us. As we passed her, I looked around sharply.

The strange feeling I'd had before at school that someone was watching me had suddenly come over me again.

But behind me all I saw were restless passengers waiting to get down the narrow aisle to their seats. Surely, none of them was interested in me.

GM and I found our seats, and I stashed my backpack under the seat in front of me. The cabin seemed kind of small and cramped to me, and I felt a fluttering in my stomach. Now that the flight was becoming real, my nerves were on me in a rush.

All too soon it was time for takeoff, and the plane began to accelerate down the runway. The sensation of being pushed back into my seat was startling to me, and I dug my fingers into my armrests. The plane tilted upward, and I glanced out the window— we were climbing steadily, impossibly in the air. Mercifully, the pressure on me began to ease, and it was not long before we had leveled off and were flying smoothly.

I had a feeling that the worst was behind me, and I breathed out in relief.

We had a long flight ahead of us.

For the most part, I dozed, but I had plenty of time to think, too, and in a rambling, haphazard way, I sifted through my memories, trying to come up with something that might help GM and me in our current predicament.

What did you do when you were being chased by a man who was already dead?

And if that man had killed my mother as Galina believed, what did he want with me? Surely, when he had taken her life, he had taken everything she'd had.

I thought back over the strange things I'd heard over the last week. Aleksandr had said there were darker things than vampires in Krov—and it seemed that Gleb was one of those darker things.

In some ways it was a shame Gleb wasn't a vampire—at least I had some idea of how to stop one—that is if popular folklore was to be believed.

But how did you stop an evil spirit in a dead man's body?

154

I frowned as an indistinct memory tugged at the back of my mind. Mr. Hightower had said something strange, too—something about a legend from the town of Krov—the legend of the Little Sun. I didn't know what that was, and I thought I might ask GM about it. Since our current circumstances were unusual—to say the least—maybe she wouldn't mind discussing it. And maybe there would be a clue in the tale somewhere.

I glanced over at GM. She seemed to be sleeping peacefully, and I hesitated to wake her.

I shifted in my seat and looked around at the cabin. The lights were off, and most people appeared to be asleep—the only sound was the steady hum of the plane's engines. It occurred to me that now wasn't the ideal time to talk to GM anyway—in the quiet cabin our voices would attract attention. I had a feeling it would be better to talk to her when we couldn't be overheard.

I settled back into my seat and tried to sleep.

Several hours later, the lights came back on and people began to stir. GM's eyes fluttered open.

"Good morning, Katie," she said. "If indeed it is morning."

"Good morning, GM."

GM asked a passing flight attendant for some water, and once she had it, I decided with some nervousness to ask her about the Little Sun. Her actions over the last several hours seemed to indicate that she had become a little more open in her attitude to the past and its superstitions, but I knew it was still dangerous territory.

"GM," I said uncertainly. "Mr. Hightower—the teacher who died—he mentioned the legend of the Little Sun to me once. He said it was from Krov. Do you know what it is?"

She sighed. "Yes, I know it. It's just a story—something parents tell their children before bedtime."

"Can you tell it to me?"

She sighed again. "Very well—there isn't much to it. According to the tale, in every generation in Krov a pure-hearted child is born who has the power to hold back the darkness and save the village—

in other words, to be a hero or heroine to the whole town. A mother would tell this to a child so he or she would go to bed on time and prove to be the heroic Little Sun."

"What do you mean by 'hold back the darkness'?" I asked.

GM shook her head. "It's nothing but silliness, Katie. The child of the tale supposedly has the ability to command a sphere of light with great power over evil. As a reference to the sphere, the child is called 'solnyshko' or 'little sun,' just like I call you. But the use of the word is common enough apart from the legend. I called your mother that, too. Many mothers use it."

"That's all there is to the legend?" I said.

"That's all I know," GM replied.

I leaned my head back against my seat. GM's story hadn't really told me much. It sounded like she was right—it was simply a bedtime story used to convince children to be good.

I would have to look elsewhere for information.

I suddenly felt once again like someone was watching me, and I turned in my seat so I could see over it. I looked around, but I didn't see anyone looking in my direction.

I remembered that the first time I had had that feeling, I had actually seen a pair of floating eyes. On impulse, I wondered if I could get the eyes to appear again—if I concentrated hard enough.

I looked around, and I willed the eyes to materialize.

Something seemed to pull me in a particular direction, and I found myself focusing on a heavyset man in a gray suit. He appeared to be absorbed in a book, so I concentrated on him as hard as I could and tried to see the floating eyes. Though it was indistinct, after a few moments of trying, I was pretty sure that I could just see a hazy image of two circles floating in the air. I concentrated harder, and the man in gray looked up at me and frowned.

I looked away, embarrassed, and I began to berate myself.

What had made me think I could will myself to see floating eyes? And why was I encouraging myself to see things that weren't there?

I had to keep my mind clear—I had enough to worry about without having hallucinations on top of everything else.

I tried to relax on the rest of the flight, but I was anxious to be off the plane. As GM had said, we were to land in Georgia and then cross illegally into Russia—though it occurred to me now that there were a lot of ways that plan could go wrong.

I wondered if GM and I could go to jail if we got caught.

At long last, the captain announced that we would soon be landing.

"Well, Katie, this is it," GM said. "First we go through customs in Georgia, and then we make our way to Krov. How is your Russian?"

I had had a Russian tutor as a child, and I had kept up with it over the years—it was something I enjoyed. "It's pretty good, GM."

Good enough, at least, for me to recognize that the word "krov" was the Russian word for blood.

Chapter Thirteen

As GM and I left the plane, I could feel eyes on me again. I turned, and I could see the man in gray walking behind me. He frowned at me, and I looked away.

I resolved to ignore the feeling of being watched if it came over me again—constantly looking over my shoulder wasn't doing me any good.

"We should converse only in Russian from now on," GM whispered to me. "I think it's best that we attract as little attention as possible."

I switched, a bit awkwardly, into Russian. I was used to listening to it, but I hadn't had much practice speaking it lately.

"Do they speak Russian in Georgia?" I asked.

"Most people speak Georgian," GM replied. "And Georgian is nothing like Russian—it's not even Slavic. But there are Russian speakers in Georgia, and we should be able to find people who understand it. As Russian speakers we won't be unusual, anyway. Besides, I know enough Georgian to get by."

We picked up our luggage and went through customs, and then we went out into the main concourse of the airport.

GM paused to read the signs overhead.

"Where are we going right now?" I asked.

"Into the city," GM replied. "I think it's best if we don't appear to be in too much of a hurry."

"Why is that?"

"It's not every day that one sneaks into Russia," GM said. "Caution is in order."

We took a train into Tbilisi, and I was surprised by how warm it was. I guessed it was about sixty degrees—definitely warmer than it had been at home. GM had steered me toward lighter-weight clothing when we were shopping, and despite her reassurances, I had been sure I would be shivering.

"You were right about the weather," I said, shortly after we had left the train.

"I can't believe you doubted me," GM said. "'Tbilisi' actually means 'warm spring' in Georgian. I wouldn't be wrong about something like that."

She gave me a serious look. "How are you feeling, solnyshko? Are you tired after the long plane trip?"

"I'm not tired at all, actually," I said.

"Well, it's about one p.m. local time," GM said. "Would you like to get some lunch?"

"Sure," I said.

We stopped at an ATM so that GM could get some local currency, and she came away with a pretty thick stack of banknotes.

"Wow," I said. "That looks like a lot of money."

"We may have need of it," GM said, tucking it away.

We found a small restaurant nearby, and GM ordered for us. While we ate our appetizer—bread with baked-in cheese called *imeruli khachapuri*—GM showed me some of the Georgian money. The coins, which she had obtained at the airport, were called *tetri*, and had lions, peacocks, and rotating wings on them. The banknotes were called *lari*, and they were all different colors—blue, brown, yellow, green, even rose. I was fascinated by the Georgian money— I had never held foreign currency in my hands before.

Shortly after GM had put the money away again, our lunch arrived. While we ate a dish of chicken and spinach, I looked around the restaurant, and I was struck very forcefully by the realization that I was in a foreign country.

"GM," I said, "do you realize that aside from my early childhood in Russia, this is the first time I've ever been out of the U.S.?"

She gave me a thoughtful look. "Yes, that is true. How do you find it?"

"It's actually pretty exciting," I said. "I just wish it were under different circumstances."

GM reached over to touch my hand. "When we sort this all out, Katie—and we will—I promise you that we will start going on proper trips. It would do you good to travel."

"Thanks," I said. "I'd like that."

It occurred to me then to wonder how GM seemed to be so comfortable traveling—and how she happened to be able to speak Georgian.

"Have you traveled much, GM?"

A strange, faraway look came into her eyes. "I did once, yes. But that was a long time ago—before you were born."

Her voice trailed off, and she was silent for a long moment. Then she sat up stiffly.

"We should settle the bill soon and be on our way."

Once we were out on the street again, GM leaned over to me and whispered.

"We'll engage a marshrutka to take us to Sochi, Russia. Then we'll rent a car there and drive the rest of the way to Krov."

"Why don't we just rent a car here?" I whispered back. "And what's a marshrutka?"

"We're going to Sochi," GM whispered, "because I think it's best not to take too direct a route—we should be careful. I've had the strangest feeling ever since we were on the plane that someone has been keeping an eye on us."

I froze. Though I had been ignoring it, the feeling that I was being watched had not left me when we'd left the airport. The fact that GM was feeling it, too, was disturbing. I couldn't help glancing over my shoulder.

GM followed my glance with concerned eyes. "But I am sure there is nothing to worry about," she said hastily. "Come, solnyshko, let's go find that marshrutka. Anyone who thinks he can follow me will be sorely disappointed."

A marshrutka turned out to be a cross between a taxi and a minibus. As GM explained it to me, the marshrutkas that ran in Tbilisi itself had fixed routes, but there were others that ran in and out of the city and had a lot more freedom in where they went. The second type could basically pick up passengers from anywhere and then drop them off wherever they wished to go. GM thought she could find one that would be willing to go all the way to Russia.

GM stopped and spoke to a number of drivers in their native tongue without success. Eventually, she stopped a man with a bright yellow marshrutka—and though I couldn't understand what they were saying—I could tell that GM thought she'd found our driver. The man was very thin, with faded blue eyes and a pleasant face, and at first he seemed to be refusing politely. But GM continued to talk, and at one point she took out a stack of banknotes. The money seemed to change his mind, and the man waved us toward the back of the marshrutka.

"Success!" GM said to me in Russian. "I have obtained a ride for us to Sochi, and the driver has agreed not to pick up any other passengers until he has dropped us off. That way, if someone is following us, he won't be able to get into our marshrutka. I feel confident we can leave him behind—whoever he is."

We drove out of the city in the marshrutka, and we were soon in the countryside. I was fascinated by the scenery, and I watched it flying by until my eyelids grew heavy and I fell asleep.

GM woke me up as we approached the Russian border, and I was instantly alert. We crossed the border without anyone even seeing us, and a feeling of excitement welled up within me as I looked out the window—this was my first glimpse of my native land in eleven years.

It was beautiful to me.

We drove on for several more hours, and I fell asleep again. When I woke up, the night was a solid black, and we were stopping for dinner in a little village that the driver knew.

Our driver had a friendly smile and seemed to be pleasant company, but I didn't speak any Georgian, and he didn't speak any Russian, so we weren't able to talk to one another. But he and GM had a lively conversation and seemed to get along very well. I figured that it was just as well that I couldn't participate—the feeling that I was being watched was stealing over me again, and I wasn't really in the mood to talk.

I told myself that after a good night's sleep in a proper bed the feeling would go away.

After dinner, we got back in the marshrutka and drove on through the night. At some point in the wee hours of the morning, we arrived in Sochi, and the driver let us off in front of a hotel.

"Unfortunately, it's too late to rent a car tonight," GM whispered to me. "We'll have to wait until morning to continue."

She and the driver spoke animatedly in Georgian once again, and she gave the driver more money and a hearty handshake. Then he drove off into the night.

We went into the hotel, and GM switched back to Russian to ask if there were any rooms available. We were in luck, and before long we were headed up to our room.

Once we were settled in, I sank gratefully onto an actual bed. It was nice to be able to stretch out after all those hours on the plane and in the marshrutka. But after all of the napping I'd done, I wasn't actually tired, and I told GM as much.

"That's jet lag," she said. "You should try to sleep now anyway—try to get your body in sync with local time."

I wanted to ask GM if the feeling of being watched had left her, but I decided against it. If she wasn't feeling worried, I didn't want to give her a reason to start now. Instead, I got ready for bed and tried to sleep.

As I lay in the dark, I felt a nervous fluttering in my stomach. We were getting ever closer to Krov. Would I really find the answers there that I was searching for?

It was hard even now to believe in that horrible white-faced creature that had attacked our home.

What did he want with me?

And had William escaped?

A sharp pain lanced through me as I thought of William. I couldn't bear to think of his being hurt, let alone—

My mind shied away from completing the thought.

A horrible sense of desolation swept over me, and tears sprang to my eyes. I felt them falling slowly down my face.

I struggled for a long time to keep my crying quiet—I didn't want GM to know that anything was wrong.

And somewhere in the night, I fell asleep.

When I awoke, sunlight was streaming into the room, and GM was braiding her long silver hair.

"Good morning, solnyshko," she said.

"Good morning," I replied. I sat up and brushed the hair out of my face.

"Are you ready to begin the last leg of your journey home?" GM asked. There was a curiously sentimental look on her face.

"Home?" I said.

"If not for the premature deaths of both your father and your mother, Katie, we would never have left Krov. It's the town you would have grown up in. Things would have been very different."

GM shrugged her mood off and went on quickly. "The weather is quite pleasant here, just like it was in Tbilisi. You won't need to dress too warmly. Sochi is a resort city."

I showered and dressed quickly, and then we packed up—a task that didn't take very long since we hadn't unpacked much to begin with. We ate breakfast in the hotel restaurant, and then GM arranged for a rental car.

Soon we were on the road again, and I was back to struggling with the persistent feeling that someone was following us. There were, of course, other cars following ours on the road, but that was only natural. All the same, I couldn't keep myself from continually turning around in my seat to stare at our fellow travelers.

"Is something wrong, Katie?" GM asked.

"No, of course not," I said.

To keep my mind off my paranoia, I picked up the paper map GM had acquired when she'd taken possession of the car, and I tried to work out our route.

"Where's Krov?" I asked.

"Behind the great gate of Kiev," GM said with a little smile. "You won't find Krov on the map—it's far too small. I picked out our route using a town nearby."

She gave me the name, and I soon located it. We had hours to go.

"Where are we going exactly?" I asked. "In Krov, I mean? And when will we go see my cousin?"

"We'll go to see your cousin eventually," GM replied. I watched as her hands gripped the steering wheel a little more tightly. "But first, we'll go to see Galina and Aleksandr. Unfortunately, they are the only people who can help us now."

"And Aleksandr is Galina's son?" I asked. I thought I'd heard that, but I wanted to be sure.

"Yes," GM said shortly.

"What is their last name?"

"Golovnin," GM said. That was what William had said, too. Again, I just wanted to be sure.

GM's replies were rather forced, so I decided to drop the rest of the questions I had about Aleksandr and Galina. Since we were going to see them, I would find out about them soon enough.

I turned to look out the window and simply watched the scenery for a long time. As I watched, civilization gave way to rugged countryside, and the cars sharing the road with us began to thin out.

Before long, we only saw cars occasionally.

As we drove along a winding road, a blue car passed us, and a little blond boy looked out the window and stuck his tongue out at us. I made a face back at him, and I saw him laugh. Then the car and the little boy zoomed off, disappearing into the distance.

GM clicked her tongue disapprovingly. "Those people are going far too fast."

"That's a serious charge coming from you," I said.

GM gave me a wry look in response.

A little while later, as we were nearing GM's town of reference on the map, we saw the same blue car again up ahead of us. This time it was stopped by the side of the road.

A woman wearing a kerchief was getting something out of the trunk, and the little blond boy was standing by the side of the road, watching us. As we passed him, the boy stuck his tongue out again and threw something onto the road in front of our car.

There was a loud popping sound and a jolt.

GM frowned. "I think we may have a flat."

"It was that little boy," I said, turning around in my seat. "He threw something at our car."

GM pulled the car over to the side of the road, and we both got out.

The woman and the boy were already back in their car, and I watched as they drove off in the opposite direction.

"I can't believe they just left us," I said.

"If the little boy threw something, I imagine his mother didn't even see it," GM said reasonably. "She likely had no idea why we pulled over."

I walked over to the road, looking for what the little boy had thrown, and I found a tennis ball-sized chunk of twisted, jagged metal. It was heavy and mostly sharp edges. I carried the chunk of metal over to the side of the road and threw it into the grass so that no one else would run over it.

I wondered—where had a small boy gotten a dangerous thing like that?

I walked back to the car, where GM was examining the damaged tire.

She looked up at my approach. "It's pretty badly torn up."

She went around to the back of the car and looked in the trunk. "Also, we don't have a spare."

GM went to her purse and got out her cell phone. After a few minutes she put it away in resignation. "In addition to our other problems—it appears that I have no service out here."

I looked around. The day was wearing away, and we were on a lonely country road. That blue car was the only car we had seen in a long time—which was one of the reasons I had noticed it in the first place.

GM looked up and down the road and sighed. "Well, Katie, we may be here for some time. I don't think it's a good idea for us to go walking around looking for assistance—it would be too easy for us to get lost. It will be dark soon, and as you can see, there are no lights on these country roads. It will be much safer to stay with the car until morning. I am glad now that I bought all those extra things back at the mall."

We stood watching the road in both directions, hoping to see a car.

But all was still.

Time passed, and as GM had prophesied, darkness was soon upon us.

"I have a feeling we won't be seeing anyone pass this way tonight," she said. "I think it's best that we get in the car."

GM got the blankets, travel pillows, and flashlights out of the trunk. Then she settled into the front seat, and I settled into the back.

"I'm not suggesting that you go to sleep right away, Katie," GM said as she passed over two blankets and a pillow. "But you should make yourself comfortable. There are many hours between now and dawn."

I wasn't particularly tired, but as neither GM nor I was in the mood for conversation, I lay down on the seat, and despite myself, began to drift off.

I was awakened abruptly when I heard a car door slam nearby. It was quickly followed by the slamming of a second door.

I sat up and turned to look out the rear window. The bright glare from a car's headlights streamed in and dazzled my eyes, forcing me to hold up my hand as a shade.

Footsteps approached the driver's side, and I heard GM's window rolling down. I looked out my own window, and I could just make out the silhouette of a man and a woman standing next to our car.

GM drew in her breath sharply. "Aleksandr? Is that you?"

I heard a man's voice. "Indeed it is I."

"Aleksandr?" I asked GM. "The one who was in our kitchen?"

"The very same," she replied.

GM got out of the car, and I quickly followed her.

Sure enough, the young man with the cinnamon hair whom I had glimpsed for just a moment in our kitchen was standing before us now. Despite the dim light, I could see that his expression was relaxed and amused as he looked at GM. His eyes shifted to me, and I felt the same feeling of strangeness I had felt when our eyes had met the last time.

Up close, his eyes were the same odd color as his hair, which only increased the feeling of strangeness, and I quickly looked to his companion.

Standing at Aleksandr's side was a young woman of about twenty-one. She was beautiful—with red-gold hair and a face that was strangely familiar.

"Odette!" I cried. I stepped forward and threw my arms around her. Though it had been eleven years since I had last seen her, I would recognize my cousin anywhere.

The young woman backed away from me and gave me a scornful look. "May I ask who you are?"

Aleksandr smiled at her. "Odette, don't you recognize them? This is Anna Rost and Ekaterina—Katie—Wickliff."

Aleksandr turned to GM and me. "Ladies, may I present to you—after an absence of many years—Odette Wickliff."

GM drew in her breath sharply and brought a hand to her mouth. "Can it be so?"

Odette turned to GM in surprise. "Annushka, is it really you?"

"Yes, my dear girl," GM replied. "I haven't seen you since you were ten years old. How lovely you have become."

"Oh, Annushka, I have missed you," Odette said.

She gave GM a hug.

Aleksandr turned suddenly and looked off into the night. He looked back at us, and a faint wariness had crept into his eyes.

"Forgive me for breaking up this fond reunion," he said. "But I think we should all be going. Just out of curiosity, what are the two of you doing out here in the dark anyway?"

Odette laughed. "Yes, don't you know that there are vampires in these parts?" Her tone was teasing, and she looked up at Aleksandr.

I shivered and looked around, but I couldn't see anything beyond the beams of light from the car behind us. I remembered that Aleksandr had also mentioned vampires back in Elspeth's Grove.

I was about to ask him if he really believed there could be vampires around us when Aleksandr answered Odette.

"The vampires are nothing to laugh about," Aleksandr chided her gently. "And there are darker things than vampires in the night. We should get out of here."

He turned to GM. "Is something wrong with your car?"

"Yes," GM replied. "We have a flat tire and no spare."

"In that case," Aleksandr said, "may we offer you a ride?"

"Thank you, Aleksandr," GM said. "That would be most helpful."

"Where were you headed?" he asked.

"We were actually headed to see you and your mother," GM replied. "It's a marvelous coincidence."

"Yes, isn't it," Aleksandr said.

"No, Annushka, I insist," Odette said. "You must come to stay with me. I have more room at my house."

"Why, thank you, Odette," GM said. "We would be delighted to stay with you."

"It's settled, then," Odette said, smiling.

"Do you have luggage with you?" Aleksandr asked.

"Yes, we do," GM said. "Quite a bit of it, actually."

"Then, please allow me to assist you with it," Aleksandr said.

Aleksandr, GM, and I transferred our things to Aleksandr's car, and then we all got in—Aleksandr and GM in the front, Odette and me in the back. We were soon back out on the road, and I was grateful to be out of our stranded car.

"Thank you, Aleksandr," I said to him. "I'm really glad you came along."

"It was my pleasure," he said.

"You seem more amused by our arrival than surprised, Aleksandr," GM said. "Did you know we would come? Even after that scene in our kitchen?"

"I didn't know, but I did hope for it."

"Oh, yes," Odette said sardonically. "Our little princess is home at last. You know, Katie, with your spun-gold hair you actually look the part."

I was surprised by Odette's tone, and I didn't quite know what to say.

Odette touched me on the arm and laughed. "I only meant that Aleksandr's mother will be very excited that you're here. She's been talking about you for years. You must not mind my sense of humor."

"So what happened?" Aleksandr asked GM quietly in the front seat. "What brought you back to us so suddenly?"

I leaned forward—I wondered how GM would handle this.

"There were disappearances," she said slowly.

"Anything else?" Aleksandr prompted.

GM shifted in her seat uncomfortably. "Our house was attacked. We may have seen him."

"Him?" Aleksandr said.

GM shook her head. "You know who I mean. The idea is just too ridiculous. I saw his funeral, after all."

"You mean Gleb Mstislav?" Aleksandr said.

"Yes," GM replied. Though it was only one syllable, it was clear she uttered it with reluctance.

"What did he look like?" Aleksandr asked.

"Horrible," GM said.

"So seeing has made a believer out of you?" Aleksandr said.

"Not necessarily," GM said stiffly. "I don't know what to think."

Odette laughed. "Annushka, do you really think you have seen one of Aleksandr's dark creatures? A dead man walking? And here I thought maybe you had come to Russia because you missed me."

I hadn't meant to say anything, but the memory of that horrifying, white-faced creature moving toward William rose in my mind, and I blurted out a question.

"How do you stop a man who's already dead?"

"That's a question for Baba," Odette said slyly.

"Baba?" I asked.

"Odette means Galina," Aleksandr said. "Some of the locals refer to her rather unkindly as Baba Yaga."

The name stirred a memory—there was a movement in *Pictures at an Exhibition* titled *The Hut on Hen's Legs*. It was about Baba Yaga and her fanciful home.

"But Baba Yaga's a witch," I said. "Are you saying that Galina is a—"

"No, Galina isn't a witch," Aleksandr said. "That's just the term some people use because they don't understand her."

He paused. "And to answer your earlier question—how do you stop a man who's already dead? As Odette said, that's one for Galina."

Chapter Fourteen

After about an hour, we reached Krov, and we drove through the town's tiny streets.

Eventually, Aleksandr pulled to a stop before a large house on a dark street, and I stared out the window in shock. I got out of the car quickly.

I found myself standing in front of a house that I had seen many times in my memories.

The rose bushes were bare, but they were just where they were supposed to be, and though I couldn't see it, I knew without doubt that there was an apple tree in the backyard.

I turned as GM got out of the car. "It's our house," I said.

She came to stand beside me, and a soft light came into her eyes. "Yes, it is."

"Actually, it's my house now," Odette said, slamming her door shut.

Aleksandr was last out of the car, and he walked up to GM. "I'll see about getting your car rescued from the side of the road in the morning. And Galina and I will come by to see you in the morning, too."

"Thank you, Aleksandr," GM said.

We retrieved our things from the car and said good night to Aleksandr. Then we went into the house with Odette.

Odette began to head for the stairs. "Would you like to stay in your old room, Annushka?"

"Yes, that would be lovely," GM replied, following her.

I paused in the hall and looked around me in wonder. I'd never dreamed that I would return to this house.

I'd been happy here—truly happy. This was the house where my family had been whole.

I stood for a long moment, just drinking everything in, and then I turned to go up the stairs. Odette was waiting for me on the landing.

"Annushka is already settled in her room," she said. "Would you like to stay in your old room, too? Of course you were so young when you left that I doubt you remember it."

"I remember it," I said.

"Well, here you are, then," Odette said, opening a door for me and switching on the light. "I'm not sure that I'll see you and Annushka in the morning, but Galina and Aleksandr should be by tomorrow to see you. You should make yourself at home."

"Thanks, Odette," I said.

She turned to go.

"Odette, I'm really glad to see you," I said.

She turned back and smiled at me. "I'm glad to see you, too. I really mean that."

Odette then disappeared down the dark hall, and I went into my room.

I set my things down and looked around the room—I was amazed by how little it had changed. My clothes, toys, and books were long gone, of course, as was the sunburst lamp that was in my room back in Elspeth's Grove. But the blue rug with the rocking horse that my mother had made was still on the floor, and my butterfly coverlet was still on the bed. The picture of the yellow bird that I had adored was still on the wall, and as I examined the wall next to the door, I found that the spot close to the floor where I had scrawled "Екатерина,"—or "EKATERINA"—in pen had not been painted over.

I smiled—the room was still mine—my name was still on it.

I even opened the closet door and looked into it, remembering how I had once locked myself inside it when I was a little girl. I had wanted to see what the closet looked like when the door was closed—to find out if it remained an ordinary closet—or if it turned into a home for monsters.

The closet had a strange, old-fashioned latch, and it could only be opened from the outside—there was no proper knob or handle on the inside. I had stepped inside the closet and shut the door by curling my fingers under the bottom and pulling until I heard the latch catch.

I hadn't realized until too late that if there was no knob I could use to close the door, that there would also be no knob I could use to open it again.

On finding myself in the dark, I had panicked. I had scrabbled at the door but couldn't find any way to open it. I had begun to scream, and my mother soon came to let me out.

She had smiled a little when I had tearfully explained what I'd been doing. But then she'd sobered and told me that I had proved conclusively that there were no monsters in the closet.

At least that was one thing I could be sure of right now—I was safe in this house. There were no monsters here.

I closed the closet door and sat down on the bed. I couldn't tell if I was tired or not—my internal clock was really off after all the traveling I'd done. I figured I should at least try to sleep so I could get myself on local time.

But I continued to sit still, and my thoughts were drawn to William. The fear I felt for him was always with me, and whenever I had time to think, it became so strong that it threatened to overwhelm me.

I wanted to know that he had survived. I wanted to know that he was safe.

But all I could do was hope for him.

I continued to sit for a long time, tormented by my thoughts, but eventually I forced myself to get up and get ready for bed.

As I lay in a house that was both familiar and strange to me, I drifted in and out of sleep. At one point, I started awake and sat up in bed. I was tense, listening.

The house was eerily quiet, and I was reminded unpleasantly of the night, not long ago, when the kost had attacked our house in Elspeth's Grove.

I continued to listen, and the house remained silent—I didn't hear anyone skittering over the roof, or rattling at the door.

At the same time I had a strong feeling that someone was stirring in the house. I slipped out into the dark hall and then went quietly down the stairs to investigate.

I found my cousin, Odette, in the kitchen. She was stirring something in a bowl, and she smiled when she saw me.

"Hello, Katie," she said. "Still not on local time, I see."

"What time is it?" I asked.

"It's just past two in the morning." She gave me an apologetic look. "I didn't wake you, did I? I was making blueberry muffins for you and Annushka for breakfast. I've never made them before, but I heard that Americans like them. You do like them, don't you?"

"Oh, yes," I said. "Thank you—that's very thoughtful. But I feel bad—you shouldn't have stayed up all night to make them. Don't you have to go to work, or school, or something in the morning?"

Odette laughed and went back to her mixing. "My parents were clever investors—they left me a lot of money that the authorities never found out about. And that has allowed me to indulge my inner night owl. I sleep very late in the morning, get up whenever I want, and do whatever I want. There's no need for me to go to a university or to go to work at all."

Odette caught sight of my expression, and she tilted her head. "You look puzzled. Why?"

I suddenly felt very unsure of myself. GM had hinted that there had been some trouble involving Odette's parents. And though I wanted to ask Odette what had happened, I didn't want to bring up memories that were painful for her. Ultimately, I decided it was better to ask.

"What happened?" I said. "To your parents, I mean."

Odette looked at me sharply, and I could see anger flash in her eyes.

"I'm sorry," I said. "Maybe I shouldn't have asked. You don't have to tell me if you don't want to."

Odette set her bowl on the table with a clatter.

"Are you serious?"

"What do you mean?" I asked.

"You're saying you don't know."

"No, I don't know."

"So, they didn't even bother to tell you," Odette said bitterly. "Do I matter so little that they couldn't even inform their precious little princess of what had happened? Did they fear to hurt your delicate sensibilities? Not one of them cared enough—not Annushka—not Galina—"

Odette broke off, breathing hard. She turned away from me.

She made an effort to compose herself. Then she gave me a wan smile. "But then, you were so young. Perhaps they thought you wouldn't understand."

Odette's calm was short-lived, however—fire quickly flared in her eyes again. "But what about you? Did you never wonder? Did you never ask?"

"Of course I wondered about you, Odette," I said. "I missed you. I thought you were wonderful. I asked GM about you all the time—"

Odette interrupted me. "GM?" She said the letters in English as I had done.

"It's what I call my grandmother—your Annushka. It's sort of an acronym. In English the letters stand for 'Grand Mother.' It's something I came up with after I moved to the U.S., and it just kind of stuck with me."

"Very cute," Odette said curtly. "So, what did your GM say when you asked her about me?"

"GM always refused to answer me," I said. "She never liked talking about the past. She said it was full of darkness and superstition."

"And what of Galina?" Odette demanded. "Did she tell you nothing?"

"I've had no contact with her," I said. "In fact, when she showed up at my house a little over a week ago, that was the first time I'd ever seen her in my life—Galina has never had any opportunity to tell me anything."

"And so all this time Galina has been fretting and worrying about you, and you didn't even know she existed."

Odette said the words more to herself than to me. She went on in the same tone. "And Annushka saw you day after day, year after year, and never saw fit to mention me."

"It was hard for her to go into the past," I said. "She had lost a lot."

Odette was silent for a long moment, and then she looked up at me. "I suppose it is left to me to explain, then."

She smiled. "I'm sorry for my outburst. How would you like some alosa tea? I know your mother used to like it. In fact, I have the very same kind she used to buy—from the very same shop. Won't you sit and have tea with me? And I will tell you about my parents."

"I would like that," I said.

Odette waved me toward a seat and got a cardboard box out of a cupboard. She set the box down in front of me.

"There you are," she said. "Alosa tea—just like your mother used to drink."

I picked up the box and examined it. The lid proclaimed the contents to be alosa tea just as Odette had said. I lifted the lid and inhaled—the scent was very spicy and exotic.

I wasn't entirely sure that I liked it.

Odette put some water on to boil, and soon she was pouring out two cups of tea for us. I was surprised to see the water turn a violent purple color.

I took a few tentative sips of the tea. The flavor wasn't bad, but it was strange. I set it down.

Odette smiled at me over the rim of her cup. "Drink up. Alosa is good for you."

I picked up my cup again.

"So, my story," Odette said. "There's really not much to tell, but it's important—at least to me. My parents were very rich once."

Odette eyed me significantly, and I took another sip of the tea.

She continued and her voice grew dreamy. "We lived in a very big house—it wasn't the biggest house in town—that was the Mstislav mansion—but it was the second biggest. You were there a few times, but you were far too small to remember it. We even had some land and horses. And I had the most beautiful clothes."

Odette sighed.

"But as it turned out, my parents had not come by their wealth through entirely honest means. The government was after them for years, and eventually they caught up with them. My parents were indicted and thrown in prison. And all their assets were confiscated—or at least all the assets that the government knew about. There was enough that was hidden to allow me to live comfortably."

Odette stopped to sip at her tea.

I was horrified. "Your parents are in prison?"

"Yes. They've still got a few decades to go."

"Odette, that's terrible," I said. "So, you've been alone all these years?"

Odette shrugged. "I wasn't entirely alone. For the first year after my parents were taken, I lived with you and your family. And then when your parents died, and Annushka left the country with you, I went to live with Galina and Aleksandr."

"Why didn't you come with us?" I asked. "Galina and Aleksandr aren't your family."

"Well, neither is Annushka for that matter. As your maternal grandmother, she's no relation to me. And my parents weren't gone—they were still alive and still in Russia—they just weren't at liberty. They wanted me to stay in this country, and Galina volunteered to be my guardian. My parents agreed, and it was made official. Before Annushka left, she made over the title of this house to Galina, and when I came of age, Galina made over the house to me—after all, she hardly needed two houses. And I had been very happy here, even though I only lived here a little while. So, that's how I came to live in this house, and that's my story."

"Oh, Odette," I said. "I don't even know what to say. Do you, do you ever—"

I hesitated.

"Do I ever see my parents?" Odette prompted.

"Yes."

"I see them from time to time. But prison is not a pleasant place to visit."

"No, I can understand that," I said. "Oh, Odette, I really wish we'd been able to keep in touch all these years. I think our being friends would have been good for both of us."

"Maybe so."

Odette drank the rest of her tea and stood up.

"I have an idea," she said impulsively. "Are you finished with your tea? Why don't we go out for a walk, and I'll show you the town when it's quiet. We can spend time together, just the two of us, before Galina and Aleksandr show up and demand all your attention."

I glanced toward the dark windows. "Now? Are you sure it's safe?"

Odette laughed. "Of course it's safe. You've been listening to the silly things that Aleksandr says. I know this village well. I'll look out for you."

I stood up. "Okay. I'll go change my clothes."

"Dress warmly," Odette said. "It's chilly here at night."

I hurried upstairs, strangely excited about spending some time with my cousin in the village where I'd been born. I felt something I couldn't quite describe—a feeling of connectedness that I hadn't expected to find.

I wondered for a moment if this was what it felt like to be home.

I hurried back downstairs, and Odette led me outside. The night was indeed cold, and the stars and the moon were bright overhead. There were only two streetlights lit on our block, so the celestial illumination was a welcome addition.

"Krov is loveliest when it's quiet," Odette said, smiling softly. "I often go on moonlit walks. Sometimes I even leave the town and go out into the countryside."

"I'm certainly grateful for your nocturnal habits," I said. "And I know GM is, too. We were really glad to see you and Aleksandr tonight. Spending the night in a car is not a lot of fun."

Odette laughed, and the sound was a little startling in the quiet. "Yes, it was lucky that we happened by. Aleksandr had asked me to go with him for a drive in the country to see the stars, and we happened to see your stranded car. He insisted on stopping to see if we could offer any assistance. Imagine our surprise when the occupants of the car turned out to be ghosts from the past."

Odette pointed. "We should turn here."

We lapsed into companionable silence, and we continued to walk until we reached a row of shops.

Odette stopped. "Do you see that shop all the way at the end? That's the one where your mother used to buy her alosa tea and where I buy the very same tea now."

I looked over at the little shop. I felt a rush of warmth come over me as I thought of my mother going there and buying her tea there regularly.

As we continued to walk, Odette pointed out the sights and told me stories of her life in the village.

As I looked around me, I was overcome by affection for this town I had once lived in. Krov was as lovely as Odette had said.

After another lapse of time during which we had simply walked—and I had let my thoughts wander—I broke the silence.

"So, are you and Aleksandr a couple?"

"Aleksandr—and me?" Odette looked at me, startled, and a smile began to quirk at the corners of her mouth. "Aleksandr is far too provincial for me. My tastes are much more sophisticated. You thought we were a couple? Just because he asked me to go for a drive?"

I was suddenly struck by a thought. "It was Aleksandr's idea to go for a drive at night?"

Odette looked at me, fire flashing in her eyes. "Yes, I've already said that. You find it strange that he would ask me?"

"No—it's just that he appeared to be nervous," I said. "He seemed to think there were supernatural creatures prowling around. Why would he ask you to go out in the night if he thought it was dangerous?"

Odette threw back her head and laughed, and the sound echoed loudly on the night air. "Oh, that. The vampires and the evil spirits and all that other nonsense? Aleksandr doesn't really believe all that stuff—not wholeheartedly anyway. Galina is the one who really believes it. And Aleksandr just goes along with it to please her and all the other superstitious locals. I told you he was provincial."

We had just reached a large, open square with a towering obelisk at its center, and Odette stopped at the edge of the square. She gave me a sly look.

"As I recall, Annushka said that she—and I assume you—had seen Gleb Mstislav at your house—the same Gleb Mstislav who has been dead for the last eleven years."

"Yes," I said uncomfortably.

"That's too marvelous," Odette said. "Would you like to see his mansion?"

I thought back to the horrible white face I had seen back in Elspeth's Grove, and I couldn't repress a shudder. "I—I don't think so."

"Don't be ridiculous, Katie," Odette said. She took me by the arm. "It's just on the other side of this square. I think seeing it will help you to feel better. It's not a haunted house at all."

Odette pulled me across the square, and from a distance I could see a long, tree-lined drive ahead of us. There were lights winking at us from between the trees.

I hesitated, and Odette pulled me forward again.

"Come on," she said in exasperation. "I thought you Americans had conquered superstition a long time ago."

We walked up the drive, and we soon came in sight of a sprawling white mansion that was lit up by spotlights. The house was much more elegant than I'd expected, and there were long, red banners hanging from every available horizontal surface.

We stopped at the mansion's wide marble steps.

"This is the Mstislav mansion," Odette said breathlessly. "How do you like it?"

"It's an impressive house," I said. "What are the red banners for?"

Odette turned shining eyes on me. "The banners are in honor of a ball that is to be held here very soon. It will be a surprise—the inspiration is Haydn's Symphony No. 94—the *Surprise Symphony*. No one knows the exact date yet. Isn't that clever?"

"A ball?" I asked. "Like a dance?"

"Exactly," Odette said. "Would you like to go? That is, if you're still here when it happens? I have an invitation, and you could come as my guest."

Once again, Gleb's pallid visage rose in my mind. "No—I couldn't. I could never go into that house—never."

"Oh, Katie," Odette said, laughing. "Gleb isn't going to be there. He's long dead. But his son, Timofei, will be there. And I've seen him before, and he is very handsome. He's only a few years older than I am. You will miss a lot of fun if you don't go. Are you going to be provincial, too?"

"Yes, I am," I said firmly.

"Oh, very well," Odette sighed. "But if you change your mind, let me know. I have a dress you can borrow. It's red—it would look lovely on you. I'm planning to wear white."

"I won't change my mind," I said.

Odette sighed again and glanced around. "Well, I believe this concludes our tour. There isn't too much beyond the Mstislav mansion—just empty fields, and those fields stretch a long way—all the way to the ruin of the old monastery. There really isn't anything else to see—that is, unless you ask the locals."

She looked at me in amusement. "Would you like to hear something fantastic? There are actually rumors that there are tunnels under those fields that lead from this mansion into the monastery. And, of course, the monastery itself is on the edge of the Pure Woods—it's a petrified forest where the locals claim all the monsters live."

Odette gave me a sly glance. "Actually, Galina and Aleksandr will probably take you to the Pure Woods once the sun comes up—you know, when it's 'safe.' It's not my kind of place, though—too natural. Shall we go home now? I can get back to my muffins, and you can get some sleep."

I agreed, and we started back. I had enjoyed my moonlit walk with Odette, but the memory of Gleb's face still lingered with me, and it had turned my blood into slow-moving ice. I felt chilled from the inside out.

I wanted very badly to crawl into my bed and pull my covers over my head.

Chapter Fifteen

T hat night, I slept better than I thought I would.

I had expected to be haunted by the image of Gleb's bloated white face, but my sleep was dreamless and heavy. I awoke when I felt sunlight on my eyes.

I got up and got dressed for the second time that morning, and then I went downstairs.

I found GM in the kitchen, washing some dishes in the sink.

"Good morning, solnyshko. Your cousin has made blueberry muffins for you." She waved a soapy hand at a big square container on the kitchen table.

I knew GM disapproved of sweets, but I could tell from her expression that she wanted me to accept this gift from our hostess.

I smiled and went to get a plate. Somehow, I knew that the plates would be in the same cupboard that my mother had kept them in— and I wasn't disappointed. And Odette even had the same china pattern that I remembered from my childhood. The kitchen was just the same as it had been when I was small—the only difference was that I could reach everything now.

"There is alosa tea, too," GM said. "Your mother's favorite."

I sat down at the table and got a muffin out of the container.

"Odette already gave me some of the tea," I said. "I woke up in the middle of the night, and I found her down here in the kitchen mixing up the muffins. We went for a walk, and Odette showed me the village."

I paused. "She also told me about her parents."

GM looked up at me sharply. "Did she? Well, now you know why you don't remember them."

"Odette was really upset," I said. "She thought that nobody had told me because nobody cared about her."

GM dried her hands and sighed heavily. "I never told you about your aunt and uncle for a reason—and it wasn't because I didn't care. I loved Odette, even though she was not my own blood, and I knew how much you loved her, too. You talked about her constantly as a child—you remembered her as a happy girl that you wanted to be like when you got older. You thought she was a real-life princess. I wanted you to continue to think of her that way. I didn't want tragedy to taint those memories."

"She was happy, wasn't she?" I said. "But Odette told me her parents were already in prison when she came to live with us."

"They were."

"So why was she happy? I remember her always laughing."

GM sat down beside me. "I don't think Odette entirely understood what was going on—at least not at first. She was nine, older than you, and in some ways, more mature. But she had always received her own way in everything. So, I think she believed her parents would be back soon—even though we tried to explain to her that they wouldn't be. She saw staying with us as a grand adventure—which I'm sure it was at first."

GM sighed again. "I can understand how a young girl might believe that everything would turn out right—and how she could become angry when it didn't."

I had stopped eating while GM was talking, and I got up now to get a glass of milk. The muffin was good, but there was something a little peculiar about the taste. I wondered if maybe Odette had used canned blueberries—I didn't know how readily available fresh ones might be in Krov.

"Where is Odette now?" I asked.

"She went up to bed just as I was coming down early this morning," GM replied. "I think it was a long night for her."

"GM," I said, as I was struck by a thought. "I know now why I don't remember my aunt and uncle, but why don't I remember Galina and Aleksandr? Galina seems to have been very important in my mother's life, and Aleksandr is her son. Surely I would have seen them?"

GM waved a dismissive hand. "Aleksandr was just a child then—he's the same age as Odette. He would hardly have come to visit us on his own."

"And Galina?" I prompted.

"I forbid her to enter the house," GM said. "I didn't like the nonsense she was filling your mother's head with. But your mother saw her behind my back—and I still don't trust Galina completely. I think she means well, but she lives in a dream world. I only came here to Krov to see her because it was the only thing I could think of to do."

GM got up and started to dry the dishes she had washed earlier.

"Our car was returned to us at some point during the night," she said briskly. "And it has a new tire on it. So, we can drive anywhere we need to now."

I was just on the verge of asking GM if we should go to see Galina and Aleksandr when there was a knock on the front door.

GM and I both went to answer it.

"Hush, boy, don't be such a fool!" Galina said sharply as the door opened.

Aleksandr looked up at us and smiled. Galina looked embarrassed.

Galina's expression changed to one of wonder as she looked at me. She held out both of her hands and stepped inside.

"Ekaterina, is it really you? You look so much like your dear mother. It's as if she lives again."

She placed her hands on my cheeks, and her eyes ranged over my face as if she feared that I would disappear.

Aleksandr stepped in after her. "I hope you ladies don't mind if we come in."

Galina shot an angry glance at him, but she quickly turned her attention back to me. "Ekaterina, you cannot know how my heart rejoices to see you here in Krov. I only pray that we are not too late."

GM made a noise that sounded suspiciously like a derisive snort. "Galina, I admit that we have come here to consult you, but I must ask you to keep the theatrics to a minimum."

Galina's expression went carefully blank, and she dropped her hands from my face.

"Of course, Annushka. I am sure that you know best."

"Well, Galina," GM said in a tone of resignation, "I suppose Aleksandr has told you that our house was attacked."

Galina nodded. "And you believe it was attacked by Gleb Mstislav."

"I dislike saying this," GM said. "But, yes. It was him. I recognized him." She shook her head, as if to ward off the memory. "When I saw him, I thought for a moment that perhaps he hadn't died—perhaps he'd actually gone into hiding instead. But his face—it was bloated and horrible. And an unnatural light shone in his eyes."

"Like green flame," Galina added quietly.

"Yes, that's what it was," GM said. "How did you know?"

"I have seen it before," Galina replied.

I hadn't seen the green flame myself, but I didn't doubt that GM had seen it. She wasn't the fanciful type—if she said she'd seen it, then it was a fact.

"There was screaming, also," GM said. "Terrible, inhuman cries."

"Annushka, you will have to accept that you have seen a kost," Galina said. "An evil spirit animating the body of a dead man. And in this case that dead man is Gleb Mstislav. He truly does walk again."

"Oh, Galina," GM said despairingly. "I don't believe in these things, yet I cannot deny what I have seen. What are we to do?"

"Ekaterina must come with me," Galina replied. "She's the only one of us who has the power to fight this evil."

Anger flashed in GM's eyes. "No. This has nothing to do with Katie. You and I will take care of this. Katie's not to be involved at all."

GM's anger was answered by Galina's. "Then why did you bring her here?"

"To get her far away from that creature. And to find answers. This is for us to solve. It's no task for a child."

"Mrs. Rost," Aleksandr interjected, "Katie really is the only one who can do this."

"Quiet, Aleksandr!" Galina snapped. "No one wants to hear from you."

For a long time, no one spoke as GM and Galina stared at one another.

"GM," I said at last, "I want to go with Galina. I want to hear what she has to say. If I can help, I want to do it."

"There, you see?" Galina said. "Ekaterina can feel it in her blood. She knows deep down who and what she is."

I wasn't entirely sure what Galina was talking about, but Gleb had threatened—and possibly even killed—people I loved. I wanted—needed—to know what was going on.

"Please, GM," I said. "Let's go with Galina and hear what she has to say. What harm can it do to listen?"

GM gave me a long look, and then she turned to Galina. "I suppose it can't hurt for us to simply listen, but I don't see why we can't talk here. There's no reason for us to go to your house."

Galina took a deep breath. "Annushka, I regret the necessity, but I am going to have to be blunt. Your negative energy will have an adverse effect on Ekaterina's abilities. Despite the fact that you have come to seek my help, you have done so reluctantly, and you do not really believe. Ekaterina needs to tap into the natural energy around us. That requires a nurturing, accepting environment—my house has that. She can't do that here with you disapproving. She will have to come with me—without you."

"Ridiculous," GM said. "Pure foolishness. It's out of the question."

"Please, Annushka," Galina said. "Let me take Ekaterina with me. I will simply talk to her, explain what's going on. And I certainly won't take her out to confront anyone or anything. Besides, it's daylight—Ekaterina is safe enough while the sun shines. When we're done talking, she can come home and tell you everything. There will be no secrets."

"Please, GM, let me go," I said.

GM glanced at me. "Well, Galina, since Katie doesn't seem to mind, I suppose it'll be all right. She can listen to you and then give me the details. It will probably be better for my temper, anyway, for me to hear the story from Katie, rather than from you. But I want it understood clearly that Katie is not to do anything. I am her grandmother. If any heroics are necessary, I will perform them myself."

Galina smiled despite herself. "You always were a mama bear, Annushka. As I said, I won't take Ekaterina out to battle anyone today. I promise you that."

"Very well. Katie may go with you. But I expect to see my granddaughter back here in one piece."

"Thank you, Annushka," Galina said. "You have done the right thing."

Galina shepherded me out, and Aleksandr followed us.

The car that Aleksandr had rescued GM and me in last night was waiting for us outside at the curb. I climbed into the back seat again, and we were off.

Our route took us through town and past the Mstislav mansion. The big white house looked even more impressive in the day, and its red banners fluttered briskly in a steady breeze.

After we passed the mansion, the landscape was much as Odette had described—we drove on through broad, featureless fields that stretched as far as the eye could see.

"This area we're passing now is known locally as the Wasteland," Aleksandr said, glancing at me in the rearview mirror. "Once upon a time there were houses where these fields are."

I glanced at Galina, expecting her to snap at him. But for once she did not rebuke him for speaking.

Aleksandr continued. "In fact, this desolate area was once a little village. Centuries ago, the village nestled between the Mstislav mansion on this side and the monastery on the other. The noble family of the great house looked after the physical well-being of the villagers, and the monastery looked after their spiritual needs—in theory anyway."

I looked out at the vast, empty fields. "What happened to the village?"

"The monastery and the mansion failed to protect their people," Galina said quietly. "Now the people are gone."

"Was the mansion known as the Mstislav mansion back then?" I asked.

"Yes," Galina replied. "The house is the Mstislavs' ancestral home. The Mstislavs actually fell into decline after the village was destroyed all those centuries ago, and the family lost the house, their position in society, and their wealth. It was Gleb who clawed his way back from obscurity—building a fortune, and then buying up the mansion and many other things besides in this town."

We drove on past more empty fields. Eventually, I spied a large stone building ahead of us, clearly ecclesiastical in nature, and beyond it was a strange white forest that looked like bleached bone.

"As you can probably guess, that's the old monastery there," Aleksandr said, pointing. "It's been abandoned for many years now. And just behind it is the Pure Woods—it's a petrified forest."

"Why is it called the 'Pure Woods'?" I asked.

"Simply because of the color—the stark whiteness," Aleksandr replied. "It is also said to be the area of greatest supernatural power in this region—both good and evil."

"Forests are some of Russia's most ancient holy sites," Galina said. "The Pure Woods is one of those sites. Your mother knew these woods well. Soon, I hope that you will know them, too."

As we drove past the white forest, we came across a small house that sat between the side of the road and the edge of the woods, and Aleksandr pulled the car into the small drive that ran behind the house.

"Welcome to our little forest abode," he said.

"Aleksandr! No foolishness!" Galina snapped. "Our work here is serious."

It was clear that her irritation with her son had returned.

We went into the house, and Galina paused just inside the door.

"Aleksandr, your presence will not be necessary. Leave."

Aleksandr gave her a formal bow, and to my surprise, he turned and left the house.

Galina turned on her heel and walked down the hall. "This way," she said.

I hesitated, and I was surprised to hear Aleksandr's car start outside.

"Aleksandr really is leaving," I said. "What's going on?"

"Please come with me, Ekaterina," Galina said shortly.

I followed her with reluctance—I was beginning to regret my decision to go with Galina.

She led me to a room that was full of books—so much so that there was barely room for a desk, two chairs, and a lamp.

Galina took off her coat and sat down at the chair behind the desk. She waved me to the other one.

I took off my coat, draping it over my arm, and I sat on the edge of the chair. I was suddenly nervous about what Galina was going to say.

She ran her hands over her face. Then she gave me a long, earnest look.

"This is difficult," she said at last. "I don't know how much like your grandmother you are. I know you expressed a desire to help when you were back at your house, but I can see skepticism in your eyes now. If your mind is closed, then this will not work. If you are realizing now that you do not wish to go on, simply tell me, and I will take you home again. There will be no further pressure from me. Take all the time you need to decide."

"I don't know what to think anymore," I said slowly.

Galina smiled at me sympathetically. "Yes, I can imagine that this is hard for you. I know your grandmother doesn't approve of sweets, but would you like some hot cocoa? I find that that always makes me feel better."

"Yes, thanks," I said.

Galina led me into the kitchen, which was small and overstuffed but scrupulously clean. As I sat at the table, she got to work with a saucepan, and soon we both had mugs of hot cocoa.

Galina looked at me over the top of her mug. "Tell me about what brought you here. How did all the trouble begin?"

I started with the visit she and her son had made to our house in the middle of the night, admitting that I'd overheard them. Then I told her about the disappearances in Elspeth's Grove and about the night that Gleb had attacked our house and GM and I had fled.

I omitted the parts of the story that had to do with William. I wasn't entirely sure why I did that, but I had a vague sense that he could be incriminated in some way if I mentioned him.

But even with the omissions, it felt good to be able to talk to someone freely about what had happened—someone who would actually believe me.

Galina took a deep breath when I had finished my tale. "You have been through a lot, my child."

Talking through it all again made me realize just how lucky I was to be alive.

It also helped me to make up my mind.

"Galina—Mrs. Golovnin—"

She smiled. "Please call me Galina."

"Galina, I've made my decision," I said. "I want you to tell me everything—even if it's hard to believe. And I want to help—I have to. I have to do what I can to stop this—this man—this horrible creature."

Galina put her hand to her heart. "My child, you don't know how glad I am that you have come to this decision. You're a brave girl."

She picked up the now-empty mugs and put them in the sink. Then she sat down again.

"From what I gather, you know very little about your mother. So, I will begin with her. Your mother and I were good friends. She was a special person—very few would recognize her for what she was. But I am sensitive—I always was. And through study, reflection, and mental exercises, I have taught myself to be more sensitive. I knew even when we were young that your mother was someone I could learn a lot from."

She paused and gave me a serious look. "Nadya had an unusual genetic background, and it is from her that you derive your unique powers. She was half-human and half-immortal, but unfortunately, anything with a body can die. Nadya's heritage was not enough to save her. Your grandfather—Annushka's husband—wasn't human."

I stared at her. "You aren't serious."

"I can assure you that I am," Galina replied.

I thought back to the creatures Aleksandr had mentioned. "My grandfather wasn't a vampire, was he?" I asked.

"No."

"Does my grandmother know that her husband wasn't human?"

Galina gave me an odd smile. "Do you know, I believe she does know deep down—but that is hardly something she would admit to."

"So, if my grandfather wasn't human, what was he?"

"He was one of the Sídh."

"Sídh," I repeated. "I don't know what that is."

Galina spelled the word for me in English. "Sometimes they are known as the Ancient Beautiful Ones. They were banished to the hills of Ireland after a battle with a race known as the Milesians—a battle which the Sídh lost. But though they were banished, they are not gone. The Sídh are older than human civilization and immensely powerful."

"By powerful," I said slowly, "do you mean that they have magic?"

"You could call it that," Galina replied. "But power is a better word for it. Some even believe the Sídh to be ancient gods."

I felt a chill steal over me. I was beginning to wish my grandfather had been a vampire. "So, what are the Sídh of Ireland doing in Russia?"

"As part of the ancient treaty that sent the Sídh to the hills, the Sídh were bound to protect particular regions of the earth from dark creatures. In this particular case, the Sídh are required to send one of their number here to Krov every few hundred years to imbue the local population with the strength to fight the darkness that lives here. In this way was the Little Sun created, and that's what your mother was."

I drew in my breath sharply. "The Little Sun? So, that legend is real?"

"Very much so," Galina replied. "The child that is born of the human-Sídh union and his or her descendants can control what is known as the 'clear fire.'"

"Clear fire," I said.

"Yes. It was a gift from the sun's elder sister, and it can only be used by someone who is both mortal and immortal—someone who stands on the boundary between the two worlds. It is a sphere of pure energy that can defeat the dark creatures who inhabit this area."

"Dark creatures?" I asked. "Like vampires?"

Galina smiled. "You seem to have vampires on your mind a lot."

I did have vampires on my mind—for a very good reason. But I couldn't admit that to Galina just yet.

"It's just that Aleksandr mentioned them as if they were real," I said. "And a real threat."

"They are real," Galina said. "They *are* a threat. They do take human life. And they do live around here. But they are not the greatest danger in the broader scheme of things, and as a result, the clear fire doesn't work on them—it wasn't designed for them. Just as there are ancient beautiful spirits, there are also ancient evil ones. The dark spirits are just as eternal and necessary as the bright ones. But though the dark ones are necessary, they are malevolent nonetheless. They seek the destruction of humanity."

"These dark spirits," I said, "are they the Milesians you mentioned?"

"No, the Milesians were ordinary humans," Galina said. "They had no special powers of any kind."

"But how could ordinary people force magical beings into exile?" I asked.

"It is a harrowing tale," Galina replied. "But not one you need to hear now. What is important is that the clear fire will help you defeat creatures like the kosts—they are an ancient and powerful evil."

"Kosts?" I asked. "You mean there are more of them aside from Gleb?"

"Unfortunately for humanity, yes. Basically, a kost is a dead man walking. It is a corpse inhabited by one of those ancient evil spirits I mentioned. The spirit takes the human body so that it can manipulate the material world, and in this state, it has unnatural and terrifying strength. The kost has a grudge against the living, and it feeds itself through human blood and fear. Death gives it strength."

My stomach began to tie itself into knots, and I felt a chill settle deeply into my bones.

"So what can we do?" I asked.

"The evil spirit that inhabits the kost cannot be killed. But the spirit can be separated from the body, and the body can be sent to its rest again permanently. This separation can be effected with the clear fire. The clear fire can also be used to seal the kost, or wall it up, within a strong chamber. That is what Nadya did—she sealed the Gleb kost within the Mstislav family crypt. The only problem with that method is that the kost remains intact and can be released. And released Gleb was.

"I need you to find the clear fire. Your mother has hidden it, and only you have the power to call it forth again. Now that your mother is gone, you are the Little Sun."

"And then once I find the clear fire, you want me to use it to stop Gleb," I said.

"Yes. You must use the clear fire to separate the spirit from the body once and for all. It is important to destroy Gleb. I don't think sealing him up again will be good enough—he will only live on and escape once you are gone."

"Do you really think I can do this?" I asked.

"You must," Galina said. "If Gleb succeeds in killing you, which he is surely trying to do, he will then go on to kill others. There is no one to stop him but you."

I was starting to feel light-headed. "So, if I find the clear fire, how do I find him—it—Gleb? The last time I saw him, he was in Elspeth's Grove."

"There will be no need for you to search for him," Galina said. "He will find you."

Chapter Sixteen

For a long time, neither one of us spoke.

"I am sorry to place this burden on you," Galina said at last. "Would you like to take a walk?"

"I think that would be a good idea," I said.

Galina led us out of the house and into the petrified woods behind it.

"The Pure Woods are safe enough while the sun is up," Galina said as we walked. "Most of the wood's dark creatures are dormant during the day, and those that are not are still sluggish and shy. The sun has great power over the denizens of the darkness."

I looked around—the woods were strangely beautiful. Sunshine filtered through the bare white branches and reflected off the smooth trunks, creating the impression that the trees were glowing softly.

The atmosphere was quiet and still, and no birds sang.

My mind roamed over all the things Galina had told me, and I struggled to comprehend it all.

Could my mother really be what she said?

Could I really be what she said?

I just didn't know.

I thought of GM, too. How could all of this have been going on without her knowledge? How could she not have known who my mother was?

"What about my grandfather?" I asked. "GM—I mean—my grandmother said he was dead. Is that true?"

"No, it isn't," Galina said. "He's still alive. But he is gone all the same."

"Does my grandmother know that he's still alive?"

Galina shook her head. "I don't know what Annushka knows. We were closer once than we are now—I was, after all, her daughter's friend from childhood. But she has certainly never confided in me."

Galina lapsed into silence, and after a moment, she went on as if she'd been reminiscing to herself.

"Things were very different in those early days. Nadya had visions from an early age, and though I was only a few years older than she was, I was sure she was the Little Sun. The legend was well known here, but not everyone had my sensitivity. In fact, the last Little Sun had died before I was born, so of course, people had already begun to believe that such a thing could not be possible."

"What did you do when you worked with my mother?" I asked. "How did you help her to develop her abilities?"

"As I said, I had studied extensively—I knew everything there was to know about what was arcane and hidden. I helped Nadya to focus her visions—to make them stronger and clearer through concentration and meditation. I helped her to interpret her visions, also. And I helped her to harness her power to use the energies of the earth."

"What do you mean 'harness her power'?" I asked. "Do you mean you were teaching her something like telekinesis?"

Galina smiled. "No. The major duty of the Little Sun is to use the clear fire. We found it here in the Pure Woods—or rather Nadya did. One day she called it forth—it was a bright, red-and-gold sphere of light—and it was unbelievably beautiful. The clear fire was difficult for her to summon at first, but soon she could call it to her from wherever she was. This forest is really its home, though."

"So, what exactly happened with Gleb and my mother?" I asked. "Not just with the crypt—but the whole thing?"

"It is a sad story, my child," Galina said. "But Nadya was proud of who she was and what she could do. I think the only thing she would regret was not having more time with you—and your dear father—although having more time with him wouldn't have been possible anyway."

She paused to gather herself. "I will tell you everything, Ekaterina. I will hold nothing back.

"As she grew older, Nadya began to have visions of Gleb, who was just an ordinary man at the time, although he was a well-known criminal—a mobster—and a very rich one. Eventually, his power on earth was not enough for him—he sought immortality. He came to this forest and sought out the darkness. The darkness came to him and gave him what he wanted—immortality for his body. But the price for that immortality was the death of his soul. Nadya saw it all in her visions.

"To the outside world, Gleb died and was buried like any mortal man. But it was necessary for him to die and be interred so that he could rise again as a kost.

"Fortunately, Nadya and I had been practicing on the dark creatures of Krov with the clear fire. We had started with the vampires—though the clear fire can't destroy them, they are none too fond of it—it reminds them unpleasantly of the sun. Nadya would use the clear fire to drive them before her. When she had grown stronger and more confident, she progressed to spirits— things I couldn't see. There were lesser spirits as well as the greater ones, and Nadya started with the lesser ones. I would watch her, and the clear fire would glow brighter and brighter as she worked. She told me she was getting stronger and that soon she would be able to face Gleb. As she worked, though, people began to disappear.

"And then Nadya herself became ill. She continued to work, but her strength was not what it was, and it was during this time that Nadya lost your father, which further sapped her strength. And finally, one night, Nadya made her fateful decision. Despite her weakness, she went out on that night—alone—to confront Gleb."

Galina stopped, and I thought I saw tears standing in her eyes.

"How did she find him?" I asked quietly.

"The kost has the power to create a field of supernatural 'static,'" Galina said. "It befuddles the senses of most supernatural creatures who would fight him, or that he himself would wish to feed upon. Nadya had the ability to see this static and not be affected by it— she described it as looking like twisting smoke. She could follow the trail of smoke to wherever Gleb was—and he knew that, so he took great care to conceal himself during the day when he was weakest. The smoke also dissipates after a few days, which made it difficult for Nadya to track him. But one day she caught sight of a fresh trail."

"I have seen the smoke myself," I said.

Galina looked at me through misty eyes. "That is an encouraging sign."

"So, my mother went out to confront Gleb?"

"Yes. Though I didn't witness it, I knew what Nadya's plan was—she would drive Gleb into his family's crypt using the clear fire. Then she would shut the door and seal it. To do this, she would wedge the lesser dark spirits into all the tiny cracks and crevices with the clear fire, and then trap them there—effectively binding the crypt closed with the power of their own evil. When Nadya recovered from her illness, she planned to unseal the crypt and drive the spirit out of the kost completely.

"But to my great sorrow, that never happened.

"The next morning I found Nadya here in the Pure Woods, and her illness was far worse—she was delirious. I took her home then. She only lasted a few more days."

"Then my mother died of a fever," I said.

"No!" Galina said sharply, and her face hardened into anger. "Gleb killed her—he poisoned her. Nadya's illness was not a natural one. Her troubles didn't look like a typical case of poisoning because of her unusual strength—her Sídh lineage gave her a powerful constitution. But her lineage did not grant her immortality, and eventually Nadya succumbed. I think it was arsenic that Gleb used—the symptoms were similar though much protracted. I don't know how Gleb administered it to her, but he had labs amongst his holdings and access to all kinds of chemicals. I'm sure he could have gotten his hands on any poison he wished to use."

Galina looked at me sadly. "So, that is the end of the story. Nadya locked Gleb up in his family crypt, and then she never got the chance to come back and drive the evil spirit out of him for good. And Gleb would have remained locked up if someone hadn't interfered. The seal on the crypt was powerful—I examined it myself. Whoever broke it used supernatural means. I suspect Gleb's son must have made a dark deal to gain the release of his father. And now the son is after you—in revenge for Gleb's imprisonment, and his own loss of position."

"Gleb's son?" I said.

"Yes," Galina replied grimly. "Once Gleb died, the government confiscated the mansion and all of Gleb's assets. Somehow the son has been buying everything back. I wouldn't be surprised to discover that he had used the occult to do it. And he is plotting with his father against you."

"Is Gleb rational then? If he can plot against people?"

"Not in the ordinary way. And he can be controlled by someone who knows how. The kost loses the spirit of the host—but the host's strong emotions will remain. And the desire to seek revenge would please the kost. Such a creature lives only to kill. It was Gleb's mistake to think he could contain an ancient evil within himself."

I shivered. This was the creature I had to stop—on my own, using a mysterious ball of light.

"Where is the clear fire hidden?" I asked.

"I believe it is here in the Pure Woods, but I don't know that for certain. If you will follow me, I will show you where I found your poor, dear mother."

Galina led me to a small, round clearing that was surrounded by a ring of tiny gray stones.

She pointed to the ring. "Your mother came here when she knew her strength was failing. It is a significant spot. Your mother was standing within that stone ring when she was first able to summon the clear fire. It's possible she has hidden it here."

I stepped into the ring and looked around. "Where would it be hidden exactly?"

Galina shook her head. "That I cannot tell you. It is beyond my knowledge. Only you have the power to sense the clear fire."

I stood very still and tried to sense something powerful in my vicinity.

I closed my eyes and waited—and hoped.

I didn't feel anything.

I stepped out of the ring. "Is there any other place the clear fire could be hidden?"

"Unfortunately, yes. It could be anywhere in these woods. And then there are still other possibilities. There are tunnels that run underground from the Mstislav mansion all the way to the monastery you saw from the road. It is my belief that when Nadya left Gleb in the crypt, that she took those tunnels to the monastery, and then came into the Pure Woods. I doubt she would have hidden the clear fire in the mansion, but she could have hidden it in the monastery or the tunnels. But I do believe that this ring is the most likely place."

"So, how do we start, then?" I asked. "How do I even begin to sense the clear fire and use it to fight Gleb?"

Galina gave me an earnest look. "Are you sure you want to do this?"

"I thought you wanted me to," I said. "You've done a lot to get me here."

"Yes," Galina said, and I was surprised to see tears come into her eyes again. "But up until now it was all theoretical. Now that you stand before me, and you are on the brink of this terrible undertaking, I wish you didn't have to do this. You remind me so much of poor, dear Nadya. I fear that I will lose you the way I once lost her."

"I want to do this," I said.

"Then I will do my best to help and protect you, my child."

Galina sighed heavily. "Unfortunately, I don't believe we have very long before Gleb tracks you to Krov. I suppose that the best place for us to begin is with your visions. Those are usually the first conduit into the spiritual world."

"I have had visions," I said. "But they don't amount to much, and they only began about a week ago. Before that I had a strange night calling—a powerful feeling that came to me every night, pulling me out into the darkness. But the night calling stopped shortly after the visions began."

Galina was thoughtful. "You have more human stock in you than your mother did—it's possible that you are not as strong as she was. Something must have triggered your visions and called out your latent abilities. What have you seen in your visions?"

I hesitated. I still wasn't sure I wanted to tell Galina about William. I was worried about him—I was fearful that Gleb had hurt or killed him—and fearful of what Galina might make of him.

I had heard so much talk of dark creatures lately—and William himself had refused to tell me what he truly was. And then a stranger had revealed William's true nature to me—a nature I had already suspected.

What if Galina thought William was evil? What if she believed he was better off dead?

I decided it was best for me to tell Galina everything—and then I would protect William from her if I had to.

"In my visions," I began, "I have seen only one person. I have seen only one face."

Galina's eyes lit up. "Ah. A face."

"And then he became real. The person I saw in my visions came to me in the flesh. His name is William. He first told me what a kost was. I think he was tracking it."

Galina nodded. "He must have been near you before you knew it. His presence must have triggered the visions."

I reached around my neck and pulled out my cross. "He gave me this."

Galina touched the charm. "Cool iron. Your William knows what he's doing. Iron scrambles a kost's senses—it makes it difficult for him to track you. It's the same for many ancient creatures of evil—iron can affect them profoundly."

She sighed. "But despite this charm, Gleb will still find you. He can use his eyes as well as any ordinary man, and he knows you are likely to come here. And his son is helping him."

"I'm worried about William," I blurted out. "When we saw Gleb—William was the one who saved us. He held the creature off so we could get out."

Galina gave me a reassuring smile. "If he knew to bring you the iron, and if he was tracking the kost, then he knows what he is doing. He will be all right."

I searched Galina's face. "What do you think about him—about William? I have to know. I don't want you to work against him, but he told me I wouldn't believe what he is—and I have reason to believe he isn't human. And my mother had visions of Gleb, and I've had visions of William. I know William isn't Gleb, but what if he is something like him?"

Galina laid a hand on my arm. "Your mother did have visions of Gleb eventually, but her first visions were very different. She herself did not understand their significance until later. Nadya's first visions were of your father."

I felt an odd tingle run down my spine when she said the words.

"Now, I think you have given us a good starting point," Galina said. "Please, step back into the ring."

I did as she asked.

"Concentrate," Galina said. "Think of your William. Try to bring a vision of him to you."

I thought of William's beautiful face, and I tried to see him clearly before me—just as I had in my last vision when I'd seen him standing next to me.

I stood for a long time, concentrating and willing his image to appear.

Eventually, I had to shake my head. Nothing was coming to me.

"It's no good," I said.

"Perhaps this is too much pressure on you all at once," Galina said. She thought for a moment. "Do you know your way back to my house from here?"

"Yes," I said. "I have a good sense of direction."

"Good. What I propose is this—I will go back to the house, leaving you here to meditate and let your thoughts flow. You may, of course, walk around as you wish and explore. In fact, I think exploring would be an excellent idea."

Galina pointed. "The old monastery is that way—that is a place you may wish to investigate. If you do go there, you can find the tunnels to the Mstislav mansion behind the altar in the chapel. You may wish to investigate those tunnels, too. You should go anywhere your intuition leads you. I will give you two hours. If you haven't returned to the house in that time, I will come find you. How does that sound?"

"I think it's a good idea," I said. "I would like to be alone for a little while."

Galina smiled. "Then I will go now. I will see you soon, my child. Just remember to relax."

Galina walked away, and once she was lost to my sight, I closed my eyes and let my mind wander. I thought of that last vision again—the one in which I'd seen William and a bright light—and I decided to focus on it.

I thought of William and the light—William and the light. For just a moment, I felt something like a spark ignite within me.

My eyes flew open, and the spark went out.

I quickly closed my eyes again and tried to will the spark to return.

But try as I might, I couldn't find the spark again.

I decided I was trying too hard, and I stepped out of the stone ring. I started to walk and tried to let my mind just wander once more.

I found that I was walking in the direction of the old monastery, and I figured that I might as well go see it. I was curious to have a look at the tunnels.

As I walked, I hoped for something to jump out at me— something that would prove to me that I could do what I needed to do.

I was finding it hard to believe that I had special powers.

Eventually, I reached the edge of the woods and came out by the monastery. The building itself was large and sprawling, and parts of it were crumbling.

It had clearly been abandoned for some time.

I wandered around the monastery until I found a way in—an open archway that had apparently once contained a door. Inside, it was dim and dusty, and I walked through several long hallways lined with bare cells and empty rooms. I looked into the rooms, but I didn't find anything of any greater interest than some moldering cloth and a few nesting birds.

After quite a few dead ends, I stumbled upon the chapel. Behind the altar and beneath two faded icons, I found a likely looking square panel. I pushed on it, and the panel fell backwards into an open space.

I realized I had found the entrance to the tunnels.

I ducked my head inside.

The opening was a little over two feet high and just wider than my shoulders, so there was plenty of room for me to wriggle through. I climbed in.

Once on the other side, I was able to stand up with no difficulty. It was dark, and a solid black expanse stretched in front of me. As I stared into the tunnel, I began to wish that I had brought a flashlight with me—there was no way I could go on without one.

I was just about to give up on exploring the tunnel when I happened to spy a small table in the gloom. On the table were several candle stubs with holders and a box of matches.

The candles and matches gave me pause. They weren't dusty, so presumably they had been used recently.

I wondered—was this tunnel in regular use?

Whether or not someone else was using the tunnel, I decided I might as well make use of the materials that were available to me.

I lit a candle and started forward into the tunnel.

As I walked along, my candle threw large, distorted shadows on the walls, and the silence and closeness of the space was oppressive. The tunnel soon began to slant downward sharply, and I stumbled as the ground fell away from my feet. My candle flickered, and I moved on with caution.

As I continued to descend into the darkness, scarcely daring to breathe, my heart began to beat faster. I pictured my mother crawling along this tunnel after she'd sealed Gleb in the crypt, making her painful way toward the Pure Woods.

Walking through the tunnel myself made it all seem real to me— I had a feeling that this tunnel had witnessed terrible things.

Eventually, I came upon a chamber that split into two further tunnels. I hesitated, unsure of which way to go.

Suddenly, I had the feeling I'd been plagued with before—that someone was watching me. I turned quickly, and the candle flickered dangerously.

I froze. I'd be lost if the candle went out.

The flame soon righted itself, throwing its grotesque shadows on the walls once more. I searched the darkness behind me, but I couldn't find any sign that I was being followed.

I turned back to the two tunnels, and I heard a noise coming from the one on the right. Was it possible that the clear fire could make a noise? The sound came again. It was hard to identify—it was resonant, yet muffled.

I went cautiously into the right-hand tunnel. The tunnel grew wider and wider, and soon I found myself in another chamber. By the light of my candle, I could see that the walls of the chamber were lined with little rooms that were hemmed in by tall, metal bars. Oddly, the rooms were boarded up behind the bars.

Cathedrals, I knew, often had small, barred alcoves that held special monuments for the graves of the more prominent people who were buried there—the bars having been added in modern times.

I figured that I was looking at the same thing here. I shivered as I realized that I was surrounded by graves.

And I wondered why someone had gone to the trouble of boarding them up.

Suddenly, I heard the muffled noise again—it sounded like a smothered cry. And it was coming from behind one of the boarded-up alcoves.

I crept closer to the alcove where the sound had come from.

"Hello?" I said. "Is someone there?"

The muffled cry grew louder, and the boards began to shake as if someone were pounding on them from the inside. The shaking boards beat against the metal bars, causing them to rattle.

I took a step back.

The cries continued.

Soon more cries rang out in the chamber, coming from the other alcoves. All around me the bars began to rattle, and the cries grew louder and louder, melding into one long howl.

Something was behind those bars. And it was trying to get out.

I turned and ran back the way I had come.

In my haste, I dropped the candle, and it flickered out. I was plunged into darkness.

The howling and rattling seemed to press in on me, and I groped in the dark, frantically trying to find the way back to the tunnel.

Something touched my hand, and I cried out, stumbling backward in my terror. I was completely disoriented in the dark, and I put out my hands in front of me. I felt my fingers brush against the cold metal of one of the barred alcoves, and I cried out again.

"You're safe," a voice whispered in my ear.

I spun around in the blackness, and I nearly fell down.

"You're safe," the voice repeated. A warm hand closed around mine and pulled me away.

I stumbled along after my mysterious rescuer and prayed that that's exactly what it was—a rescue—and not a new threat.

A tiny hope sprang up in my heart—perhaps it was William, miraculously come to save me as he had done once before.

After what felt like an eternity of stumbling blindly through the darkness, I spied a square of light up ahead—I realized with relief that it was the entrance to the chapel.

"Out you go," whispered the voice, and the warm hand released mine.

I wriggled out through the opening and turned to face my rescuer.

He wriggled through after me and stood up.

I was startled. "Aleksandr?"

He gave me a wry smile. "You sound disappointed."

"No," I said. "No, I'm just surprised. I'm glad you're here. You came along at exactly the right moment."

Aleksandr was staring at me steadily, and I suddenly felt strangely suspicious. "Why are you here? Did Galina send you to check on me?"

An odd light crept into his strange, cinnamon eyes. "No. She doesn't know I'm here."

Something about his tone made me feel uneasy. "Aleksandr, what's going on here? What were those things down in the tunnels?"

Aleksandr continued to stare at me.

"Katie," he said at last, "I have to tell you something very difficult, and I don't know if you'll believe me. And if you don't, I'll have to make you believe me. And to do that I'll have to show you something that humans usually find frightening."

Aleksandr's use of the word "humans" sent a chill through me. I took a step back and tried to look surreptitiously for the door.

Aleksandr watched me for a moment. Then he continued. "Katie, Galina can't be trusted. What just happened here confirms that to me. I don't want you to see Galina anymore. And if somehow you do see her again accidentally, promise me you won't eat or drink anything she gives you."

I began to back away from him steadily. "What's going on?"

Again the odd light was in his eyes. "I can see that you don't believe me. I'm sorry about this, Katie. But it's important for you to stay away from Galina Golovnin."

I felt panic welling up within me. "Why are you acting this way? Why don't you want me to see your mother?"

"Well, to begin with," Aleksandr said, "she isn't my mother."

I watched in horror as Aleksandr's shape wavered and then changed.

Suddenly, standing before me was a tall man with bright green hair and a bright green beard—and both hair and beard appeared to be made of grass. His skin was unnaturally pale, and his eyes were a green even brighter than his hair and beard. Where Aleksandr had stood, there now stood a stranger.

I froze. "Aleksandr, how did you do that?"

The man started toward me. "I am not Aleksandr."

I started to back away again.

The man stopped. "I see I have upset you, Katie."

"How do you know who I am?" I asked.

The man laughed. "We are better friends than you know. I am the one who dropped the photo on you in the Old Grove."

I stared at him. "You did what?"

"I dropped the burnt photo on you. I was trying to give you a clue without scaring you. I saw Gleb and his keeper out there on Sunday burning a huge fire—the one the two human boys were arrested for. That night, the keeper was burning that same photo from one of the stolen yearbooks—the photo with you in it."

"Why would he burn a photo of me?" I asked.

"It was part of a ritual, to get Gleb to track you and catch you. Gleb and his keeper are the ones who burglarized your school. They stole the records to find a student with the last name 'Wickliff' who had a guardian with the last name 'Rost.' And then they stole the yearbooks so that they could obtain a photo of you. The photo was then burned, and Gleb caught the scent of the people in it. But Gleb, being the poor old kost that he is, was terribly literal—he had to grab people in the order in which they appeared."

I remembered that there had been four people in the photo—and that I was the last.

The man continued. "I've been following you ever since Galina and I came to your house in Elspeth's Grove. I actually arrived a little before she did—that's how I got to see Gleb and his keeper get up to their tricks." He tilted his head to one side. "Not being human has its advantages. I don't need a plane to travel. I *can* take one, but I don't *need* it."

"So, if you aren't human," I said. "What are you?"

The green-bearded man smiled. "You haven't figured it out? Katie, I practically told you when you were sitting on the stairs eavesdropping."

He paused expectantly.

When I didn't reply, he sighed. "Oh, very well. I am the Leshi."

He held his arms out and his shape wavered once more. He turned back into Aleksandr. Then he wavered again, and the green-bearded man reappeared.

"You are the Leshi," I said slowly. "The same creature I looked up on the internet—the forest spirit who protects woodlands and animals and can change his appearance."

The man bowed. "I can be any shape I wish. I can be as small as a blade of grass or as tall as the tallest tree."

I glanced down at his feet. "I read that your shoes would be on backwards—but your shoes are on the right way."

The Leshi smiled. "Sorry to disappoint."

"So, there is a real Aleksandr Golovnin somewhere, isn't there?" I asked.

"Yes," the Leshi replied.

"And you've been impersonating him the whole time I've known you?" I asked.

"Yes."

"Does Galina know who you really are?"

"Yes."

"She never told me that."

"There's a lot she hasn't told you."

I walked over to the altar and leaned against it. "This is a lot for me to take, Aleksandr—Leshi—what do I call you exactly?"

"I can sympathize with you," the Leshi said. "Encounters with the supernatural are often difficult for humans—even for ones with your exotic background. And just call me 'Leshi,' although when we're back out in public, it would be best to continue to call me 'Aleksandr.'"

I nodded.

The Leshi went on. "I like Galina, I really do. But all the creatures in this area, including humans, mistrust her. Even the vampires suspect her. I'd held out hope that they were wrong, but it looks like I was the one who was wrong."

"The *vampires* suspect Galina?" I said.

"Yes," the Leshi replied. "In an odd sort of way, they help to protect this region, though, of course, they also prey on it. The situation is a little complex."

"I see," I said.

"But it turns out the vampires were right to be suspicious," the Leshi said. "After all, Galina did send you here—right into a trap."

"A trap?" I asked.

"Yes, of course. What do you think that was down in the tunnels?"

"You think Galina sent me into that purposefully?"

"Think about it," the Leshi said. "First, Galina banishes me from the house so I can't overhear your conversation or see what she does."

"When did she—"

"When she said 'leave'—it was a direct command. It's a Leshi thing—trust me, it works on me.

"Then she takes you out to the Pure Woods, suggests that you visit the monastery, and then tells you how to find the tunnels—where you very quickly fall into a trap. It's lucky for you that I was able to pick up on you again in the woods and follow you."

I began to feel like I was sinking—what the Leshi was suggesting about Galina made sense.

"But why would Galina send me into a trap?" I asked. "And what was down there in the tunnels?"

"What was in the tunnels, I do not know. But I am reasonably certain that it would not have been good for your health. As for Galina, I do know what could be motivating her—Gleb and his keeper took her son—the real Aleksandr."

"Gleb took her son?"

The Leshi nodded grimly. "Yes, he did. Some time before Gleb left for the U.S., he and his keeper kidnapped the real Aleksandr. They are using him as leverage—if Galina does what they want, Aleksandr will be returned unharmed. If not—"

The Leshi shrugged. "There are few humans who can fight off a kost."

"What do they want Galina to do?" I asked.

215

The Leshi gave me a wry smile. "They want her to deliver you to Gleb. Galina told me so herself. Gleb's people approached her first, before she came to see you. She claims she refused them, even though they had Aleksandr. I think the keeper was the one who came up with the actual plan—Gleb doesn't do much these days but moan and follow orders."

"Who is this 'keeper'?"

"There is someone with Gleb who seems to be controlling him. He—I'm assuming it's a he, though I don't know for sure—is very clever. He has some kind of power to block me, so I can't see who it is. But someone is definitely working with Gleb—engineering all this trouble."

I thought of the two men I had seen in the cave back in the Old Grove—one swathed in furs—probably Gleb—and the other whispering, weaving words that swirled around in the cave chamber. Surely, he was the one controlling the kost.

"I think I've seen them," I said. "The kost and the keeper together. But I didn't see the keeper's face."

"That's a pity," the Leshi said.

"So, what do we do now?" I asked.

The Leshi cast a nervous glance at the opening to the tunnel. "I'm afraid it's not safe to stay around here. I don't know how long what's down in the tunnels will stay down in the tunnels."

He quickly kneeled down and replaced the panel that covered the entrance.

Then he held his arm out to me. "I think I should get you back to your grandmother."

Chapter Seventeen

"Ridiculous."

GM's voice was low and steady, but her eyes flashed fire. I could tell that she was furious, but she was making an effort to appear calm because we were in a public place.

GM, the-Leshi-as-Aleksandr, and I were all walking toward the shops near Odette's house. Back at the monastery, I had half-expected Aleksandr to transform himself into some fabulous monster and fly us to safety. Instead, we had simply walked out of the monastery to Aleksandr's car, which was parked nearby. Then he had driven me back home.

GM had wanted to hear about Galina as soon as Alexander and I had walked through the door, but I had suggested that we all go out for a walk instead. I wanted to talk to GM away from the house—I didn't want Odette to overhear our conversation and think I was crazy.

To my relief, GM had wanted to do some shopping and had agreed.

I had also asked Aleksandr to stay with us for a little while—after I was done with GM, I still needed to talk to him.

Aleksandr and I had agreed on the car ride over that we wouldn't tell GM about Galina's trap, or tell her who he really was—telling her about the clear fire would be hard enough.

And I wasn't worried that Galina would come looking for me if I didn't return. Now that I knew what she was up to, I had a feeling she didn't actually expect me to return anyway.

I had just finished telling GM about the clear fire—and about my Sídh ancestry—and the result was pretty much what I had expected.

"Ridiculous," GM said again. "Beyond ridiculous."

I watched her face as she worked to contain her ire.

"The nerve of that woman," GM said in a low, angry voice. "She actually told you that my husband wasn't human?"

"Yes, she did."

"Unbelievable. Irresponsible. To tell a girl that her deceased grandfather is still alive. Katie, I am truly sorry that you had to hear that. Your poor grandfather has most definitely passed on. The whole town attended his funeral."

GM snorted. Then she turned to more practical matters for a moment. "Let's turn into this little shop here. I want to buy some of that alosa tea that your mother used to like."

We all went into the shop, and a little bell jangled.

"Preposterous," GM hissed, as she walked down an aisle. "And—as if insulting your grandfather's memory wasn't enough—the woman wants you to find a magic, glowing ball and attack a madman with it."

GM stopped and grabbed a box of tea with some violence, crushing it in the middle. "If I ever see her again, I will tear her apart."

She then stormed off to the cashier, and Aleksandr and I hurried after her.

GM released her grip on the tea, and the badly crumpled box landed on the sales counter in front of a surprised clerk.

"Just the tea, thank you," GM said.

She led us next to a butcher's shop so she could buy lamb to cook for dinner, and then we went on to a greengrocery so she could buy vegetables. She continued to mutter imprecations against Galina the entire time.

"I will tell you this, Katie," GM said as we exited the grocer's. "Galina will never be permitted to darken our door again. And I have come to a decision. I will stop this Gleb—I will do it myself. Do you know—I don't believe for one moment that he is undead. He did look horrible—that much I will grant him. But I don't believe any longer that he died. He's been hiding all these years—like I thought at first. And that ghastly, bloated face of his? Drugs. He's a horrible, crazy drug user."

She paused on the street and turned. "If I recall correctly, the police station is up that way. If I didn't have this lamb to get home, I would march down there and report Gleb right now."

"Mrs. Rost, if you will permit me," Aleksandr said, "I will see your granddaughter home and take your groceries with me. Then you will be free to go to the police."

"Why, thank you, Aleksandr," GM replied. "That is an excellent solution. You know, you are far more sensible than your mother is. I will go, then—Katie, I will see you back at the house."

GM handed Aleksandr her bags and then marched purposefully down the street.

I watched her as she stormed off. "Are you sure this is a good idea? Aren't the police just going to laugh at GM when she tries to tell them that a dead man is trying to kill her granddaughter? There aren't even any disappearances here to investigate—except, of course, for Aleksandr's, and you took care of that one."

"I don't think it's such a terrible idea," Aleksandr said. "It is true that the police, in all probability, will not believe her story—but they are likely to remember it. Then if something does go wrong—and I'm not saying it will—but if it does, the police will already have the idea planted in their minds that it could be Gleb. Even as an ordinary man, he was quite a terror in these parts. Besides, your grandmother's mission gives us a chance to talk without her being around. I believe you said you had some questions for me?"

"Yes, I did," I said.

"Then ask away."

We started to walk back toward the house.

"What I'm most worried about is Galina," I began.

"That's a good place to start," Aleksandr replied, "especially since she tried to lead you into a trap this morning."

"What I mean is, if I can't trust Galina, can I believe anything she's told me? Can I believe any of that stuff about my background—about the clear fire—about the legend of the Little Sun? I find it hard to believe I'm who she says I am."

Aleksandr smiled wryly. "I'm afraid it's all true. You are everything Galina said—and the clear fire is real. I am very old, and the Pure Woods has been my home for a long time. I saw your mother and Galina working out there when they were children, and after they grew older, I actually introduced myself to them. I have personally seen your mother with the clear fire."

"Do you know where it is now?" I asked.

"I believe the clear fire is in the stone ring in the Pure Woods," Aleksandr said. "But it's in a place I can't see. My powers are limited."

"I don't suppose it's simply buried in the ground?"

"Not a chance. Wherever it is within the ring, it can only be accessed through supernatural means."

"Could Galina really help me to find it as she claims?"

"As our unlucky stars would have it, yes. Galina can genuinely help you to sharpen your powers, and if you went back to her, she would probably give you a story that would make her sound innocent. And then she would start to work with you again. But in the end she would betray you—she would give you up for Aleksandr. She loves her son as much as she despises me."

"She does seem to dislike you, doesn't she?" I said.

Aleksandr grinned. "Indeed she does. I actually find it very amusing."

"Why does she go along with the impersonation, then?"

"I was the one who came up with the idea," Aleksandr said. "I wanted to keep an eye on her, and she wanted to keep her son's disappearance secret—she feared any interference from the police might cause Gleb to harm Aleksandr. And she does have a point—Gleb always was rather shy with authority figures."

"Can't you just charge into the Mstislav mansion and get Aleksandr back?" I asked. "Can't you turn into an elephant or something and knock the walls down?"

Aleksandr shook his head. "Unfortunately, no. First of all, I don't know where Aleksandr is. I have searched the Mstislav mansion from top to bottom, and Aleksandr isn't there. And second, as I may have mentioned, my powers are limited. I have the ability to disguise myself—I can make myself appear as an elephant—but I don't actually have the power of an elephant. I only have the strength I have in my real form—and I am no stronger than an average mortal man.

"And if that weren't enough, I can be bound. If someone sprinkles me with ashes created by burning the petrified wood from my forest, then I will freeze up completely—like a statue. Burning petrified wood is not an easy task, mind you. It's basically stone. But such a thing can be done through supernatural methods."

We had reached Odette's house, and we went inside. Aleksandr set GM's purchases down in the kitchen, and I began to put everything away.

"Since we're on the topic of my abilities," Aleksandr said, "or in some cases, my lack thereof, there is something I've been meaning to show you in the interests of full disclosure. But we'd better keep an eye out for Odette—this isn't something she should see."

I stepped out into the hall and glanced around.

"I don't think Odette's here," I said.

"Good," Aleksandr replied. He smiled.

Then he vanished.

I looked around, startled. "Aleksandr?"

Suddenly, Aleksandr reappeared. "That's one of the ways I was able to follow you—in addition to changing my appearance, I can make myself invisible. And here are some of the disguises I used—the only trouble I have is getting the eye color just right. It's usually a little too bright."

As I watched, Aleksandr turned into a teenage boy in a white T-shirt and jeans—I remembered seeing him the day the addresses for Irina's parents had mysteriously fallen out of the sky. Then he turned into the businessman in the gray suit that I had seen on the plane. Finally, he turned into the little boy who had thrown the chunk of metal at GM and me from the side of the road.

"You flattened our tire!" I said.

The little boy turned back into Aleksandr. He grinned mischievously. "Yes. It was regrettable but necessary."

"And the woman with you?"

"Was Galina. A kerchief makes a better disguise than you might think. Also, I have a little ability—a very little ability—to disguise the things around me. I was able to change the color of my car and tweak Galina's features just a bit."

"Then you and Odette didn't find us by accident," I said.

"No. I had been following you and your grandmother for some time, but I wasn't entirely sure where you were going. I was fairly certain you were going to Krov, but I had to make sure of it. And what better way for me to make sure of it than to drive you there myself? I thought bringing Odette along would make you less suspicious—she, of course, didn't know anything about it."

Aleksandr gave me a serious look. "I wanted you to see all this so that you'd know you could trust me. I spied on you, but I only did it to keep you safe. I'm going to help you in any way I can."

"Thanks, Aleksandr—Leshi."

Aleksandr smiled. "Well—now that that's over with, I'd better be on my way." He turned to leave the kitchen.

I followed him. "Where are you going?"

"I'm going to explain to the untrustworthy Galina that she is to stay away from you. I'm sure Gleb and his people will tell her soon that her trap has failed."

Aleksandr paused at the front door. "Be careful, Katie. I'll keep an eye on you when I can."

He turned to go.

"Aleksandr, wait," I said. "I have one more question. Back at the monastery, you said not to eat or drink anything Galina gave me."

He turned back. "Yes, I did say that. You probably don't need to worry about that now. I doubt you'll be seeing her."

"But I've already had something to drink at her house," I said. "She gave me some cocoa before we went out to the woods."

Alarm flickered in Aleksandr's eyes.

"What's wrong with drinking something at Galina's house?" I asked.

"To be honest, I don't know," Aleksandr replied. "It's a warning I was given by the vampires to give to you—to the Little Sun. As I said, the vampires suspect Galina—they suspect her of duplicity in any matter that concerns Aleksandr, either directly or indirectly. And they suspect her of something else, too, but they wouldn't tell me what it was. Vampires can be frustratingly enigmatic."

"Is there something I should do, then?" I asked. "In case the drink wasn't right? Is there some kind of herb I should take?"

"I'm sure everything will be fine," Aleksandr said. "But if you start to feel ill, you can give me a call. Do you have something I can write with?"

I quickly found him pen and paper, and he gave me his number.

"That's my cell phone," he said. "Galina doesn't know about it."

I had to smile. "Who knew that forest spirits had cell phones?"

Aleksandr grinned at me and left.

I went back to the kitchen and sat down at the table—I had a lot to think over. I had only just found out that I had to find the clear fire.

And now the one person who could help me to find it and use it had turned out to be someone I couldn't trust.

I had only been sitting for a few minutes when I heard the front door open and then slam closed. GM soon marched into the kitchen.

"How did it go with the police?" I asked.

"Some people have very closed minds," GM said curtly. "Some people do not know enough to listen, even when they are told the facts very plainly and clearly."

She went to the refrigerator and snatched a note off it. "What's this?"

"I don't know," I said. "I didn't notice it before."

GM looked it over. "Odette says she's going out and won't be back till later." She sighed. "At least that will give me a chance to complain about the police without poor Odette having to overhear it."

"It was that bad?" I said.

"It was worse," GM replied grimly. "You should have some tea with me, solnyshko. This has been a trying day for you, also."

As GM got out her tea, she clicked her tongue in irritation. I could see from the label that her smashed box actually contained chamomile—in her anger, she must have picked up the wrong box at the store.

She sighed again. "I suppose I'll have to use Odette's tea. I hope she won't mind."

GM soon had two cups of tea brewed up for us, and once again, I found the strange taste and color of Odette's tea to be a little off-putting. I decided that I really didn't like alosa.

After the tea, we had lunch, and then I went up to my room. I sank down on the bed.

I was tired, and I needed to think. I had to find the clear fire, and Aleksandr believed it was in the stone ring in the Pure Woods. But I had been in the stone ring myself, and I hadn't seen or sensed anything there at all.

I decided to close my eyes and let my mind drift. Galina had said that my mother eventually developed the ability to call the clear fire to her at will. I doubted I would be able to do that—I really didn't know enough about the clear fire to even attempt it. But maybe I could still sense something, even if I wasn't in the stone ring.

As I let my thoughts wander, I began to feel that the answer was already there in my mind—if only I could find it.

At one point, I felt the spark ignite within me that I had felt back in the stone ring—but it was only for a moment, and then it went out again.

It wasn't much, but I was encouraged by it.

I was hopeful, if a little tired, hours later when I came down for dinner.

"I hope you had a good rest and are feeling better," GM said as I came into the kitchen.

"I do feel better," I said. "How about you?"

"I am always well," GM said firmly.

I glanced around. "Where's Odette?"

"She's not back yet." GM waved a hand at the table. "I made the lamb specially for her because I knew it was one of her favorites from when she was a girl. But lamb tastes good as leftovers, too, so maybe she can have it later."

GM smiled, but I thought she looked a little sad.

After dinner, GM and I went for a walk. I was done with my meditations and soul-searching for the day, and I needed to clear my head. I was also out of ideas at the moment—I had to hope that something would come to me in the morning. In the meantime, I was considering asking Aleksandr to take me to the Pure Woods tomorrow. Maybe I could try to get the inner spark I'd felt to return to me there.

And then there was William.

I missed him more with every passing hour—his absence was a constant ache that never left me. And I had no way of finding out what had happened to him.

I thought back to what Galina had said—about my mother's first visions being about my father, and I felt a strange fluttering in my stomach as I thought about it.

I wondered what such a thing could mean.

"Are you all right, solnyshko?" GM asked.

I blinked, startled out of my reverie. "What was that?"

"I asked if you were all right. You had a funny expression on your face. I would almost call it dreamy."

I felt a blush rising to my cheeks. "I was just thinking. Things have been so—so strange lately."

"Do not worry, Katie," GM said. "I will take care of this situation. So what if the police won't listen? Who needs them? I certainly don't. I will take care of this Gleb—this madman—all on my own."

I had to smile at GM's speech.

We continued to walk until the sun set, and then we returned home by streetlight.

Shortly after we got back, Odette came in, her arms laden with bags. Her hair had been trimmed and styled, and she smelled like strawberries. She swirled into the kitchen where GM and I were sitting, dropping her bags onto the table and herself into a chair.

She smiled at us over her purchases.

"How are you this evening, Odette?" GM asked.

"Tired but happy." Odette sighed contentedly. "I spent the whole day shopping, getting my hair done, my nails."

She turned to me expectantly. "Can you guess why I had to do all that, Katie?"

"No—I have no idea."

Odette's eyes shone. "They have sprung the surprise! The Mstislav ball is tomorrow night. Now that it's upon us—wouldn't you like to go with me?"

Once again Gleb's bloated face rose in my mind. "No, thank you, Odette. I don't think I'm really up to going to the Mstislav mansion."

"If you're worried about a dress, I bought several of them weeks ago. I told you I have one you could wear."

"No, really—I just couldn't."

I caught GM's eye. I could tell she agreed with me.

I glanced over all of Odette's bags. "If you have a dress already, why did you have to go shopping?"

Odette laughed. "Katie, there's more to your look than a dress. You need makeup, jewelry, shoes, an evening bag, a wrap. And sometimes you need to bring home a few options so you can decide on just the right ones."

She looked up at me appealingly. "The ball will be too wonderful. Are you *sure* you won't come?"

"I'm sorry, Odette. I can't."

She looked over her bags and sighed again. "I guess if you aren't going with me, then I'll have to take Aleksandr—I can hardly go alone. At the very least you'll have to help me make the final decisions on my outfit."

"Sure, I can do that."

Odette's face suddenly lit up. "Oh! And the most exciting news is that the Mstislav private jet landed at their airfield late last night. The Mstislav family must be in residence at this very moment."

I felt a flash of panic run through me.

Gleb must be back in Krov.

I glanced over at GM. I could tell by her expression that she was thinking the same thing.

Odette seemed to be unaware of the effect her words had had on GM and me. "Would you like to see what I bought?"

"Of course, dear," GM said politely. "But first, I made lamb for dinner tonight. Would you like me to heat some up for you?"

Odette waved a hand. "You are kind, Annushka, but I stopped for dinner on the way home." She pulled a bag toward her. "Now, wait till you see these earrings."

I stayed with GM and Odette the rest of the evening, and Odette's cheerful chattering helped to take the edge off my fears.

But I was fearful all the same, and I could feel my stomach tying itself into knots.

When I finally decided to go up to bed, GM stopped me in the hall and gave me a hug.

"It will be okay, solnyshko," she whispered in my ear. "Do not fear this Gleb. I will take care of him."

I went upstairs and got ready for bed, but I lay awake for a very long time. Eventually, I heard both Odette and GM come up for bed, and I heard the house settle into silence.

But sleep still eluded me.

Gleb Mstislav had returned and would be after me soon—if not this very night—and I still had to find the clear fire.

I tried to turn my concentration inward and find the spark within me again, but all I managed to do was make my stomach hurt.

Find the clear fire, I told myself. *Find the clear fire.*

As the night wore on, I began to feel feverish, and I thought longingly of my mother—if only she were here to help me.

I wished I could go down the hall to my parents' room like I did when I was small and tell my parents that I was scared. And then I could just ask my mother where the clear fire was.

I smiled to myself as I thought of my mother—she would probably tell me, as she always did, that it was behind the great gate of Kiev.

Something clicked in my mind, and I sat up. A rush of excitement ran through me.

I knew exactly where the clear fire was.
It was behind the great gate of Kiev.

Chapter Eighteen

After changing into warmer clothes, I slipped out of the house and ran through the bright moonlight toward the Pure Woods. I was frantic to get to the stone ring.

I ran past the shops and the Mstislav mansion with its banners and spotlights. I ran on to the blighted fields of the Wasteland.

I ran until my breath was ragged and my sides were sore. Eventually, I was forced to walk, and I cursed my own exhaustion.

I began to fear that I would never reach the stone ring, and that Gleb would detach himself from the darkness and overtake me. The air around me seemed to be full of grotesque shapes, and every sound I heard made me jump.

I continued to walk past empty, featureless fields that seemed to stretch forever. Just when I thought I couldn't go on any longer, I saw the large, rambling shape of the monastery silhouetted against the moon. Beyond it, the Pure Woods reached its ghostly white arms to the sky.

I got out the flashlight that I had brought with me and plunged into the woods. The flashlight's powerful beam illuminated the forest floor for me, and I was able to make quick progress. I silently thanked GM for picking out good equipment.

When the flashlight's beam lit up the stone ring, my heart began to beat faster.

I switched off the flashlight and put it away. Then I stepped into the ring and closed my eyes.

I took a deep breath. I knew I was right.

I had to be right.

I turned my attention inward and searched for the spark. At the same time, I began to sing the melody from *The Great Gate of Kiev*—it was the same theme that ran throughout Mussorgsky's *Pictures at an Exhibition*, tying the entire piece together. The melody was strong and beautiful, and I knew now that there was a reason my mother had worked so hard to get me to remember it.

She had known that I would need it someday.

As I continued to sing, I concentrated harder, delving deeper within. I felt the spark I was searching for ignite within me. I caught the spark and held it with my mind, willing it to grow brighter. And grow brighter it did.

I felt a fire erupt within me.

My eyes flew open.

There in front of me, hanging in the air, was a sphere of red and gold. I caught my breath—it was a strange and impossible thing. The sphere was translucent, yet somehow opaque, and it shone with a light that was brighter than any I had ever seen before. Despite the brightness of the light, I found I could gaze at it comfortably, and the air around the sphere seemed to resonate with a sound I couldn't hear but could only feel.

I had found the clear fire.

There was a gasp behind me, and I turned, no longer afraid of what might be lurking in the night. I was suffused now with a deep calm unlike any I had ever experienced.

The sphere illuminated the area around me, and a tall form stepped into the stone ring. I saw the face I had most hoped to see in all the world.

William was standing before me, his face alight with wonder—it was the same image I had seen in my last vision.

Following an instinct I didn't quite understand, I placed my hand under the clear fire and willed it to rise up into the air.

William watched the sphere fly up a few feet and come to a stop over our heads, bathing us both in red-and-gold light.

Then he looked back down at me.

Before I knew it, William's arms were around me, and mine were around him. Wherever his fingers touched, I could feel a tingle run through me.

I could hardly believe that he was safe. I held him tighter to make sure that he was real.

"You're alive," I whispered.

"I'm hard to get rid of," William replied.

I blinked in surprise and looked up at him. "You speak Russian."

"So do you."

I was puzzled, but it wasn't important. What mattered was the fact that he was here.

"William, I was terrified I'd never see you again," I said. "What happened back at the house? How did you get away from that horrible creature?"

"We fought, and he got away," William said. "But at least I stopped him from chasing after you that night." He gripped me firmly by the arms. "What are you doing here? Don't you know this is the last place you should be? Gleb has returned to Krov, and I'm here hunting him. You have to get out of Russia right away."

"I came here to find this." I gestured up at the clear fire. "Though I had no idea until this morning that such a thing even existed."

William stared up at the glowing sphere. "What is it?"

"Oh, William," said a new voice. "Do you really not know?"

William and I both turned.

Standing just outside the stone ring, staring at us, was a man. It was a man I had seen before—he had chin-length hair, a short beard, and strangely antique, almost medieval clothes.

And there was a hint of amusement in his clear, light-colored eyes.

William quickly moved in front of me. "You stay away from her."

"The little one is safe," the man said lightly.

"Get out of here," William growled.

"As I said, the little one is safe. We have not had much success feeding on your kind. Or in turning them either, though as you well know, there are exceptions."

William turned to me, startled. "My kind?"

"Yes, William," the man said patiently. "She is part Sídh. Your senses are not as keen as they should be—otherwise you would have detected that fact yourself. That's what you get for not feeding properly."

William looked at me as if I had betrayed him.

"William, what's wrong?" I asked.

He did not reply.

"You must not blame her," the man said. "From what I understand she didn't know herself until recently."

I felt a little stab of panic run through me. The idea that this strange, light-eyed man had heard news about me was not a pleasant one.

"You know about my Sídh blood?" I asked.

"Yes, Katie Wickliff, we know you are the Little Sun. Why else do you think I came to visit you in your so-charming small town?"

The look on William's face changed to shock. "Katie's the Little Sun?"

A tiny smile curved the man's lips. "Such a pity. Not truly one or the other, yet you could be stronger and sharper than both if you chose. Please try to think, William. Why do you imagine that Gleb Mstislav has been tracking her?"

I watched as the lines in William's face hardened.

I turned to the strange man before us. "Who are you?"

The man gave me a stately nod. "My friends know me as Innokenti."

Feeling deeply uneasy, I asked him my next question, though I already suspected the answer.

"What are you?"

"I am a vampire," Innokenti said simply, and he smiled broadly so that I could see his razor-sharp teeth.

Fear lanced through me. William I knew and trusted. But this vampire was somehow very different from William—and William didn't seem to trust him, either.

Innokenti tilted his head to one side. "You know, little one, I think you may not quite understand us. Ultimately, we are a help to humanity. And your friend William here is a vampire, too—at least, he is after a fashion. His situation is rather complex."

I looked up at William. "I already know you're a vampire. And I trust you."

William's face seemed set in stone. He didn't answer me.

I turned back to Innokenti. "Why are you here?"

He glanced up at the clear fire. "I was attracted by the bright light, and I had to see what it was. Speaking of bright lights, would you mind dimming that thing? It hurts my eyes."

I didn't know how to do what Innokenti asked, and I stared at him in a way that I hoped looked defiant. From what I'd heard, I understood that the clear fire wasn't harmful to vampires, but I'd also heard that they didn't like it and could be driven away by it. It seemed to me that the clear fire was the only defense I had against Innokenti—and I didn't want him to see that I didn't know what I was doing.

So I didn't move.

"Very well," Innokenti said. "If it makes you feel safer, leave it on. But I can assure you that you have nothing to fear from me or from others of my kind. On the contrary, I am very pleased that you have made your discovery. A kost, when he is unleashed, will make no distinction between the supernatural and the mundane. He preys just as freely on vampires as he does on more fragile humans."

Innokenti turned his attention to William. "You see? This all works to the good—you need not look so miserable. Our Little Sun here has found what is known as the 'clear fire.' You have heard of it, I am sure, but few have been lucky enough to see it. I have seen it, and I know what it can do. Katie's purpose is the same as yours, William. The two of you should work together."

I seized on Innokenti's words—the vampire seemed to know quite a bit about the clear fire. I still didn't feel entirely safe admitting to him that I didn't know how to use it, but at the same time, I felt questioning him would be worth the risk.

"Galina Golovnin," I said quickly, before I lost my nerve.

Innokenti looked at me inquiringly.

"Do you know her?" I asked.

"Yes."

I went on in a rush. "Galina said I can use the clear fire to separate the evil spirit from the body of the kost and stop it for good. Is that true?"

Innokenti inclined his head. "Yes. There are two ways to stop the kost—one is open to you, the other to William. With the clear fire you can drive out the evil spirit—but you must first make it glow with the fire of a thousand suns. That takes a great deal of power."

Innokenti's eyes flicked to William, and then back to me. "As I said, the other method is open to William—he must physically wrestle the creature back into his grave. Gleb died, was buried, and rose again as a kost. He must be forced back into the Mstislav crypt and then into his own stone tomb—not an easy task, considering the kost's power. No human could do it, nor could an ordinary vampire. In ancient days, we would have said it required the strength of a hero."

Innokenti's eyes flicked to William once again. Then he smiled at me—his smile was a disturbing thing.

"As for Galina," Innokenti said, "be careful how much you associate with her."

I remembered what Aleksandr had said. "You don't trust her?"

"No."

"Why not?"

"In our capacity as the protectors of the Pure Woods and the people of Krov, we vampires watch everything. We knew of your mother. We knew who and what she was. We watched her as she worked in these woods. We also watched her grow sick and weak. But her illness was not natural. The Sídh do not succumb to sickness the way ordinary mortals do—and that includes the half-Sídh. Your mother was poisoned, and she was poisoned on a regular basis. Her Sídh strength protected her for a time, but her body eventually failed. Unfortunately, anything with a body can die.

"Galina told everyone that your mother was poisoned by Gleb, though she claimed she didn't know exactly how he accomplished it. But we watched your mother everywhere she went, and we kept watch over everyone who passed by her house. Neither Gleb nor any of his agents ever went anywhere near your mother."

"Then you think Gleb couldn't have poisoned her," I said.

"Exactly so. We think the poisoner was someone she knew well—someone she saw every day. You and your cousin were surely too young. Your father died weeks before your mother did—so if he were the poisoner, her symptoms should have subsided. But they actually grew worse. That leaves your grandmother and Galina.

"Now, we can't entirely discount your grandmother. However, it's a rare woman who would poison a grown daughter—especially when she had been a loving and attentive parent in that daughter's childhood. To us, the likeliest suspect is Galina. She had plenty of access to your mother, and she's always had a kitchen full of strange items. In addition, Galina, more so than anyone else, would know what would work on an unusual person like your mother."

"That can't be true," I said, shocked. "You have to be wrong. Why would Galina do something like that?"

Innokenti shrugged. "Who can know the human heart? I suspect it was jealousy. Galina had studied the supernatural for a long time, and she'd always wanted to have a higher purpose—to be special. Your mother actually was special."

"I don't believe it," I said.

"It gets worse, little one. We believe that Galina has been secretly working for Gleb for a long time—working to get to you. And someone opened the Mstislav crypt and let Gleb out. Though we don't know who was responsible for committing that vile deed, we do know that Galina has the right type of knowledge to accomplish the task."

"A vampire could open the crypt," William said in a cold, distant voice.

"True," Innokenti replied. "But none of our number would do such a thing. After all, Gleb can destroy us, too. The spirit within Gleb is far older than we are."

"I don't believe it," I said again. "I haven't known Galina for a very long time, and she may be guilty of some wrongdoing, but after the way she talked about my mother, I can't believe that she would've hurt her. I also can't believe she would've let Gleb out of his crypt."

Innokenti spread out his hands. "We are not agents of the law. We do not gather evidence. We do not put people on trial. In our capacity as protectors, we watch and observe. We don't *know*—but we do suspect."

"You said something like that before," I said. "What do you mean by your 'capacity as protectors'?"

Innokenti smiled broadly, showing his teeth. "As vampires, we have certain gifts—advantages that humans do not have. For example, we have greater speed and strength, we have heightened senses, we have remarkable powers of persuasion. And there are darker things than vampires in these woods—things that are hazardous to human life. We can't handle everything, but we do keep many truly horrible creatures in check—creatures I hope you never have the misfortune to encounter."

"So, you're saying you're beneficial?" I asked.

"We like to think so," Innokenti replied. "We consider our condition a noble calling. As I said, we have advantages that humans—including special humans, such as yourself—do not have."

There was a feral gleam in Innokenti's eye as he spoke, and I began to feel distinctly uneasy.

"So, little one, if I were you, I would be careful how you speak about us."

"Don't threaten her," William said sharply.

"I am threatening no one," Innokenti replied mildly. "I am simply offering advice. There are many vampires in these parts, and it isn't wise to offend us. In fact, our ranks have been growing—there are new converts every day. That means something is coming. When supernatural conditions grow more hazardous for humans, our kind grows thirstier. I have seen it before."

Innokenti gave me a piercing stare. "So, yes, little one, I do believe we vampires are beneficial. In fact, I myself once gave you a warning about betrayal—a warning that you would be wise to heed."

I felt like my line of questioning was a dangerous one, but I also felt compelled to go on.

"You say you're beneficial to humanity, but you still—" I stumbled over my words. "You—you actually feed on humans, don't you? Sometimes you even kill them?"

"Yes, we do," Innokenti said. "There's a price to be paid for everything."

The vampire glanced up at the glowing sphere above us. "Well, you two seem to have everything in order here, so I will take my leave. Incidentally, if I were you, I wouldn't attempt to fight the kost tonight. Don't seek him out in his own lair—he isn't alone. Wait till he comes for you. He will be alone then."

Innokenti gave me one last disturbing grin. "And make no mistake, little one, he will come for you. Good night."

Innokenti sketched a courtly bow and then melted into the darkness beyond the stone circle.

After the vampire was gone, I felt myself breathing easier.

And yet, there was still a vampire standing next to me.

I looked up at William. His face was set in stone, and he was turned away from me.

"William," I began, "I don't entirely understand—"

He turned to look at me. His eyes were desolate.

I drew in my breath sharply. It hurt me to see him in so much pain.

"William," I said quietly, "Innokenti said you were Sídh. But I know that you're also a vampire. How can you be both? What are you exactly?"

"I am cursed," he said bitterly.

"Cursed?" I said.

He looked away. "The funny thing is that I was suspicious of you at first because of Galina. I thought you were going to help her to help Gleb. And that nearly tore me apart because of the way I felt about you. That first time I saw you at your house after the visit from Galina I—"

William broke off.

I remembered that I had seen a figure in the shadows that night.

"That was you," I murmured.

William looked up at me. "And now I find that the truth is even worse. You're one of them. You're Sídh. I'm cursed and you know it. How you must have laughed at me."

Once again, he looked away.

I put a hand on his shoulder. "William, I didn't know I was Sídh until today—I'd never even heard that word before. Galina told me this morning that my grandfather was Sídh, and that I was born to use this strange light that sits above us. But I don't know what I'm doing, or what being Sídh could possibly mean. And I don't believe you're cursed."

I could feel the tension in William's shoulder relax, and he turned to look at me.

He took both my hands in his, and his eyes were earnest and searching. "You shouldn't say that I'm not cursed—not yet. I want you to know the truth—even if you despise me for it."

William paused, and my heart ached for him.

"I was Sídh once," he said, "though I can barely remember that life. I was attacked one night by a vampire—one both very ancient and very powerful. He attempted to turn me and it worked—after a fashion. Vampire blood does indeed course through my veins. I can feel their hunger, but I don't need to indulge it. I don't need human blood to live—though Innokenti and the others tell me I would be stronger if I took it."

William paused again, and his expression hardened.

"But despite the fact that I don't need human blood, I'm not the same as I was. And the Sídh wouldn't take me back after the attack—I was no longer pure. The Sídh avoid me, shun me. They stole my memories, and they banished me. All I have left is my name and a few of my strongest core memories—including a vague remembrance that I was once happy. The vampires found me wandering and brought me here. They tried to make me one of them."

William laughed harshly. "From what I understand, there is an ancient enmity between the Sídh and the vampires. But even though I was once one of the Sídh, I will help the vampires to protect their people. They asked me to help them combat Gleb and his kind, and I accepted—they seem to have known that he would escape the crypt one day.

"I am now cursed to roam the day and the night, cut off from everything I once loved."

William continued to hold my hands, but his gaze faltered, and he looked down.

"I don't believe you're cursed," I said.

William's hands gripped mine convulsively, and in the next moment, he pulled me into his arms. His body was warm—very warm, and I could feel all his longing and loneliness in the way he held me.

"Would you run if I tried to kiss you?" he asked.

"No," I said. "Never."

He kissed me then, and I could feel fire run through my veins. I clung to him. I never wanted the kiss to end.

Far too soon, William stepped back and took my hands again. "I'm forgetting myself. It's not safe for you out here."

"But I'm with you," I said.

He shook his head. "You're not safe even when you're with me. I'm not confident that I can fight off what awaits you in the dark. You should send the clear fire back to where it came from, and I should get you home."

Still holding William's hands, I closed my eyes and concentrated on the clear fire. I began to sing.

I had a strong feeling that William's presence would help, rather than hinder, my newfound abilities.

And I didn't want to let go of him—ever.

I bent my mind toward sending the clear fire back to its hiding place. After a moment of intense inward concentration, I felt the light go out above me, and I opened my eyes. William and I were now standing in the darkness.

I felt a tiny surge of hope—I had successfully managed to find the clear fire and send it away again—all on the same night. Maybe I actually could use it to fight Gleb.

"I should get you home," William said again.

He started to pull me forward.

"William, wait," I said. "I can't see. Let me get out my flashlight."

"You don't need it," William said. "The trees here have a natural luminescence. Your eyes will adjust to their light after a moment.

Until then, I can see well enough for the both of us. I can guide you."

I took his arm, and we moved quickly through the woods. Soon I could make out the ghostly white trees all around us, and I realized that William was right—there was enough light for me to see by.

The woods were even more beautiful at night, and though the circumstances were less than ideal, I was enjoying just being in William's company.

Eventually, we reached the edge of the Pure Woods, and William led me behind the old monastery to a parked car.

"You know how to drive?" I said.

William gave me his little half smile. "Of course. I'd hardly take you to a car if I couldn't."

"But your background is so—exotic," I said. "It's hard for me to imagine you doing something as normal as driving a car."

"The memories are dim," William said. "But as I recall, when I first encountered humans, their most advanced form of travel was the horse. I've had plenty of time to learn."

We settled into the car, and I gave William directions to Odette's house. Then we drove swiftly through the night, and I had the very disorienting feeling that we were going at a dangerous speed.

I avoided looking at the speedometer. I didn't want to know for sure.

As we pulled up to the house, I felt my heart sink, and I glanced over at William.

I didn't want to say good night to him.

We both got out of the car and stood in the light of the two working streetlights. William took my hands and then let them go. I felt the loss of his touch keenly.

"You should go in and go to sleep," he said gently. "Gleb will not harm you in the night. I will see to that."

I was suddenly worried. "You're not going to try to fight Gleb tonight, are you?"

William gave me a small smile. "Innokenti said not to."

I relaxed. "Then I will sleep soundly, knowing that you will be safe, too."

I walked up to the house and went inside.

But once I'd closed and locked the door behind me, I couldn't help hurrying to the window and looking out through the curtains to see if William was still there.

He was, and his head was bowed—dejection was written in every line of his body. I let the curtain drop, and I hurried to the door.

But by the time I'd opened it, he was gone.

Chapter Nineteen

I tried to sleep through what was left of the night, but my dreams were troubled and broken.

I was worried about William, and the feverishness I had felt earlier had returned.

I kept waking up—my skin was hot, and my throat was dry and sore. My hair clung damply to my face and neck, and my limbs and chest were beginning to ache. My covers seemed to hurt me any place they touched, so I threw them on the floor.

It was impossible for me to find a position that was comfortable. I turned from side to side, and I threw my pillows on the floor, too.

There was a gentle knock on my bedroom door, and I ignored it. I didn't want to talk to anyone, and I had an idea that if I could just get some unbroken sleep, that the pain and the fever would go away.

The door opened, letting in the light from the hall, and I shut my eyes tightly. I hoped that if I pretended to be asleep that whoever it was would go away.

"Katie, are you all right?" asked a soft voice.

I opened my eyes. It was Odette.

I turned away from her.

Odette came into the room. "Katie, what's wrong? I could hear you crying from my room."

I hadn't realized that I'd been crying. I passed a hand over my eyes, and my fingers came away wet.

"And why have you thrown all your covers on the floor?" Odette asked. "The night is too cold for you to sleep without them."

She pressed a hand to my forehead, and her hand felt like ice against my hot skin. I pulled away from her.

"Oh, Katie, you're burning up," Odette said.

She bent down and picked up my pillows, which she placed under my head. Then she picked up my covers.

"You don't have to have the heavier ones," Odette said soothingly, "but you should at least have the sheet."

She drew the sheet up over me and then folded up my other covers and placed them at the foot of the bed.

"I'll be right back. Don't throw away your pillows or your covers while I'm gone," she ordered gently.

Odette returned a few moments later with a cool, damp cloth that she pressed to my forehead and the sides of my face. I wasn't exactly comfortable, but I was starting to feel calmer.

"You should have something to drink," Odette said. "Would you like some tea?"

"No," I said quickly. "Nothing hot."

"Perhaps you are right," Odette said. "I will bring you something else."

She left the room and soon returned with a glass of water. I sat up and drank it, wincing at first at the coldness of it. But soon the coolness began to feel soothing.

"Oh, Katie, you are terribly unwell, aren't you?" Odette said. She gave me a stern look. "Now this is important—keep drinking liquids and get some sleep. If you do that, you'll feel better in the morning."

"Isn't it morning yet?" I asked. I had been outside in the forest for a long time, and then I had slept—though I hadn't slept well. It seemed to me that it had to be morning by now.

"I suppose it is, technically," Odette said. "It's about four in the morning. But dawn is still a little way off."

She glanced at my empty glass. "I'll get you more water, and I'll tell Annushka that you have a fever." She paused at the door. "Remember what I said—sleep and you will feel better."

Odette left, and after a few minutes, I heard GM hurrying down the hall.

She rushed into the room and laid a warm hand on my forehead. "Oh, Katie, Odette was right. Your forehead is on fire."

GM glanced around the dark room. "It looks like Odette has done everything just right to make you comfortable. You keep drinking water, and I will get you some juice, too, if you would like. Just try to relax, and I will sit with you. You tell me if you need anything."

GM's presence made me feel even calmer, and I closed my eyes and lay back against the pillows. Odette soon came in with a clinking pitcher of ice water and a folding chair for GM. Other than that we were undisturbed, and before I knew it, I had drifted off to sleep.

When I opened my eyes again, the room was much brighter. Though the curtains were still drawn, I could tell the sun was out. I breathed in deeply and put a hand to my face. My skin was still hot and feverish, and my limbs still ached. But somehow I felt better— like the pain and the fever didn't matter.

I felt like I should get out of bed.

I looked over at GM. She was sitting by the bed in her folding chair, and her eyes were closed.

"Good morning, GM," I said.

Her eyes flew open, and she sat up. "Katie, you're awake. How are you feeling?"

"Much better."

GM was clearly relieved. "Oh, solnyshko, you don't know how happy I am to hear that. It was terrifying to have a fever in this house ag—"

She broke off.

I sat up and took a deep breath. My chest wasn't as sore as it had been, and the chills I had felt had gone away.

My mind was clearing, too—things were not nearly as hazy as they'd been for the few hours I had been awake earlier.

My thoughts immediately turned to William—and the way he had looked last night. The look on his face had really frightened me, and I wished I knew where he was.

I remembered suddenly that I had called for William once, and he had come to me out of nowhere. It occurred to me that I could try calling him again.

I wanted very badly to call him right away, but I hesitated. GM would surely not be happy to see William, and his presence would be hard to explain. I would have to wait until tonight after she had gone to bed to try calling him.

And I realized I would have to go out myself tonight, too—I had to go back to the stone ring and retrieve the clear fire again—I was going to need it. Now that Gleb was back in Krov, he would be after me—Innokenti had said as much.

As if seeking reassurance, I fumbled at my neck for the iron charm that William had given me, and I wrapped my fingers around it tightly. I knew that by wearing the charm I could throw Gleb off my trail, but I also knew that Gleb knew this town well and knew where my mother had lived.

Charm, or no charm, this house would be one of the first places Gleb would look for me.

And I couldn't let him come here. I had to go out myself and find Gleb before he became a threat to GM and Odette.

But the work I had to do was hours away. In the meantime, I figured I should rest—with any luck I would continue to feel better. Perhaps my fever would be gone by the time the way was clear for me to go out.

The light behind the curtains continued to die away, and GM soon brought dinner up to me—more juice and broth. I was glad that she hadn't brought anything more substantial—I still wasn't in the mood for solid food.

"Is Odette back yet?" I asked, as GM settled my tray.

"No," she said, frowning. "I do wish she would come home soon." GM leaned over to feel my forehead. "You do look a bit better, but you're still burning up. I wish I knew how high your temperature was."

After dinner, I fell asleep again, and I was awakened some time later by a telephone ringing downstairs. The phone continued to ring for several minutes, and I tried to tune it out.

But try as I might, I couldn't block out the sound.

The phone continued to ring.

It suddenly occurred to me that something might have happened to GM, and I quickly got out of bed. But as my feet touched the floor, I found myself swaying dizzily, and I had to force myself out of my dark room and down the hall. I had just reached the top of the stairs when the ring of the phone was cut off abruptly.

"What do you want?" GM snapped. "Of course I knew it was you. We have caller ID, you know."

There was a brief silence.

"What do you mean your son's gone?"

Another silence.

"Galina, you're talking nonsense as usual."

GM paused once more.

"I cannot possibly leave here. Katie is ill. You'll have to call the police—there's nothing I can do."

I heard the front door open, and someone bustled in.

"Annushka, I'm home!" Odette called cheerfully. "Annushka!"

"Odette, please do not shout," GM said, her tone changing. I could picture her making an effort to compose herself for Odette. "I will be with you in a moment. I'm on the phone with Galina, and I'm trying to get rid of her."

"What does Galina want?" Odette asked.

"Galina claims that Aleksandr was just taken forcibly from their home and that she herself has been injured. She wants me to come over to see her. I'm trying to get her to call the police instead."

"Oh, no," Odette said. "You know Galina doesn't trust the police. You must go to her—help her. If you are with her, maybe you can convince her to be sensible."

"It's out of the question. I can't leave Katie." GM's tone changed again. "Yes, you heard me correctly, Galina," she snapped. "I'm not coming."

"Go to Galina," Odette urged. "I'll stay with Katie."

"What about your ball?"

"The ball is not important," Odette said firmly. "This is an emergency. I'll stay here and look after Katie. Galina needs you."

"Well, thank you, Odette, you're a thoughtful girl." GM's tone grew sharp. "Galina, I'm coming over to help, but I want you to know that I do it against my better judgment."

GM put the phone down rather more forcefully than was necessary, and moments later, the front door slammed.

The sound jolted me out of my daze—I had frozen when I'd heard that Galina was on the phone, and a strong sense of uneasiness was growing on me. I was surprised to hear that Galina was claiming that Aleksandr had just been abducted—especially since Galina knew very well that the real Aleksandr had been abducted some time ago.

I wondered—did Galina mean that someone had taken the Leshi? That didn't seem very likely. And why was she claiming that she herself was injured? That didn't seem very likely, either. I had to stop GM from going to Galina's house.

I started down the stairs, leaning heavily on the banister.

Odette was in the hall surrounded by bags—no doubt the result of her day's shopping.

She looked up at me and smiled. "Katie! I see you're doing much better."

"Odette," I said urgently, "we have to stop GM. We have to go after her right now. Something's not right about that phone call. It's a trap. Galina isn't—"

I stopped. Odette was staring at me, looking startled.

"Galina isn't to be trusted," I finished.

"What? Katie, how could you say something like that?"

I reached the bottom of the stairs with difficulty, and I stood for a moment, trying to figure out what to say. I wished now that Aleksandr and I had let Odette in on our conversation about Galina the other day. She had no idea what Galina was really like.

"Odette, I don't have time to explain everything," I said. "But Galina's dangerous, and whatever she's planning won't be good for GM. You have to believe me."

Odette laughed. "Galina dangerous? Don't be ridiculous. I've known her ever since I was a child. She is as good as good can be. Who told you something so absurd?"

"Aleksandr, for one," I said. "And GM herself doubts her. And then there are the—"

I came close to saying "vampires," but I stopped myself just in time. "Then there are the people in town. They all suspect her."

"Nonsense," Odette said. "Have you really been listening to those people? I've told you how superstitious this place can be."

"Yes, Odette, but—"

She gave me a level look. "Katie, please believe me. Galina is not dangerous, and she is not going to hurt Annushka. Trust me."

I began to feel a bit foolish. I was dizzy and weak from the fever—maybe I wasn't thinking straight.

"I suppose you're right, Odette. I don't know what I was thinking."

She smiled. "Of course I'm right. Now, you, Katie, are looking much better than you were this morning. You do feel better, don't you?"

"Yes, I do."

Odette gave me a knowing look. "You know, I can see it. You want to go to the ball with me. Don't try to tell me you don't. I can see it in your eyes. And now that you're better, there's no reason why you can't go."

"But, GM wouldn't like it."

"Annushka won't mind," Odette said, "especially not now that you're well again. Actually, she'd be happy you were out enjoying yourself. Think of it—the beautiful gowns, soft lights, lovely music, handsome young men. Deep down, you really want to go, don't you?"

I pictured the things she mentioned, and I found myself longing to go the ball. "Yes, I would like that."

Odette smiled. "Wonderful! Thank you, Katie. I'm so glad you're going with me. Let's go upstairs and get dressed."

Odette gathered up her bags and hurried upstairs. I followed her much more slowly.

"This way, Katie! Come up to my room!"

I made my way laboriously to Odette's room. Her bedroom was all the way at the end of the hall, and it was the same room that she had had as a child when she'd stayed with us—even though she now owned the house, she hadn't moved to any of the larger bedrooms. I hadn't been in Odette's room since I'd arrived at the house, and as I went in, I looked around in surprise.

She hadn't changed her room at all from the days when I had lived with her.

Odette's little rag doll still sat in her own rocking chair in the corner, and pairs of shoes that would have fit Odette's feet when she was a child sat in a row under her bed. Childish drawings she had done on construction paper still hung on the walls, and a picture of a ten-year-old Odette sat on the dresser.

It was not a room that belonged to someone of Odette's age.

Odette dropped her bags on the floor and went to her closet. She pulled out a floor-length red gown and held it up to me. As she did so, she rested her hand on my shoulder for a moment, and I felt something tickle my neck. I ignored it.

"I know this will look lovely on you," Odette said, "and we're about the same size. I told you I had a dress you could borrow."

She put the dress into my arms and then piled a number of glittering things on top of it.

"Now, go get dressed and put on your makeup," Odette said. "And run a brush through your hair. It's fine if you just leave it down—it's such a pretty color. When you're done getting ready, go downstairs. Quickly, now. We don't want to be late."

I went to my room to do as she asked, and soon as I was able to manage it, I was standing at the bottom of the stairs, waiting for Odette.

I was just beginning to feel myself nodding off, when I heard a rustle of soft cloth, and I looked up. Odette was descending the stairs.

She'd left her red hair long and flowing, and her ivory skin was luminous. She was wearing white, and she gave off a palpable aura of glamour.

"Odette, you look like an angel," I said as she reached me.

Odette laughed and threw a wrap around my shoulders. "Thank you."

She went to the door, and I followed slowly. I was still feeling weak, and my dizziness hadn't been helped by my recent exertions—light though they were.

"Odette, wait," I said. "I'm out of breath. I don't think I can take walking to the ball. I should stay here."

"Don't be ridiculous," Odette replied. "We aren't walking—we're taking a cab. I called one while you were getting dressed."

She opened the door, and I could see that a cab was already waiting for us.

"Come on, now." Odette ushered me out into the night.

We rode through the dark, and before long, we were deposited in front of the Mstislav mansion. The sprawling white house was lit up by multiple floodlights, and the red banners that I had seen earlier were fluttering in a robust breeze—it was almost as if the house itself realized that a celebration was under way.

Throngs of well-dressed people were climbing the wide marble steps of the mansion, and the jewelry of the women glittered in the light. We went to join the crowd.

A man took Odette's invitation at the door, and we were permitted entry into a vast hall. Though a haze was starting to descend on me, I could see dimly that most of the guests were making their way through the hall to an even larger room beyond.

Odette frowned and looked around. "Where's Timofei? He should be here to greet his guests."

"Who's Timofei?" I asked.

"Timofei Mstislav—I told you about him. He's the son of Gleb Mstislav. I wanted you to meet him—he's very handsome. Let's go look for him."

Odette moved on into the next room, and I trailed after her. It was very warm in the mansion, and I began to feel light-headed. I lagged behind Odette, and I soon lost sight of her in the crowd.

Before long, I stopped trying to follow Odette completely, and I found myself leaning against a nearby sculpture of a Greek goddess. I closed my eyes.

Having a place to rest felt good, and I let my body relax. The sound of the crowd began to fade, and I soon sank into blissful darkness.

"Oh, Katie, I'm so sorry."

My eyes flew open, and I was startled to see Odette standing in front of me. I glanced over at the goddess. I had no idea how long I'd been hanging onto her.

"You must be tired after your recent illness," Odette said. "And I can't find Timofei anywhere. How about I take you somewhere so you can rest, and then I'll keep searching for him?"

I nodded my agreement, and Odette led me through the house, this time going more slowly so that I could keep up.

After we'd walked through countless rooms and halls, Odette stopped by a door at the back of the house and lit a candle. Then she led me outside.

I followed Odette to a door in the ground—which she opened—and she led me down a flight of stairs into a dark room. I shivered as I looked around—Odette's candle was the only source of illumination.

Odette led me down another flight of stairs and into a long, black hall. She opened a door in the hall and ushered me into a cold, stone chamber that was full of large, stone boxes.

A chill ran through me then that had nothing to do with my illness.

I realized that the stone boxes all around me were just the right size to hold coffins.

And in the area that I could see by candlelight, there was a thick, black smoke whirling around in the chamber—it was a smoke I had seen before.

"Odette, what is this place?' I asked.

"This is the Mstislav crypt."

I was horrified. "Why would you bring me here?"

"It really is too funny," Odette replied. "Some of the locals are saying that an undead Gleb Mstislav was sealed in this crypt. They're also saying that someone let him out."

I shivered. "I'd heard that."

"Did you hear who did it?" Odette asked.

"I heard it was Galina," I said.

Odette laughed. "Galina doesn't have the power to break a seal like the one that was on this crypt. It would have to be someone like you who did it—someone with real power."

My mind was cloudy. "I don't understand what you're saying, Odette. I didn't open this crypt."

"I'm saying you're not the only one with power anymore," Odette replied. "I have power now, too. I'm the one who opened the crypt."

"You?" I was sure I'd heard her wrong. "How could you open the crypt?"

Odette smiled. "I'm a vampire."

Chapter Twenty

I stared at Odette.

"You're a—"

"Vampire," Odette finished for me. "I even have the teeth."

She gave me a mirthless smile.

"So, that's why you've been gone during the day," I said slowly. "You weren't really out shopping all that time."

"No," Odette said.

Some instinct made me reach for my iron charm. But my neck was bare.

Odette laughed. "I took the cross back in my room. It doesn't bother me, but it might distract Gleb a little. You didn't even notice when I did it. And you know why you didn't notice? Because I didn't want you to. I wanted you to be distracted. Just like I wanted you to come to this ball. I can persuade you to do anything I want."

I couldn't believe what I was hearing. "Odette, how did this happen to you? Were you attacked?"

"No—I wasn't attacked," Odette said, suddenly angry. "I *chose* this. All I ever heard about growing up was you. How wonderful you were. How special you were. How much Galina wished you lived with us so she could teach you. I tried to get her to teach me instead, but she said she could teach only you. She said only you had the right powers. Well, I have powers now, too."

"You *volunteered* to be a vampire?" I said.

Odette was triumphant. "Timofei approached Galina—he asked her to help him free Gleb and catch you. Galina turned him down. Then he approached me—and I said yes. But I didn't know where you were, and I didn't have any abilities of my own. So, I haunted the Pure Woods until I found a vampire. And I was in luck—I found an old one. My blood is strong—like I said, I have powers now. I was the one who unsealed the crypt that had held Gleb for so many years. And when you showed up in Krov, I was delighted—I could now deliver you to Timofei, too. I'm the one who told him you were here so he knew to come back. I'm the reason Timofei and Gleb are in Krov."

"Then, Galina really is innocent—of everything."

"I told you that," Odette said. "How dare you insult my foster mother?"

"But what about the poison?" I asked. "I heard my mother was poisoned and that Galina was suspected."

"Galina didn't poison your mother," Odette said dismissively. "Gleb did. In fact, he used the same poison on her that I gave to you."

"You—you poisoned me?" I said.

"The alosa tea was poisoned," Odette replied, "just like it was in the old days. Gleb owned the company that produced the tea your mother bought. When he found out she bought it, he had an extra element introduced."

"That's insane," I said. "Gleb would have poisoned everyone who bought the tea. There's no way he could have known which particular box my mother would buy. It wouldn't have worked."

Odette smiled. "You don't know what the poison was. It's something that only works on the Sídh. Normal people wouldn't be affected by it—although I suppose they wouldn't be too happy if they knew what they were drinking."

"What was the poison?" I asked.

"Vampire blood," Odette said.

I felt a wave of revulsion wash over me. "Vampire blood?"

"In the old days, Gleb had vampire volunteers donate the blood," Odette said. "Then it was freeze-dried and added to the loose tea—he didn't really need a lot. And when you came to my house, and I needed to weaken you, I simply added some of my own blood to the tea. My blood was much fresher though—I let it dry on the leaves. I also added some blood to those blueberry muffins."

"That's why I'm ill," I said. "I'm sick just like my mother was."

"Yes, you are," Odette said. "And ingesting my blood also makes you more susceptible to my powers of persuasion. It's too bad—now that you know about the tea, you'd get better in a few days if you stopped drinking it. But I don't think you're going to get that chance. I'm going to get Timofei now, and then he'll get his father. I haven't met Gleb yet—but I'll get to meet him soon. And so will you."

Odette smiled. Then she blew out her candle, and the crypt was plunged into darkness.

I heard the crypt door shut with a heavy clang, and then a key scraped in the lock.

I was trapped.

I stood still, breathing raggedly. Gradually, my eyes grew accustomed to the darkness, and I could see white smoke whirling furiously, silently in the otherwise black crypt. The smoke was thickest around one tomb in particular.

On shaking legs, I crept close to it. I had a bad feeling about that tomb.

The heavy lid of the tomb was lying on the ground, and the tomb itself yawned open. I looked inside.

As I had feared, the deep, dark recess of the tomb was full of the writhing white smoke. Other than that, it was empty.

I drew back from the lip of the tomb, and in the dim, ghostly light provided by the smoke, I could read the name that was engraved on the side: Gleb Mstislav.

This was the tomb into which Gleb had been placed after his human life had ended. It was also the tomb out of which he had risen as one of the undead.

And soon, he would be back to this place for me.

I could see my way to the door of the crypt, and I hurried over to it in a panic, running my hands over the heavy stone door. But no matter how I scrabbled at the stone, it remained immovable, and there was no way I could scratch or dent it—much less break it down. There was no way I could get out.

I sank to the floor. This crypt would be my final resting place.

I thought then of William and how much I loved him—I would give anything to see him one last time.

I leaned my head against the stone door. If only William were just on the other side—then I could at least hear his voice.

"Katie Wickliff summons you," I whispered.

The words escaped my lips before I even realized what I was saying.

I scarcely had time to draw in another breath when there was a loud banging on the other side of the stone door.

I jumped back in fear. Odette was back already—with Timofei and Gleb.

"Katie!" cried a voice. "Katie!"

I drew in my breath sharply—the voice sounded like William's.

I was afraid my terror was making me imagine things—what if I wasn't hearing William at all?

The banging grew louder.

"Katie! Katie, are you there?"

The voice still sounded wonderfully familiar. "William?"

"Katie! Katie, I'm here! Stand back. I'll get you out!"

I quickly moved backward.

The banging on the door grew even more intense. The door's hinges soon began to protest loudly—then they gave way under the strain.

The stone door fell heavily to the ground, throwing up a great cloud of dust. I could just make out a tall silhouette in the doorway.

"William?"

"I'm here, Katie."

I stumbled toward him.

William wrapped his arms around me, and I felt relief flood through my body.

"Lean on me," he said. "I'll get you out of here."

"William," I breathed. "I thought I'd never see you again."

He placed his hands on my face and looked me in the eye. "Katie, I will always come for you."

He took me by the hand then and slipped his other arm around my waist. "I have to get you out of here. Quickly now."

William led me out of the crypt and along the hall. The way was dark, but I trusted him to guide me. William began to move with greater speed.

"Where are we going?" I whispered.

"This hall is actually a tunnel that leads all the way back to the old monastery," William said. "I'm going to get you out through there. I can't risk taking you out through the Mstislav mansion."

I gripped his arm convulsively. "William, Gleb Mstislav is here. And that was his crypt we just left—with his tomb."

"I know," William said. "Don't worry."

"William, I can get the clear fire from the stone ring. I don't think I can stop him on my own, but if you work with me, maybe we can stop him together."

William's arm tightened around me. "No. You can't be in danger. I'm going to face him alone."

"William—"

"Katie, please. Don't ask me to put you in harm's way."

I could hear the fear in his voice, and I fell silent. I wasn't going to try to reason with him anymore.

But I also wasn't going to give up.

We continued to move swiftly through the dark, and at one point, William stumbled.

"Are you all right?" I asked.

"It's nothing," William said. We hurried on.

Just as I was beginning to believe that the darkness would stretch on forever, I sensed a change in the air. Even without being able to see it, I could tell that we had entered a wider space—we had left the tunnel and entered a much larger chamber.

"We're nearly there," William murmured. "Hang on, Katie."

Suddenly, a great gust of wind flew past us, bringing with it a horrible chill.

Light flared in my eyes, blinding me, and the acrid scent of a burning flame rose up under my nose.

I blinked and my vision cleared. I looked around. Somehow, candles had been lit all around us.

William and I were standing in the same chamber that I had been trapped in when I'd lost my candle and the Leshi had rescued me—it was the chamber with the barred and boarded-up alcoves.

Muffled cries rose up from behind the boards, and the bars began to rattle. The cries grew louder, blending into one long howl that swirled all around us.

There was another gust of icy air, and Odette was suddenly standing right in front of me, holding a candle once again.

Beyond her, I could see the opening that led to the other side of the tunnel—and the way out.

William gripped my hand. "This way."

He moved swiftly to go around Odette, but she moved even faster. Her form blurred suddenly, and she flashed ahead of us. In an instant, Odette was standing in the entrance to the tunnel, firmly barring the way.

"Odette, please," I said. "Let us go."

"Get out of our way," William said. "I don't want to be forced to go through you."

Odette arched an eyebrow at him. "Are you sure you're feeling up to that? I heard last night was pretty rough for you."

I turned to look at William. Now that I could see him in the light, I could see that he wasn't looking good. His skin was ashen, and there were dark marks under his eyes—less like dark circles and more like bruises. There were also long, red lines like claw marks running across his face and neck.

"William, what happened to you?" I said.

It was Odette who answered. "I was told he tangled with Gleb last night. And I also heard it didn't go very well for him."

A stab of fear ran through me. "William, are you all right? Just tell me you're all right."

"Get out of our way," William growled at Odette.

"You won't get very far," Odette said with a malicious smile. "Timofei has arrived."

At her words, the howling all around us abruptly stopped.

"Hello, Katie," said a man's voice.

I turned.

Standing on the other side of the chamber was someone I knew. It was Mr. Hightower.

It was suddenly hard for me to breathe.

"But you're dead," I said.

"No," he replied. "Not so much."

"But the police found your body."

"They found a body with my ring. It was a prop. Ostentatious for a reason—to throw the police off so they wouldn't continue to look for me. Can you guess who the body really was?"

I suddenly felt very cold. "It was Mr. Del Gatto."

"I told you you were a good student," Mr. Hightower said.

"And you are actually Gleb's son, Timofei Mstislav," I said slowly. "You were the one the Leshi called Gleb's 'keeper'—the one he couldn't see."

"Yes. And I have the Leshi now, too. He's frozen with ashes from the Pure Woods."

"I'm the one who actually brought the Leshi here," Odette interjected sharply, looking at me. "I attacked him and Galina just minutes before I came home. I knew the diversion would get Annushka out of the house, and I had to get her out so I could get rid of you. Now when you go missing, I'll get to have her all to myself."

"Welcome to my surprise ball, Katie," Timofei said, spreading out his arms. "Do you know what the occasion is? I'm celebrating freeing my father and getting rid of you—the Little Sun."

He turned to look behind him. "You've already met, I know. But allow me to formally introduce my father, Gleb Mstislav."

Timofei began to whisper. Just beyond him I could see the dark entranceway that led back into the tunnel. As I watched, a greater darkness detached itself from the shadows and moved into the chamber.

Shrouded in a hood and surrounded by swirling black smoke was an immensely tall figure. The figure raised its head and pulled the hood off.

It was Gleb—but he was many times larger than he had been before.

His face was huge—horrible, bloated, and white. His eyes were lit by a malevolent green flame, and the sickly scent of the grave clung to him. His enormous hands had rust-colored stains under the gray nails, and I had a terrible feeling that the stains were blood.

Gleb was like a nightmare that had broken through into reality.

I heard a gasp, and I turned. Odette was staring at Gleb with a look of pure horror on her face.

Timofei's father was apparently not what she'd expected.

"My father has been on a strict diet lately," Timofei said. "It was necessary for me to enforce that to keep him under control. But last night I let him feed as much as he wanted. Now he is much stronger, much more powerful—as this young man here discovered when he confronted us."

Gleb's eyes oriented on me, and I could see hatred burning there.

Timofei began to walk toward us. "Since I couldn't let my father have your friends back in Elspeth's Grove, Katie, I brought them all here and saved them till tonight. That way my father can feast on all of you together."

He turned. "Odette, break these boards down. It's time to unveil the prisoners."

I glanced at Odette. She was staring fixedly at Gleb.

"Odette!" Timofei shouted. "The boards!"

Her eyes shifted to him. She didn't move.

"I'll do it myself," Timofei said in disgust.

He picked up a hammer and began to pry the nails out of one of the boards. The nails and the board soon rattled down behind the bars. I could see a familiar face peering out at me.

"James?" I said.

"Get out of here, Katie!" he shouted. "Get out of here, all of you! He'll kill you!"

Timofei continued to pry the boards away from the other alcoves to reveal Irina and a man I assumed was the real Aleksandr. In a third alcove, I could see the green-haired Leshi standing unmoving, staring straight ahead. He was covered in ashes.

Timofei turned and began to chant something to his father.

Gleb suddenly sprang toward me.

William jumped in front of me to meet Gleb, and the two of them slammed into one another with terrifying force. Gleb wrapped his massive arms around William and lifted him bodily off the ground. William cried out and pushed against Gleb's grip.

Gleb was trying to crush him.

William managed to break free, but Gleb caught him again and threw him against the far wall.

Gleb turned back to me.

William ran at him and knocked him down, but Gleb soon caught him in his punishing grip once again and lifted him off the ground.

If this went on much longer, William was going to be killed.

I had to do something.

I ran toward the tunnel that led back to the monastery—my only hope was to get the clear fire.

But I was forced to stop short.

Odette still stood in the entrance, barring the way.

Seeing me seemed to shake Odette out of her stupor, and she drew in a deep breath and let it out raggedly. There was a strange, mute appeal in her eyes.

"Odette," I said, "I saw your face when Gleb came in. This isn't what you wanted, is it?"

She winced.

"Odette, let me go," I said. "Let me get the clear fire and use it to stop Gleb. He's a killer. And he'll kill you, too."

Odette's face suddenly twisted into a snarl, and I stumbled backward, terrified.

Someone grabbed me by the hair and wrenched my neck back painfully.

"You're not going anywhere," growled a voice.

I twisted my head. Out of the corner of my eye, I could see that I was caught in Timofei's grasp.

Panic welled up within me.

With a suddenness that knocked the breath out of my body, I was thrown out of the way.

I twisted around to see Odette grabbing Timofei by the throat and hurling him against a wall. Then she turned toward me, grabbed me by the wrist, and dragged me into the tunnel.

Odette's fingers were icy, and her grip was like iron, and all around us was darkness. We hurtled along the tunnel at an inhuman pace, moving so fast that my feet left the ground.

I threw my free arm across my eyes—I had a sudden fear that I might collide with something in the dark.

Within moments, Odette burst through the panel that led into the monastery, somehow miraculously avoiding the stone wall that surrounded it. We tore through the monastery quickly, and we were soon out amongst the spectral trees of the Pure Woods.

Odette released me at the stone ring. I fell to the ground, and she stood staring at me, her eyes blazing.

I scrambled into the stone ring and closed my eyes. I began to sing. I concentrated with everything I had in me on finding the clear fire.

I felt the spark ignite somewhere within me and spread outward. Then I felt a bright light on my face.

I opened my eyes and saw the clear fire floating before me.

"Odette, thank you," I breathed. "Now we have a chance to—"

I looked around. "Odette?"

The stone circle and the forest around me were empty. Odette had gone.

I hesitated for a moment, unsure of what to do next. I very genuinely knew nothing about the clear fire, or how to use it—I didn't even know how to take it with me.

I would have to work off of instinct.

I stared at the clear fire and willed it to move. Then, I held out my hand with the palm up, and the clear fire came to rest just above it. I continued to concentrate on the clear fire, and I took a few steps forward. I was relieved to see that the clear fire moved with me, hovering over my palm.

I cupped my other hand around it as if I were trying to support something fragile. Then I stepped out of the stone ring, still concentrating.

I moved forward more quickly, and the clear fire continued to move with me.

I began to run through the woods back toward the monastery, keeping an eye on both the clear fire and the trees.

Now, I only hoped I could reach William in time.

My lungs began to burn as I ran, and my hair and dress clung to me damply, but I pushed myself to move even faster. Eventually, I reached the monastery, and I hurried through its empty halls to the chapel. Then I plunged into the dark tunnel with the clear fire floating before me.

As I ran along the tunnel, my fear for William hit me full force.

What if I couldn't do anything with the clear fire to help him?

What if I was too late?

Just as my panic threatened to overwhelm me, I reached the point at which the tunnel split in two, and I ran into the right branch.

I forced myself to move even faster.

I ran until I reached the chamber where I had last seen William, and the sight that met my eyes when I entered froze my blood. Timofei was chanting, and black smoke was whirling furiously around Gleb's hulking form. Gleb had his massive foot on William's neck and was bearing down with all his considerable weight.

William was holding Gleb's foot with both his hands and pushing back, but it was obvious that he wouldn't last much longer.

"Gleb!" I screamed. What was it Innokenti had said? I needed to make the clear fire burn with the fire of a thousand suns to drive the evil creature back.

I rushed forward and concentrated every particle of emotion and will I had into the clear fire. I ordered it to attack Gleb.

The clear fire began to glow more brightly, and it soared toward Gleb. I could see his strange eyes of green flame turn toward the sphere. A strangled growl escaped from his swollen lips, and he stumbled backward heavily.

William staggered to his feet.

Out of the corner of my eye, I saw movement, and I turned my head to see Timofei rushing toward me. I couldn't move, or I'd risk releasing Gleb, and I couldn't hold Timofei off with the clear fire.

I braced for whatever he would do.

But William appeared in front of me in an instant. He caught Timofei and threw him across the chamber.

Timofei's body hit the stone corner of the tunnel, and there was a horrible cracking sound.

He fell to the ground and lay still.

Oblivious to his son's fate, Gleb continued to growl and gurgle, never taking his eyes off me. He prowled around at the edges of the clear fire's aura, trying to get around it.

I tried to infuse the clear fire with even more power, but I didn't seem to have much of anything left in me.

William rushed forward and grappled with Gleb. I willed the clear fire to move closer to the kost, and he stared at it with hate-filled eyes. Eventually, William wrapped his arms around the creature and began to push him back.

Gleb let out an inhuman roar and redoubled his struggles, but no matter how violently he resisted, his feet continued to slide backward on the stone floor.

I followed the two of them as they fought, pouring everything I could dredge up into the clear fire. I began to feel a deep, terrible strain as if I were burning out my own soul.

But I kept going.

William pushed Gleb back inch by inch, until they reached the entrance to the tunnel that led back toward the Mstislav crypt. Gleb fought back with sudden force, and William lost his hold on him.

Gleb lunged toward me, but William caught him once again and swung him around. With his head down and his shoulder braced against the creature, William pushed him into the tunnel. Gleb was forced to double over in order to fit inside.

I followed, fighting to keep up my concentration on the clear fire—I could feel my strength steadily draining away.

While Gleb raged and struggled, William slowly wrestled him down the tunnel, smoke whirling around them furiously.

At long last, William forced Gleb over the broken door into the Mstislav crypt.

Gleb's flame eyes rolled wildly in his head as he saw himself being pushed back toward his own tomb.

Gleb intensified his struggles and let out a roar that seemed to shake the stones of the crypt. I reached within myself to pour what was left of me into the clear fire. William let up on Gleb for a moment, and then gathered himself and slammed his shoulder into Gleb, driving him back through the smoke and up against the empty tomb.

With a sudden, powerful lunge, William forced Gleb's head into the tomb. Gleb began to shrink in size.

With a roar of his own, William picked Gleb up bodily and threw him into the tomb.

In the light of the clear fire, William and I watched as Gleb flailed, trying to grasp the edges of the tomb and haul himself out. He screamed and writhed and stared at us in hatred, but the eerie fire that burned in his eyes flickered, and the energy that animated him began to fail.

The light in Gleb's eyes went out, and he sank back into death.

William picked up the stone lid of the tomb and let it fall heavily back into place.

Gleb was finally gone.

My strength was gone at last, too, and I felt myself falling. The clear fire above me went out, and we were plunged into darkness.

I felt William lift me up and carry me out of the crypt. I wrapped my arms around his neck and rested my head on his shoulder. I closed my eyes.

Where we were going, I didn't know, but I could feel the fever and the pain in my limbs returning with even greater force. I felt the world around me waver.

After a little while, I heard gasps, and I opened my eyes. William had brought me back to the Mstislav ball, and we were moving through a crowd of well-dressed people, all of whom were staring at us in shock.

I imagined that the two of us didn't look very presentable—and I had probably ruined Odette's beautiful red dress.

William set me on a couch and sat beside me, holding me close.

I thought to myself that being in William's arms was the best place in the world to be.

Then I felt the world fade away.

Chapter Twenty-One

Two days later, I was reclining on the couch in the living room at Odette's house, propped up on some pillows.

The night of the Mstislav ball, I had been rushed to the nearest hospital, and GM had joined me there. My fever had broken the next morning, and I had been pronounced fit and allowed to leave. GM had brought me back to Odette's house, where she had fussed over me and worried about Odette.

Odette had not returned home, and the last place anyone had seen her was at the Mstislav mansion.

"I can't imagine what could have possessed Odette to drag you to that ball," GM had said over and over again.

I hadn't told GM what Odette had become, nor had I told her that Odette was the one who had attacked Galina and the Leshi-posing-as-Aleksandr.

As for William, he had seen that I was taken to the hospital, and he'd let everyone know that there were prisoners in the tunnels. Then he had disappeared.

The police had arrived at some point that night and freed Irina, the real Aleksandr, and James. And I figured that William himself must have freed the Leshi from the ashes—no one mentioned seeing a man with green hair and a green beard at the Mstislav mansion.

Irina, Aleksandr, and James had been questioned by the police, and then allowed to go home—I knew that Irina and James had actually flown home this morning. I myself had been questioned back at the hospital.

From what the police had determined, Timofei had kidnapped the four of us and planned to kill us, and we had been rescued by William—our stories all matched. William was still a person of interest to the police—but they had been unable to find him.

Timofei's body had been found down in the tunnels and had been buried in the Mstislav crypt.

The police had not believed Irina, James, or Aleksandr when they had told them about the horror that had kidnapped them—the reanimated Gleb Mstislav. But the police did go to the trouble of opening his tomb, and they found exactly what they'd expected to find—Gleb was lying silently in his grave just as he had been for the last eleven years.

I didn't even mention Gleb when I talked to the police. I knew they wouldn't believe me.

GM and I were staying on in Krov for a few days, rather than hurrying home. I was feeling better, but GM wanted to make sure that I was genuinely strong again before she moved me.

I knew she was also hoping that there would be news of Odette.

Irina, James, and Aleksandr hadn't been able to give a clear account of what they'd seen of her down in the tunnels, and the current rumor was that Odette had been murdered by Timofei and her body hidden.

I wished I could tell GM that Odette was still alive—after a fashion—but my version of Odette's fate would not have been comforting or believable to her.

I wondered if Odette was in the Pure Woods—and I wondered if William was there, too.

I felt a deep, horrible ache whenever I thought of him.

After I had been sitting for some time alone with my thoughts, GM walked into the living room with a laptop.

"I have something for you, Katie."

She set the laptop down on a nearby table and turned it on. "I know you don't have your phone with you, so I borrowed this from Aleksandr. Your friends at home will surely know by now some of the things that have happened here. And they will just as surely have heard some wild tales that are not at all true—rumor is often swifter than fact. I thought you would like to let them know that you're all right."

"Thanks, GM."

"Would you like some tea, solnyshko?"

"No!" I cried.

GM looked at me in surprise.

"I mean, no, thank you. No tea. I don't think that alosa tea of Odette's is good anymore. I think it's spoiled. You should definitely throw it away."

GM patted me on the knee. "I will bring you some water, then. You should continue drinking liquids. I'm sure you're still not properly hydrated after your fever."

She left the room, and I logged onto my email. Charisse and Simon seemed to have sent me a hundred messages each, and I read through them quickly. Simon seemed to be pretty panicked—he said over and over again that he hoped I was okay. Charisse said the same thing—and she also said she was sorry about our argument. She said further that she and Branden had decided not to go to New York— but I knew that that hadn't really been her idea anyway.

Quickly, I wrote back to them, letting them know that I was okay.

I also told them how much I missed them.

GM came back into the room and set a glass of water down next to me. Then she sat down in a nearby chair with a cup of tea, and I felt a flash of panic. But I relaxed when I spotted the tea's pale amber color—GM was drinking her own chamomile and not the tainted alosa.

I looked back at the laptop screen. While I was looking forward to going home again, my thoughts drifted back to William.

Though he had taken care of me on the night of the Mstislav ball, he'd been badly injured himself, and the same fear was never far from my mind—what if William had suffered more than he could bear? The longer he was missing, the worse my fear had grown.

A sudden hope rose in my heart. Maybe William had survived. Maybe he was even nearby—hiding in the shadows just as he had been the very first night I'd seen him.

I darted a glance at GM. "GM, did anyone stop by at the hospital, or here at the house and ask to see me? Maybe while I was asleep?"

She looked at me over the top of her teacup. "I was wondering when you were going to ask about that. I didn't know who he was, but I had a feeling that you would."

"He?" I said eagerly.

"Yes, 'he.' How did you manage to meet a boy here in the last few days? I could have sworn you were never alone for more than a few minutes. He never said anything to me, but I did see him haunting the halls in the hospital near your room. And I saw him on the street here yesterday morning."

I caught my breath. "You saw him here? How did he look?"

There was a knock on the front door.

GM rose. "I'll get that. I have a feeling you may get the answer to your question."

I followed her. The mere possibility that William had been nearby had set every nerve in my body tingling.

GM opened the door. William was standing on the other side.

"William!" I cried. Only GM's presence stopped me from rushing into his arms.

"So, you are William, are you?" GM said. "It's nice to know your name."

"GM, this is William Sursur," I said. "William saved my life down in those tunnels."

"And Katie saved mine," William said.

GM seemed unimpressed by our announcements. "You may as well come in, William. I am Anna Rost, Katie's grandmother."

The three of us went into the living room, and we all sat down. I looked at William, and he looked back at me. Neither one of us spoke.

"Oh, very well." GM picked up her tea and rose. "I'll be in the kitchen so you two can talk. But I won't be far away. The two of you should keep that in mind."

GM left the room.

I looked William over. His skin still had an unhealthy pallor, but he was no longer ashen. The red marks that had stood out so starkly still ran across his face and neck, but they were much less angry-looking now. And the dark marks under his eyes had disappeared.

"You look better," I said.

"So do you," he replied, and he gave me his little half smile. "It means a lot to me to see you safe and well."

"GM—my grandmother—said someone was haunting the halls of the hospital near my room. Was that you?"

"Yes."

"Why didn't you talk to me?"

"I knew I shouldn't."

"Why?" I asked.

"Why?" William said in disbelief. "Katie, you know what I am."

"I never wanted you to stay away," I said. "I was worried about you. You looked bad to begin with, and then after you fought that creature—"

A shiver ran through me. "I was afraid that you'd been killed. I needed to know that you were okay."

"I'm sorry," William said quietly. "It never occurred to me that it would matter to you."

"Of course it matters to me," I said. I looked at him sharply. "What changed your mind about talking to me? Why did you come here today?"

"I had to see you one last time before you left."

"What if I don't want it to be the last time you see me?" I asked.

"It has to be."

"The night before the Mstislav ball," I said slowly, "you took me home from the Pure Woods. I looked out the window at you before you left, and you looked really, deeply unhappy. What was wrong?"

"I knew I was going to go after Gleb," William replied. "And I knew that if I succeeded in destroying him that I would never see you again. But I certainly couldn't hope that I would fail. Gleb was too dangerous to let go for even a day."

"So, you *were* going after him," I said. "But you let me believe that you weren't going to do that."

"I had to," William said. "The alternative was to let you be used as bait for Gleb. I couldn't let that happen."

"William, everything you've said makes it sound like you do want to see me. And I want to see you, too."

"Katie, I'm the only one like me," William said. "And I can barely remember most of my life."

"I'm the only one like me, too," I said. "And I didn't even know what I was until I got here."

William shook his head. "Though you have Sídh blood, you're really human at heart. You deserve a normal, happy life with your own kind."

"What could possibly be worse?" I asked suddenly.

"What do you mean?"

"What could be worse than what we've already been through?" I asked. "You say you're cursed. Well, maybe I am, too. I'm not entirely human, and I had an insane, murderous undead creature after me. Maybe I'm just as cursed as you are. Cursed people should stick together."

A smile quirked at William's mouth, and I felt hope stir in my heart.

"You have a point," William said. "We have been through a lot together in a very short time. But you live in another country—you have a home and school and a whole life ahead of you there. I live here in Russia. I haunt the Pure Woods. There's no way we can see each other again."

"There are woods not far from my house in Elspeth's Grove," I said. "You could do your haunting there."

William laughed, despite himself. "You have an answer for everything, don't you?"

He stood. "Katie, you are very young. And though I look young, I am not. You don't really understand what you're saying. You think that you're in love with me. But at your age, love flares up like a lit match and then goes out. You'll forget about me completely in a few months' time, and that's exactly the way it should be. I only came here to say goodbye."

I stood up quickly. "But you do feel something for me, don't you?"

"Yes, I do," William said. "But this can't be."

He leaned over and kissed me on the forehead. Then he turned to go.

"William—" I began. Words failed me.

He stopped and looked back at me. Then he walked out.

I sat down. I felt unpleasantly like I was drowning.

GM returned a short time later. She took in the expression on my face and sat down next to me.

"Things did not go well with your young man?"

"He said he lives here, and I live in another country. So we can't be together."

"He's the same one, isn't he?" GM asked. "He's the one who got us out of the house in Elspeth's Grove."

"Yes," I said. "He followed Gleb to the U.S. That's how he knew to get us out."

"So, he had a mission when he came to our country. But his home is here?"

"Yes."

"Then it is true, solnyshko. The two of you will have to be apart."

I did not reply.

"I'm sorry, Katie. In time things will look brighter to you—though I'm sure that doesn't seem possible now. You have been through a very trying experience, and your emotions are running high. Please just give yourself some time."

I nodded and rested my head on GM's shoulder.

That night at dinner, GM announced that we were leaving Russia.

As she buttered a slice of bread, GM gave a despairing shake of her head. "I'd hoped to hear news of Odette before we left, but that doesn't seem likely to happen any time soon. The poor child. I hate to leave her like this."

GM looked at me. "But you have to get back to school, and this is not where we live—not anymore. Galina has said that she'll keep me apprised of any developments."

"First you borrow Aleksandr's laptop," I said. "And now Galina is going to keep in touch. Are you and Galina getting along now?"

"Yes, I think so," GM said. "Of course there are things we will never agree on. But maybe the past doesn't need to be a complete blank."

She looked around the kitchen. "We should give the kitchen a good cleaning tonight. We don't want Odette coming back to an untidy house."

Later that night, I climbed the stairs to my room to pack. We were going to drive back into Georgia tomorrow, and then take a flight to the U.S. the next day.

I paused on the landing and looked toward Odette's door. On impulse, I went into her room.

Odette's closet was still standing open, and there were dresses lying on the floor. In amongst the tangle, I spied something gleaming dully, and I bent to pick it up. It was my iron cross.

I curled my fingers around the charm.

"Come back, Odette," I whispered.

I looked around her room, which was still a little girl's room. I hoped Odette would come back to it again after we were gone. She could live in this house forever now—she would be forever young and forever beautiful.

The next morning, GM and I left for Georgia, and the morning after that we left for the U.S. I was back to speaking English again.

On my return home, I had the police to deal with once more. But Irina, James, and I all had matching stories, and Mr. Del Gatto's body was finally identified properly. The police even found the accomplice Timofei had hired to pose as an agent to Charisse, and it turned out that he'd approached Simon about a phony video game tournament, too. Apparently, Timofei had wanted my friends to be distracted so that they wouldn't be paying attention to me like they normally might—he wanted as few witnesses around me as possible. But the accomplice hadn't done anything more than pretend to be something he wasn't—he hadn't been involved in the kidnappings or in Mr. Del Gatto's death. The case was closed, and quite a few people turned out for Mr. Del Gatto's funeral.

As I went back to all the old, familiar places, I saw that Gleb's smoke had disappeared both from my house and from the town— I was grateful that the nightmare really was over.

In a few days, I was back at school. Charisse and I were friends again, and Charisse and Branden had definitely decided to stay in town—at least until graduation. Simon was happy to see me, and I was happy to see him, but I kept a bit of distance between us. It wasn't fair for me to let him think we could be anything more than friends—especially not when my mind was always on someone else.

No matter where I was, or what I was doing, I never stopped thinking of William.

The days passed and before I knew it, it was Halloween. Though I wasn't feeling particularly festive, I agreed to go to a Halloween party in a group with Simon, Charisse, and Branden. I hoped the party would be a good distraction. Maybe for one night, I could forget about William.

I had another reason for going, too—the party was being hosted by Irina's father. It was well known in Elspeth's Grove that Mr. Neverov threw a formal Halloween costume party every year. But this year he'd allowed Irina to invite guests, too, and she had included me. Irina and I were getting along better than we had in a long time.

While I waited for Charisse to pick me up on Halloween night, I helped GM give out candy to the children who rang the doorbell.

It had been years since I'd had to come up with a Halloween costume, and unfortunately all the easy ones I could think of reminded me unpleasantly of the recent past—ghost, witch, vampire.

I'd had enough of darkness lately.

I'd managed to find an old pair of wings that had been part of a sugar plum fairy costume that I'd worn years ago, and I also found a dress in my closet that was pretty close in color to the wings. I decided to go as a butterfly.

The doorbell rang once again, and GM answered it with her candy bowl ready.

Instead of a group of children, it was Charisse. She was holding a bouquet, and she was wearing a veil and a long white dress under her coat.

"Don't you look adorable," GM said. "Surely, you deserve some candy."

"No, thanks, Mrs. Rost," Charisse said. "Is Katie ready to go?"

"I'm ready," I said. "I'll just get my coat."

Putting on a coat while wearing wings proved to be unworkable, so I ended up taking off the wings and just carrying them instead.

As I walked with Charisse to her car, I glanced over at her. "Why are you going as a bride?"

She lifted the hem of her skirt to show me her shoes. She was wearing sneakers.

Charisse smiled. "I'm a runaway—a runaway bride, that is. It was Branden's idea."

I got into the car and saw that Branden was going as a green-faced Frankenstein's monster with bolts in his neck. Simon was wearing a long tunic and had a white shield with a red cross on it—it turned out he was going as a knight from one of his favorite video games.

Charisse drove us to Mr. Neverov's house, and it took her a little while to find a parking spot—the entire block seemed to be taken up already by Mr. Neverov's guests.

Eventually, Charisse found a place to park, and the four of us walked up to the imposing house. There were candles in all the windows, and intricately carved pumpkins lined the paved walkway up to the door.

Charisse knocked, and the door opened to reveal Irina in a sequined gown and a sash that read "MISS AMERICA." Next to her was Ms. Finch with a pair of cat ears nestled in her sleek hair.

"Thanks for coming to our party," Irina said.

Once Ms. Finch had ascertained that we were, in fact, on the guest list, we were allowed in.

I looked around. The lighting was low, and the crowd was dressed in very impressive costumes. Black-cloaked servers moved amongst the guests, serving food and drinks.

The effect of the party was very elegant, and for one terrible moment, I was reminded forcefully of the ball at the Mstislav mansion. But I pushed the memory aside.

I reminded myself that I was safe now.

One of the black-cloaked attendants came up to us and offered to show us where we could put our coats.

As we followed the attendant, Irina called after us.

"Simon, remember you promised me a dance tonight!"

The four of us shed our coats, and I put my wings back on.

Very soon a buffet table was revealed, and not long after that, a big ballroom with a parquet floor was thrown open, and dancing began. I danced with Simon, Branden, and even Charisse.

At one point, while out on the dance floor, I noticed a tall figure in a tuxedo that made me draw in my breath sharply.

I thought for just a moment that I had seen William.

The night wore on, and while Simon was dancing with Irina, and Branden was dancing with Charisse, I escaped out onto a terrace at the back of the house.

I was alone there, and the night air was cold and clear.

For just one moment, I considered calling William to see if he would appear.

"May I have the next dance?" said a voice behind me.

I froze. The voice sounded a lot like William's.

Was I starting to hallucinate again?

"Katie?" said the voice, and it was just as wonderfully familiar as before.

I felt panic rise up within me—what if I started seeing and hearing things just because I wanted them to be true?

"Katie, will you look at me, please?" The voice that sounded like William's had a note of despair in it.

I turned. Standing before me was the man in the tuxedo that I had spotted earlier on the dance floor. He looked like William—and he looked real. But the last vision I'd had of William had looked real, too.

I was afraid to believe it was him and have him disappear.

"Katie, will you say something?"

"Is it really you?"

I reached a hand out toward him, half-expecting to encounter empty air. But his shoulder, when I touched it, was solid and unyielding.

I looked up at him, scarcely daring to breathe.

"It is you," I whispered.

William gave me his half smile. "Yes, it's me. But you haven't answered my question. May I have the next dance?"

"I don't want to go back to the dance floor," I said. "I'm afraid if we move from this spot that you'll disappear again."

"Then we'll dance here."

"In that case, you may have the next dance."

William took one of my hands in his and slid his other hand around my waist, just under my butterfly wings.

We began to move in a dance with no music.

"What brought you back to me?" I asked.

William was silent for a long moment.

"I tried to stay away," he said at last. "But I lost a battle with myself. I couldn't stand to be alone, knowing that I could be near you instead."

"I never wanted you to stay away," I said softly.

William looked down.

"I have something terrible I have to tell you," he said. "I have a confession to make."

He looked back up at me. "I love you."

Happiness surged through me. "That's not so terrible."

William stopped the dance. "Look at me, Katie. I was bitten by a monster. I was banished by my own people. I'm a half creature—not really one thing or the other—not pure. I'm loved by no one."

"Stay here," I said. "And be loved by me."

"Katie, I came here because I couldn't stop myself. But you shouldn't talk about loving me. You're too young to understand what that means. All I want is to see you and talk to you from time to time. I can't ask any more of you than that."

My heart began to beat wildly. "So, you will stay?"

"Yes," William said quietly.

Joy welled up within me. "Then I will be in love with you whether you want me to be or not."

"Katie, trust me, your feelings will change. You'll meet someone else someday—someone like you. And you'll fall in love with him. And I will be destroyed. But I know that going into this."

"Shall we bet?" I asked.

Puzzlement flickered in William's eyes. "What do you mean?"

"Do you want to place a bet on whether or not I'll fall in love with someone else?"

"I already have," William said. "And I've bet my life."

"I'll bet my life, too," I said.

His hand gripped mine convulsively. "No. You can't bet that."

"It's too late," I said. "I've already made my decision."

His eyes roamed over my face.

"We'll see what happens," he said softly.

"Yes, we will," I replied. "I love you."

William touched my face. "And I love you."

Then he bent his head, and our lips met in a kiss.

Thank you for reading!

Thanks for reading *Pure*! If you enjoyed it, please leave a review at your choice of retailer:

Amazon
Apple
Barnes & Noble
Google Play
Kobo

Thank you very much!

Excerpt from Pure Series: Book 2
Firebird

Chapter One

It was Sunday morning, and I was going to meet William.

And I was nervous.

A feeling of uneasiness had been growing on me steadily within the last month, and just as steadily I had pushed it aside. But the feeling was stronger than ever this morning, and this time I couldn't block it out.

And so I hesitated before the door.

Things are normal now, I said to myself sternly. *You no longer have visions. All of that is over.*

I *wasn't* having a vision, but there was a feeling—a barrier—something solid but invisible standing in my way. The way this strange feeling overwhelmed me reminded me of how I had felt when I *had* had visions—it overpowered my senses and threatened to blot out the reality in front of me.

This particular feeling warned me not to leave the house.

But I was determined to go—I wasn't going to let fear run my life—no matter what had happened in the recent past.

All the same, I couldn't help stepping quietly back to my grandmother's office at the front of the house and peering in through the open door. GM was sitting with her back to me, her head bent as she perused a letter, her long silver braid flowing like liquid silk down her back. I had already said goodbye to her, but I had a strong urge to say it again—as if it would be the last time I would ever see her.

Don't be ridiculous, I said to myself. *What could happen in a sleepy small town like Elspeth's Grove?*

But my own memories of a little more than a month ago rose up like an uneasy spirit to answer me.

I saw a livid face, burning eyes—I heard inhuman cries—

I shut my mind against the memory and hurried out the front door before I lost my nerve.

The morning was clear and cold—it was just past Thanksgiving—and a brisk wind kicked up, whipping my pale hair across my eyes. I pulled the strands of hair away from my face carefully.

As I pulled my unruly hair back and secured it, I wondered what advice my mother would have given me on a day like today—a day on which, if I admitted it to myself, I could feel danger in the air.

I tried to close my mind to it, but the strange feeling remained.

I hurried on toward Hywel's Plaza, which was surrounded on all sides by trees, and as I entered the wooded area, I was struck by the eerie calm of the place. There were no sounds of birds or other animals—it was as if the woods were watching, waiting for something. There were no people or houses nearby, and I broke into a sudden, panicked run.

What do you think is in these woods? I asked myself, and I found I couldn't answer my own question. I just knew that I wanted to get away from the silence and the trees as fast as I possibly could.

I ran for what felt like an eternity before breaking out suddenly upon a clearing.

Stretched before me was a vast sheet of ice, surrounded by a low wall. A roof made of pipes and angles, supported by thick metal poles, extended protectively over the ice, and black matting had been laid down between the ice rink and the skate house. The rink was brand-new and had only been open for about a week.

Loud, cheerful music suddenly filled the plaza, and I could see that skaters were already out on the ice. All of the sound and motion was a pleasant contrast to the watchful silence of the trees. As I stood looking out over the big white sheet of ice, the sun dipped behind a thick bank of solid gray clouds, and its harsh glare was blunted, suffusing the area with a muted, gentle glow.

The area around the rink was fairly crowded, and the atmosphere was cheerful, happy, relaxed. And in the midst of the crowd I spotted a familiar, well-loved figure.

I hurried forward.

William turned and smiled his crooked half smile.

A casual observer would describe William as tall, lean, dark-haired—maybe eighteen or nineteen years old. The only thing that might be said to be unusual about him were his eyes—blue was not an unusual color, but the intensity of the color in his eyes wasn't quite human. There were other words, too, that had been used to describe him—c*ursed, damned, outcast*—words that had real, if melodramatic meaning. There were still other words that described him—fantastical words but real nonetheless. On this particular morning my mind shied away from that last group of words—as if thinking them could somehow bring about disaster.

"You had me worried, Katie," William said as I reached him. His voice was colored as always by an accent that I could never quite place. "I was beginning to think you weren't coming."

His tone was light, but there was an undercurrent of tension in it.

I glanced at him sharply, and I could see faint lines of strain around his eyes. I was late, and that was unusual for me—but it seemed to me that William was anxious over more than just my lateness. Or was it my imagination? I shrugged the feeling off—I figured I was just projecting my own recent paranoia onto him.

"Sorry," I said. "I just got started a little later than I meant to."

William held out his hand, and I took it, marveling anew at the tingle that ran through me whenever he touched me. His skin was warm, and his hand was pleasantly calloused. I didn't want to think about anything but how wonderful it was to be with him. As I had done for the past month, I decided not to tell him about the strange feeling of dread that had stolen over me.

We started toward the skate house.

"Were you worried about trying to skate today?" William asked.

"No," I said, making an effort to be relaxed. "I wasn't worried about skating."

A strong gust of wind swirled around us then, causing me to stop and turn toward William. William slipped his arms around me, and I leaned against him.

There was laughter out on the ice, as skaters found themselves pushed around involuntarily by the wind.

We stood together until the wind died down, and then I went closer to the ice to watch the skaters for a few minutes—I had never actually been ice-skating before.

A little girl with braids and red mittens went flying by on miniature skates, her cheeks flushed with happiness. An even smaller girl with equally pink cheeks gave a tiny shriek and chased after the bigger girl. I wondered if the two of them were sisters.

The atmosphere at the rink seemed so happy and normal that it was hard for me to credit my fears of only a few minutes ago. Surely there was nothing dangerous in the woods that surrounded us.

"Do you think you can do that, too?" William had come up to stand beside me, and he was smiling at me now.

I glanced back at the two little girls who were now on the other side of the rink.

"I think so," I said, smiling back at him.

We turned once more toward the skate house.

As we reached the door, William stopped and looked around suddenly, as if he'd heard something. His eyes narrowed warily.

"What is it?" I asked. "What's wrong?"

"It's nothing," he said. He gave me a reassuring smile.

"Are you sure?" I asked.

"Yes," he said. "I'm positive—it's nothing."

I knew William could hear things I couldn't, and I felt a flash of panic that I quickly pushed aside. I told myself to relax—just because William had heard something that had distracted him, didn't mean it was something dangerous. I would have to make an effort to get my imagination under control.

We continued on into the skate house and emerged a short time later with skates on our feet.

A gate stood open in the rink, and I walked over to it and paused with one hand resting on either side of the gate. The ice stretched out in front of me, white and unforgiving.

Now that I was about to step onto it, the rink suddenly seemed much bigger than I had realized, and the ice itself seemed to glow faintly, as if it were pulling all available light into its depths. It almost didn't seem real.

I was seized powerfully by nerves.

At the same time, I felt something like relief. The fear I was currently feeling was born of the moment—it had nothing to do with the fear that had very nearly prevented me from leaving the house that morning. It was a perfectly normal fear.

As I stared at the ice, however, I suddenly saw a dark figure appear in the white surface—right by my feet. The figure was black and shifting and vaguely human in form. It looked like a human shadow, but it wasn't mine—and it was definitely something that shouldn't have been there. At first there was only one—and then there was another and another. The figures seemed to swim under the surface of the ice itself—dark phantom shapes that twisted and turned, as if they were trying to escape.

I backed away from the ice.

William was standing right behind me, and I bumped into him.

"Are you all right?" he asked. He took my arm, and we stepped away from the gate.

"There's something out there—under the ice," I said. "I can see—things."

"Those are just shadows," William said reassuringly. "It's nothing to worry about. The ice can play tricks on your eyes if you're not used to it. You'll adjust."

I looked back out over the ice again, and the strange shapes I'd seen had disappeared. Maybe William was right—maybe I'd just seen shadows.

"Go on out, Katie," William said. "Don't worry. I'll be right here to catch you if you fall."

There was more laughter from the ice rink, and I looked around. Out on the ice there were parents helping their young children, older children racing each other, smiling couples holding hands. Everyone and everything seemed so normal and down-to-earth that I wanted to join them.

For just a moment, I wished that I could be normal, too.

I stepped back to the gate. Two skaters suddenly zipped past me at what seemed like alarming speed, and I felt a little tingle of nerves again. I told myself I would be fine as long as I didn't see any more dark shapes in the ice.

"Like I said, I'll be right here to catch you," William murmured.

I waited till the way was clear, and then I stepped out onto the ice. Almost immediately I began to slip, and I grabbed frantically for the wall, catching it just in time to prevent myself from falling.

I clung to the wall, my heart pounding.

William glided around to my side and leaned against the wall, his lips twitching suspiciously.

"You're laughing at me," I said.

"No, no, I'm not," William said, but his smile grew broader. "I'm not laughing at you, really."

I continued to cling to the wall.

"So, what do I do?" I asked after a moment. "I don't actually know how to move away from here."

William reached over and helped me to prize my hands away from the wall. Then he pulled me to a standing position. As he did so, I noticed with some irritation that his shoulders were shaking with silent laughter.

Over the next hour—with William's help and with much stumbling on my part—I managed to make it all the way around the rink several times—and I even managed to move away from the safety of the wall. We kept going, and eventually, I raised my head and looked around. I realized I was moving along with everyone else on the ice and having a good time.

William gave me his crooked smile. "You're glad you did this now, aren't you?"

I could feel the cold air nipping at my cheeks, but the rest of me was comfortably warm. And William was beside me.

"Yes," I said quietly. "I'm happy I did this. And I don't just mean the ice-skating."

Other Books by Catherine Mesick

Firebird, Book 2 of the *Pure* series

Dangerous Creatures, Book 3 of the *Pure* series

Ghost Girl, Book 4 of the *Pure* series

Coming soon!

Little Sun, Book 5 of the *Pure* series

About the Author

Catherine Mesick is the author of *Pure*, *Firebird*, *Dangerous Creatures*, and *Ghost Girl*. She is a graduate of Pace University and Susquehanna University. She lives in Maryland.

Visit the author's website at catherinemesick.com and her Facebook page at facebook.com/PureBookSeries. You can also connect with her on Twitter at twitter.com/CatherineMesick.

www.ingramcontent.com/pod-product-compliance
Lightning Source LLC
Chambersburg PA
CBHW022142170626
46807CB00005B/2039